Revenge Is Better

By

Keith Pulver

To my wife and family

Prologue

There was blood dripping from the six-inch serrated hunting knife as it was pulled out of the lifeless body of Charlotte Mobbs and plunged back in again. The rage continued to be intense and savage even after inflicting a fourth stab wound, such was the anger in the person holding the knife.

The person holding the knife was the usually calm and mild tempered Professor Emerson Noble, an eminent professor of orthopaedic surgery specialising in sports injuries.

The professor woke up, sweating profusely, it was a nightmare. It was a recurring nightmare which he had been having nightly for the past few months. Only this time it was different. Usually in his nightmare, he would be alone in the room with Charlotte Mobbs, but this time there was someone else in the room with him. He could not make out who it was.

Chapter One

Manhattan, New York

Linda Crossland was feeling dazed as she picked up her mobile phone from the kitchen table. She focused her eyes and looked through her contact list until she found the initials ESDA, it was short for the Empire State Detective Agency. She pressed the dial button and waited for a few seconds until her call was answered.

"You have to help me!" she said in a panic to the female voice who answered the call. "My husband is dead and I think that I may have killed him, I'm at our house in W24th Street."

The voice at the other end of the call was Hannah Cozin, the owner and co-founder of the Empire State Detective Agency. The number which Linda Crossland had called was Hannah's personal mobile number, a number which she only gave out to a few people.

Linda had believed that her husband, Mike, had been having an affair and had employed Hannah to find out if it was true.

Hannah was just finishing writing up her notes on a previous case when she received the call from Linda. "I'll be there in twenty minutes," she told her. "Don't touch, or move, anything and stay exactly where you are, until I arrive." She continued Hannah immediately got up from her desk and spoke to her assistant Ava. "Ava, hold all of my calls, I've got to go out and probably won't be back until tomorrow," she said. Hannah looked around the room and took a back pack, which was hanging on the coat rack by her office door, she filled it with a few items which her experience told her what she might need. She took the lift from her 10th floor office in the Empire State Building, down to the ground floor and hailed a cab from the entrance in 5th Avenue.

Hannah Cozin arrived at Linda Crossland's house in W24th Street within fifteen minutes. The dark red door of the red brick four-storey townhouse was slightly ajar as Hannah let herself in, carefully and slowly. She walked in to the kitchen and saw Linda, staring at the body of Mike, lying on the floor with a blood-stained shirt and a pool of blood spreading wider on the floor. There was a gun-shot wound in his chest but no sign of a gun. Hannah could see that Linda was still dazed and thought that she may have been drugged. She took out a mobile drug testing kit from her back pack and tested Linda. As she suspected, the test was positive for an opioid based, sleep-inducing drug. She checked Linda's hands for gunshot residue, but there was none.

Hannah knew straight away that Linda could not have killed her husband, she also knew that Linda did not even own a gun. Hannah called Lieutenant Krakowski a police officer she had worked with before, and knew she could trust,.

"I'll be there in ten," he said, after Hannah explained the situation to him.

Hannah had been investigating Mike and had found out that Linda's suspicions were correct. He was having an affair with Holly, a woman almost half his age. The affair had been carrying on for several months and Hannah had photographic proof. She had photographed them, through a motel window, having sex. Hannah had shown the photos to Linda only the previous day, and now Mike was dead. It could not be a coincidence.

Hannah gently pulled her camera out of her back pack and took photos of the crime scene, whilst she waited with Linda until Lieutenant Krakowski arrived. Whilst they were waiting, Hannah called her team of computer experts and asked them to scan the local street cameras for the last week to see if they could see anything unusual. They were used to receiving this type of call from Hannah and were on the case, immediately. Within seconds they had hacked into the CCTV system and accessed all of the cameras in the street, as well as the surrounding streets and avenues. They had seen a man entering in to the town house in W24th Street, one hour before Linda had called Hannah to say that her husband was dead. The man had arrived in a yellow taxi and the number was clearly visible on the roof of the taxi. The

3

team of computer experts accessed the taxi company records and found out where the driver had picked up the fare. They traced the address and found out that the property was owned by Holly and her husband. They relayed this information to Hannah.

A few minutes later, Lieutenant Krakowski arrived and walked in to the kitchen where he was met by a grief-stricken Linda and Hannah, who had already solved the crime. Hannah told the Lieutenant the results of the drug and gunshot residue tests which she had carried out on Linda. She also told the Lieutenant that the husband of the girl who Mike was having an affair with had been spotted entering the building only an hour earlier.

Lieutenant Krakowski called his assistant detectives to go to Holly's house where they found her body lying on the floor, also with a gun-shot wound, dead. An all-points bulletin was issued for the arrest of Holly's husband. Hannah put her arm around Linda to try and console her but her job was done. She was good, not just good but the best.

Chapter Two

Professor Noble

Professor Emerson Noble had a clinic and surgery in the famous Harley Street, in the West End of London, where he would see his patients.

He had achieved all of the awards going in his profession. He was a Fellow of the Royal College of Surgeons as well as being the author of several books on the subject which he loved, including the future of surgery.

He had recently lectured in front of a worldwide audience of thousands, both in the auditorium and via online screens.

Professor Noble was in his late fifties but looked younger. He was a handsome man, his hair was light brown, almost dark blonde, but greying slightly with no hair loss which was good for a man of his age. He was a kind and gentle man with piercing blue eyes, which most people commented on when them saw him as they were so distinctive.

He was a muscular man and would train in the gym in his house, where he would lift weights and use the rowing and running machines. He used to row at Cambridge University, including taking part in the annual Oxford versus Cambridge boat race, on the River Thames. He studied medicine at Cambridge and achieved a first-class honours medical degree.

After Cambridge, he continued with several years of further training in surgical specialities during which time he acquired the Membership of the Royal College of Surgeons and later became a Fellow.

Exactly why he had the knife and was stabbing Charlotte Mobbs so viciously, in his dream, was completely out of character. However, in his mind, it was what she deserved after everything that she had done to him, and others, she had created this nightmare. She had ruined his career and almost his life.

Chapter Three

TWO YEARS EARLIER

Professor Noble had just finished giving a lecture on new techniques and technology in orthopaedic surgery, in front of two hundred paying professional surgeons and anaesthetists at a specially adapted area in the Natural History Museum in Kensington, London. It was part of his and their ongoing professional development within the medical industry. He had talked for an hour using information from his lap top computer, showing images directly on to the large screens in the room. He knew most of the people in the room, they were of all ages and genders. Some of the attendees worked with him and others from his building. The Q & A section at the end took longer than expected and he received a long round of applause once he had finished.

The professor had practised as a consultant in both NHS and private clinics before starting his own clinic in Harley Street over twenty years ago. His clinic was on the first floor of a six storey Grade ll Listed terraced property, originally built as a house but now arranged as six separate clinics; one on each floor.

The specialists and consultants in the other clinics were from varying areas of medicine from an ophthalmology clinic, breast augmentation, and open-heart surgery, amongst others. He knew the other consultants in the building well and had made many good friends, including Professor Clement Tomkins who was the consultant in charge of the open-heart surgery clinic on the ground floor.

Professor Tomkins was younger than Professor Noble, by about ten years. To look at them, you would have thought that they were about the same age, as Professor Noble kept himself in shape whereas Professor Tomkins liked to eat and drink to excess, as well as take drugs, and it showed. Professor Tomkins' hair had greyed and thinned, his face and stomach had grown in recent years. He was out of condition and he knew it, but he did not seem too worried by this. He walked with a slight limp but no-one seemed to know why. Professor Tomkins was jealous of Professor Noble but did not let on. Professor Noble employed four staff members including an administration team of two, an anaesthetist and a surgical assistant, Doctor Helen Harris.

Doctor Harris was in her early thirties, she was a very attractive person with a kind face, amazing brown eyes and medium length brown hair which settled just below her shoulders. She was an extremely competent surgeon in her own right and was happy to work with Professor Noble to gain as much experience as possible. Her goal was to open her own clinic and progress to become a professor.

On Professor Noble's client list there were many top athletes from a range of sports, from Olympic Gold medallists and tennis players to rugby and football players. He had recently carried out the most sophisticated operation on the knee of the most famous footballer in the world, Kyle Scott, the captain of England and the scorer of the winning goal in the recent World Cup final. The operation was a success and made sure that Kyle Scott could continue playing his sport for several more years. The success of the operation led to more referrals for the professor and even more recognition within his profession. Professor Noble lived from Monday to Friday in his penthouse apartment on the top floor of the most exclusive apartment block in Knightsbridge. The flat was only a few years old and cost several million pounds, part paid for from his earnings from his clinic and part with a mortgage, as advised by his financial adviser for tax reasons. The apartment had a large roof terrace which overlooked the serenity of Hyde Park at the rear, whilst the front overlooked the hustle and bustle of Knightsbridge with Harrods and Harvey Nicholls a stone's throw away. His main property was a superb six bedroom detached house in The Bishop's Avenue, Hampstead, an exclusive road close to Hampstead Heath with mostly very large houses. Some of the older houses had been knocked down and redeveloped in to prestigious flats. Professor Noble lived in the house in Hampstead with his wife,

7

Elizabeth. Elizabeth was a few years younger than the professor and had looked after herself very well, she did not look her age. Elizabeth had brown hair which came down to just below her shoulders and beautiful hazel eyes, she had a great figure and was also incredibly sexy. The professor knew that he was very fortunate to be married to such a lovely and sexy person and also to live in the beautiful homes. It was his career that had paid for all of this through his hard work and he was a self-made millionaire.

Elizabeth and Emerson Noble had been married for twenty years, it was each their second marriages and both had grown up children who had since left home – a boy and girl each, now in their late twenties. Their children's careers had also been successful, with his son, Russell, the CEO of a private bank in the City of London – the youngest CEO in the history of the bank. His daughter, Judith, was a director of an insurance broking company. They both had gained many friends and contacts in high places over the years – their father had always told them how important that was. Elizabeth's children were famous celebrities in the catering world. Her daughter, Jackie and son, Steven, had opened their own restaurant, La JaSte, together, in Mayfair and had earned a Michelin star of which they and their entire family were very proud.

Emerson's parents had died when he was twenty years old and he had grown up with no mentors. He had a brother, Nigel, who was a few years older than Emerson. Nigel was an accountant who had had his own accountancy practise for several years. Nigel always helped Emerson with his accounts and advised him on many tax saving investments, but had recently retired.

Chapter Four

Emerson and Elizabeth Noble had lived very nicely due to the success of the professor's surgery. They had great five-star holidays including the Maldives, Mauritius and the Seychelles as well as city breaks in Paris, New York and Amsterdam, amongst others. They travelled first class and stayed in five-star hotels. They dined out in top Michelin star restaurants at least once a week, including La JaSte, as well as many other restaurants close to the professor's apartment, in London's West End, such as Le Gavroche, The Ivy Club and a private table at Alain Ducasse's restaurant in The Dorchester Hotel, in Park Lane. The professor paid for all of this with his Black American Express Centurion Card made from anodised titanium. He had had this card for several years – it is an "invitation only" card and not one that could be applied for. The Centurion Card was offered to him following several years of Platinum Card membership. He remembered being so very excited when the offer came through, that he accepted immediately. They had access to all VIP events including the Wimbledon tennis finals, Cannes Film Festival private parties, Royal Ascot where they would be in the box adjacent to the Royal Box where Her Majesty Queen Elizabeth was only a few yards away. A private box for all events at Wembley Stadium and at Lords cricket ground, amongst others.

The professor had owned several fast sports cars over the years including Aston Martins, Ferraris and Jaguars but in the past few years his attention was brought to the future of the electric vehicle and had acquired a Tesla Model S saloon. He was the first person in the UK to buy one having put a deposit down and waited two years before delivery. The reward for this was being handed the key, which was shaped like the car, directly from the company owner and billionaire, Elon Musk, in a handing over ceremony at The Crystal Building in London Docklands. The speed of the Tesla was so much faster than any of the other cars that he had driven in the past and the acceleration was instant. It was like being in a go-kart, whereas there was always a lag in a petrol engine car, and the Tesla was so smooth. He had recently exchanged his original Model S for a new one which had a yoke steering wheel, like an aeroplane. The acceleration was immense at less than two seconds from start to 60 mph, not that you could use this in the clogged-up street of London. There was no congestion charge to pay as the car was electric. There was also no petrol needed and he had set up a charging point in the garage of his house in The Bishop's Avenue. Elizabeth drove a new Range Rover which she didn't really need as it was such a large vehicle. The only times she used it was to go to Waitrose for food shopping, or to her local yoga and Pilate's sessions, which she went to twice a week. Elizabeth's interest was in her designer handbags, she had amassed a collection of several Chanel bags and also exclusive limited-edition bags from Hermes. She also loved her designer shoes with the red sole shoes of Christian Louboutin being amongst her favourites. Professor Noble also had a Private Pilot's Licence; he had a keen interest in flying due to the fact that his father used to fly Spitfires in the second world war.

The professor's flying interest was purely for fun. He had learned to fly in a Cessna 152 single engine plane, over twenty years earlier, at Biggin Hill airport located to the south east of London in the London Borough of Bromley. After obtaining his private pilot's licence, he progressed to flying a twin-engine Cessna 310, which he kept in a hangar at Elstree Aerodrome in Hertfordshire, just to the north west of London, as it was the most convenient private airport close to his home in Hampstead. He would routinely fly Elizabeth to Le Touquet, France, or Newquay in Cornwall, for a romantic picnic on the beach and return the same day. They even flew to Paris for shopping trips, weather permitting. Sometimes the professor would fly alone, the feeling was so relaxing flying above the Hertfordshire towns, it was his way of relaxing at the weekends, after the demanding days of surgery. Another way of letting off steam for the professor was to go to see his favourite football team, West Ham United, play. They had never been as successful as some of the other more famous teams such as Manchester United or Liverpool or even Tottenham and Chelsea but there was something about them that he just loved. They were a household name in the 1960's, when he was growing up, having won several cup competitions. They also produced many fine young players, including Bobby Moore, Geoff Hurst and Martin Peters, all of whom played for England in the 1966 World Cup final at Wembley. Their names would stay in the mind of the young Emerson for decades.

As soon as he was in a position where he could afford it, he bought a season ticket and then a private box, at the stadium for himself and his brother, Nigel. West Ham moved from their old stadium in Green Street, Upton Park in east London to the former 2012 London Olympic Stadium in Stratford. He bought another private box in the new stadium, now called The London Stadium. The box and seats were the best in the stadium, being directly in line with the half way line and close to the area where the director's and family of the players seats were. He would try to get to as many games as possible although his work often prevented that. He did indeed live an expensive lifestyle, but this was all about to change.

Chapter Five

There had been a complaint to the Royal College of Surgeons following a recent operation which the professor had performed. Following the successful surgery of the footballer, Kyle Scott, Professor Noble carried out a similar surgery on a general member of the public, Kirk King, but there was a problem, the operation was not successful. The professor had operated as usual but during the operation his hand twitched slightly and he accidently cut in to a nerve, close to the knee of Mr King. As a result of this, Mr King could not walk unaided, he would have to use a walking-stick for at least six months whilst the nerve repaired. Fortunately for Mr King it would be temporary, and not for the rest of his life. Mr King was a roofing contractor and would not be able to work for a total of nine months, including three months of regular physiotherapy. He made a formal complaint to the Royal College of Surgeons, claiming medical negligence and sued for damages of over one million pounds.

As is common practice, all clinics have to take out a form of insurance known as professional indemnity insurance where, in the case of negligence, the insurance will pay in the event of a successful claim. The insurers in this instance were a very large insurance company with offices worldwide, with their head office being in New York. They provided professional indemnity insurance for most professions, but they specialised in medical negligence insurance. The premium for the insurance was in excess of one hundred thousand pounds a year and this was only the second claim that the professor had against him in thirty years. The first claim was over fifteen years earlier when a similar error occurred during surgery and again, in that instance, there was no long-term damage to the patient. The claim paid was in the low thousands of pounds. As part of their protocol the insurers insisted that an investigation was undertaken and an appointment was arranged. The person leading the investigation was Charlotte Mobbs, from the General Medical Council, a public body that maintains the official register of medical practitioners within the United Kingdom. by controlling entry to the register, and suspending or removing members when necessary.

Charlotte Mobbs and her team arrived at nine o'clock in the morning, on the date arranged. Initially, they went to the wrong building. It was lucky that the professor was looking out of his window as he saw a few people who he did not recognise, mingling outside of the adjacent building. He was waiting for them so he went down and asked them who they were, sure enough it was the team of investigators. After the initial frivolities were out of the way and coffee was offered, they were down to business. Charlotte Mobbs was in her early forties and had a reputation within the General Medical Council as being a ruthless investigator. She was not tall, only about five foot two inches in height, but a very confident person. She had a rounded face and shoulder length mousey coloured hair. She wore a two-piece trouser suit which was tight and showed off her stomach bulges more than she would have hoped. Charlotte Mobbs was not slim and she knew it. She had tried to lose weight but with no avail as she enjoyed so many sweet things. She would devour a whole packet of biscuits with the several cups of tea, which she would drink each day with sugar. It was a bit of a surprise that she would have worn clothes that highlighted her weight gain, rather than try to conceal it.

Professor Noble noticed that Charlotte Mobbs seemed to be a slightly nervous person. Her hands twitched slightly and she touched her face more than usual. He noticed that she bit her nails to the quick, it was a very unpleasant sight. In contrast to this, he also noticed that she was very health conscience and kept a small bottle of hand sanitiser gel in her hand bag. She used this several times during the meeting, especially after touching the desk or papers. Mobbs had a team with her on the investigation including an accountant, Clementine Follows, an older lady in her seventies. Clementine Follows did not have the same weight problem that Charlotte Mobbs had, in fact the opposite. She was very thin and looked as if she may have anorexia, or a similar eating disorder. Follows looked like she should have retired years ago but she could not afford to retire. She was also a jobsworth and was deliberately uncooperative during the investigation, acting in an obstructive and unhelpful manner throughout the meeting. Clementine Follows wore a flower power style of clothing which reminded her of the days in the fifties and sixties in which she grew up. She had grey and thinning long hair which was yellowing from the tar in the copious cigarettes that she had smoked throughout her life, and still did. She came across as being a bit eccentric and did not seem to understand the type of system that the professor used for his accounting. Her role as an accountant was to ask for a two-year cash flow projection and 12-month business plan budget. The third person in the team was a member of the professional indemnity insurance company, James Hopkiss. Hopkiss was in his late thirties; he was a tall, slim, good-looking and confident man wearing a very smart Savile Row hand-made tailored suit. Professor Noble estimated that the suit cost in the region of a thousand pounds, as it was a similar style to some of the professor's own suits. Hopkiss also wore a pair of Church's shoes and a tailored Eton shirt, with an open collared neck and no tie. The professor estimated that the total cost of James Hopkiss' attire was just under two thousand pounds.

Hopkiss had climbed the ladder of the insurance company very quickly and straight to the top - he was on the board of directors and he dressed to impress. He did not impress the professor as the professor knew that James Hopkiss was not there today to be nice, it was to intimidate him. The professor had had the same investigation carried out when the first claim was made against him, just over fifteen years earlier. The previous claim was not as serious but, as well as the insurers' paying out compensation to the claimant, the professor received a hefty fine. He also received a warning, which was the normal course of action, followed by an increased insurance premium and excess. The increased premium was "purely a coincidence", according to the insurers and apparently reflected the current market conditions. The professor knew that it was another way for the insurers to punish him further and get some money back from the claim that they had paid.

The team of investigators were there until seven o'clock that evening and returned for three more days. All file notes were read and re-read thoroughly, along with notes from similar surgeries undertaken by the professor over the past few years. All of the professors' surgeries were filmed as part of the professors' own insistence, this one was no exception. It was compelling evidence against the professor and showed the exact moment that the error was made when the scalpel nicked the nerve. It did not look good.

Upon leaving after the final day of what seemed like interrogation to the professor, James Hopkiss gave the professor a nasty scowled smile. He pointed his finger at the professor. "You're finished, Noble," he told him, in the most unprofessional way. Professor Noble could not believe how unprofessional James Hopkiss had been throughout, and how any insurance company could employ someone like this.

A few weeks after the investigation Professor Noble received the letter that he had been dreading. He had expected a hefty fine and a further increase in the insurance premium as previously, but no...The letter he received from Charlotte Mobbs was far from that. "I recommend that the insurers do not continue to insure either you or your clinic, with immediate effect." The letter stated. "You will no longer be allowed to carry on with surgery for a period of two years and after that time, it would have to be under strict supervision." The letter continued. In effect, Professor Noble's career was over as in two years' time he would be over sixty years old and there were many younger surgeons coming up through the system. The letter also went on to say that there was no challenge to this decision. Professor Noble could not believe the content of the letter which he had received, this was only the second complaint against him in thirty years. Noble spoke with several of his colleagues, in the industry, and not one of them could believe how unfair the punishment was. All of them would have expected a fine, but not a full ban. Something was clearly not right and the professor was determined to find out what was going on.

Professor Noble asked his daughter, Judith, to try to get insurance through other insurance companies. It was not her line of expertise but, as tends to be the case, if one insurer refuses to insure you then the others follow suit, like lemmings or baby ducks in a row. No other insurance company would insure him. As a result of this, Professor Noble could not carry on his practice, something which he had nurtured from a start-up clinic to become the successful clinic that it was today. He was forced to close the clinic and make the staff that he employed, redundant. He felt that he had let his team down and he spoke with the consultants in the other clinics in the building in Harley Street, including Professor Tomkins, to see if they would take on his staff as they had been so loyal to him.

Luckily, they did, although it was probably not luck but the amazing work references which the professor had given them. The two administrative staff went to work in the breast augmentation clinic whilst the anaesthetist went to the ophthalmology clinic. Doctor Harris went to work with Professor Clement Tomkins, in his open-heart surgery clinic on the ground floor. They were all re-employed in the same building as before.

As far as the professor was concerned, he would not be working. He had however, amassed a vast fortune over the years and knew that he would not have major financial issues, at least for a few years. Both the house and apartment were heavily mortgaged but there were only a few years left until the endowment policies, taken out twenty years earlier to pay off the capital amounts, would mature. He knew that he and Elizabeth would have to cut back on their luxury lifestyle and after a meeting with their financial adviser, Mark Ballak and his now retired accountant brother Nigel, it was decided that they would sell the lease on the Harley Street offices, to another surgeon – for this they made a good profit. It was also believed that there were sufficient reserves to last about five years before the money would start to run out. He rented the apartment in Knightsbridge to a wealthy business man from the Middle East. The income covered the monthly mortgage payments, even showing a profit.

Chapter Six

SIX MONTHS AGO

It had been eighteen months since the professor received the devastating news about being refused insurance to carry on working. It was proving more difficult than either the professor or his wife had thought to reduce the outgoings to a manageable level, but they did their best. Once word got out about his situation, the seminars stopped and no one wanted to read his books any more. It was very demoralising for a person of such a high standing to be reduced to this. Many of his so-called friends had moved on to befriend other people – it really was a way of finding out who your true friends were. They had reduced their restaurant visits from every week to once a month, they had stopped the VIP hospitality and stayed in most weekends. Instead of going out to eat they would invariably get take-aways of either Indian food from The Veeraswamy restaurant, an excellent Indian Restaurant just off Regent Street, or even fish and chips from the award winning Sea Shell restaurant in Lisson Grove in the Marylebone area of London. There were nearer restaurants to their house but it was food that they liked and until things were absolutely desperate, they did not want to give up everything that they were used to. They would still go to La JaSte and would be treated well by the owners who, after all, were their children.

Fortunately, the apartment over-looking Hyde Park was self-funding as it was rented. The value of the apartment had risen significantly so, if he needed to sell it, he would make a nice profit although a large part of any profit would have to go to the Government in Capital Gains Tax. In order to maintain his Private Pilot's Licence, it had to be renewed annually by flying a minimum of twelve hours a year. One hour of this had to be with a dedicated instructor and at least three take offs and landings, as required by the Civil Aviation Authority. Professor

Noble maintained his licence as the cost was minimal and there was an annual medical which he wanted to keep taking. The Cessna was paid for in full and the storage charge at Elstree was paid in advance for five years, including servicing. He had invested his money wisely whilst he was earning well and this helped him maintain some of his previous lifestyle without having to find additional funds. Elizabeth had changed her car from the gas guzzling Range Rover to a Tesla Model Y. It was slightly smaller than her husband's Model S; the monthly cost was less and, like the Model S, the cost of electricity was far lower than the cost of the petrol that she had used in the Range Rover.

Professor Noble had kept in touch with his many surgeon colleagues and friends and he was offered a part-time job by his friend, Luke Randall. The work was initially at a desk, with the intention of starting to carry out surgery as a junior surgeon under full time supervision; as per the letter from Charlotte Mobbs, at a leading teaching hospital in London. It was a nine to five job, three days a week. He still had lots of time to spend with his wife, family and the remaining friends who hadn't lost contact with him. It was a job and, although the pay was far less than the professor had been used to earning, it kept his mind occupied. Luckily, he had such a strong relationship with Elizabeth, that she was there to support him through all of the rough times and sleepless nights which he had suffered since the day he received the letter from Charlotte Mobbs. It gave the professor time to think. To think about the wrongs that had been done to him by a team of just three people. Charlotte Mobbs, James Hopkiss and Clementine Follows. Three people who had ruined his career and his way of life. It also gave him time to look in to the private lives of those three people, he was thinking of ways in which he could obtain his revenge on them for what they had done to him. It was the thought of this which kept him strong and determined to carry on. He had used his spare time to search through the many medical journals available and the internet and, with social media abundant, it was easy to find out more information about the main investigator, Charlotte Mobbs. Mobbs had accounts with most of the social media and liked to post photos of her cats, of which she had three – all black but with such different features that it was easy to tell them apart.

She was divorced from her wife, had no children and lived alone in a large detached house amongst a similar style and age of houses in one of the best roads in Mill Hill, in the north west London suburb of Barnet.

Professor Noble had decided what he was going to do. It was a drastic choice but one to which he had given a lot of thought and realised the potential consequences. He knew that he would have to plan meticulously. He manged to obtain access to Charlotte Mobbs' work schedule by using the password code on his computer to access the staff roster at the General Medical Council. Her work profile was all about setting professional standards of doctors, surgeons and specialists – she thought of herself as the "industry police". He had also obtained information including floor plans and photographs of Charlotte Mobbs' house using one of the numerous web sites where properties are listed for sale. He saw that she had bought her house only a few years ago, for over a million pounds. Professor Noble would drive past her house in Mill Hill on his way to Elstree aerodrome and sometimes park his car around the corner to see if she was at home to try and trace her movements. He had done this on many occasions, including on one occasion where he had actually seen Mobbs getting out of her car, she didn't see him. He saw that Mobbs' property was large and had a monitored security alarm system. The house had its own driveway and garage and he noticed a very expensive brand new white Mercedes C Class Cabriolet in the driveway. Professor Noble knew what Mobbs' salary pay grade was and something was clearly not right. He was determined to find out what was she doing in order to be able to afford the house and car - it could not just be based on her salary. Professor Noble decided to look in to this further but he was also looking in to the two other people who had brought down his career, Clementine Follows and James Hopkiss. He was starting to plot his revenge.

19

Chapter Seven

Clementine Follows

Clementine Follows was not as easy to find, she was an elderly woman and it seems that she did not like the internet or social media. Professor Noble knew from his conversation with her when she came up to his clinic that she lived in a market town in East Anglia on the east coast of England, but no more than that. He looked on line at many search engines and typed her name in followed by East Anglia. The search result came back with only one result from a local newspaper, the East Anglia Gazette. The newspaper was published weekly and this article was about an eccentric elderly female accountant who had recently been struck off from the accountancy profession for unstated reasons. Professor Noble thought that this must surely be the same person. He telephoned the local journalist Patrick Hendrick, who had written the article, and found out that Clementine Follows had been struck off for falsifying the accounts of several firms and was lucky not to have been put in to prison for her crimes. Professor noble hadn't told the journalist why he was interested in Clementine Follows, but as all good journalists would do, he thought that there may be another side to the story. Patrick Hendrick intended to find out why this man from London wanted to know so much about an old lady in an old age home.

Clementine Follows had sold her possessions, including her home, to fight the law suits against her. She had lost as she had no defence against the crimes which she had committed. Follows was now in a government run warden assisted living home for the over 60's. It had been provided to her by the state and was on the outskirts of Bury St Edmunds. Patrick Hendrick refused to give out Clementine Follows' address but Professor Noble's online research suggested that there was only one such facility in Bury St Edmunds. He decided to take a look for himself. He put the address in the sat nav section of the 17-inch screen in his Tesla and it told him how long the journey would take – it also advised him that he would have to stop for a top up charge in the services at Bishops Stortford on the M11 motorway, near Stanstead Airport. The route took him along the M25 and M11 motorways, stopping for a charge to the car battery of 30 minutes in the Tesla owned Supercharging network, this added over 150 miles to the depleted battery range. During the thirty minutes there was time for a toilet break, coffee and a pastry. He particularly enjoyed a warm pain au raisin from Pret a Manger. After his break, he continued the journey on the M11 motorway, past Cambridge, which he knew so well from his college days, and then along several A roads, past Newmarket, until he reached the outskirts of Bury St Edmunds to see for himself. The assisted living home was a run-down block of flats, built in the 1960's of grey concrete panels and resembled a London local authority estate. He found out that Clementine Follows' flat was on the ground floor of the three-storey block and had direct access to a small private patio which opened on to communal gardens. The gardens were overgrown and generally badly maintained. Professor Noble waited for a while and finally saw an old woman shuffling slowly along from her flat to the garden area, using a Zimmer frame. She sat down on a shaky chair at an old wooden slatted table, in the garden. The woman only vaguely resembled the accountant who had visited his clinic less than two years earlier. She had already been old and very thin when he met her in his clinic, but now she had the appearance of being at death's door. Her thin grey nicotine-stained hair was even thinner than when he had last seen her. Her clothes were too large for her as she had clearly lost even more weight. She had aged considerably in the short space of time between her visit to his clinic and now, presumably due to the stress and strains of the court cases against her. Professor Noble walked over to Clementine Follows in her garden and sat down in the chair next to her. "Remember me?" he asked the old woman. Clementine Follows looked carefully at him through squinted eyes, her decades of looking at accounting books and figures had taken a toll on her eyes. She eventually recognised him and the first words she spoke were damning. "It was criminal what that woman did to you," she said with a croaky voice. A voice which he hardly recognised from the woman who he had met in his clinic. "She and her team of associates are up to no good," she continued. "They have done this, and other worse things, to many other professional people and must be stopped". Professor Noble assumed that Clementine Follows was referring to Charlotte Mobbs and James Hopkiss. He tried to ask her questions but Clementine Follows had fallen asleep whilst sitting in her chair. The professor left; he had decided that Karma had taken over and that he would leave her to die alone and in misery. He drove back home in the comfort of his car, with the words which Clementine Follows had said going round and round in his head. It made him even more determined to carry out his revenge on the people who ruined his name and career. On his way home he telephoned Patrick Hendrick from his hands-free car phone. He told the journalist that he had been to see the old woman in the warden assisted home. Professor Noble explained that he was involved in one of her cases and was curious as to what had happened to her. He asked Patrick Hendrick to advise him of any changes, the journalist seemed only too happy to assist. The professor didn't have to wait long. It was only a week later when he received a call from Patrick Hendrick, saying that Clementine Follows had been found dead in her apartment. She had died of old age and no suspicious circumstances. There had been a funeral, but no-one had attended. Professor Noble felt sorry for Clementine Follows for a moment, but only a brief moment, as he remembered the hard time she had given him during their meeting. A few days after the funeral had taken place, the journalist called Professor Noble. A sealed envelope had been left in Clementine Follows' flat and was found by the warden, whilst she was clearing out the flat. It had the professor's name on the envelope. The warden didn't know who the professor was, but remembered the article in the local newspaper and called Patrick Hendrick. The conversation between Patrick Hendrick and Professor Noble was brief. The journalist advised the professor of the envelope and, on the professor's instruction, he opened the envelope. Inside the envelope was a single piece of white un-lined paper. On the paper were the following words, written in bold letters. "TAKE DOWN CHARLOTTE MOBBS BEFORE SHE RUINS MORE PEOPLE'S LIVES, SHE IS CROOKED". Hendricks was intrigued by this. He didn't know who Charlotte Mobbs was, but Professor Noble knew exactly who she was and what it meant. Patrick Hendrick asked Professor Noble if there was a story for him to write. "As soon as I can tell you, I will, I promise" the Professor said to Hendrick.

Chapter Eight

James Hopkiss

James Hopkiss was more difficult to find as his insurance company was based in Manhattan, New York. Professor Noble asked his daughter, Judith, to find out information about him as she was high up in the insurance business, being a director of an insurance broking firm. Judith confirmed that James Hopkiss was indeed on the board of directors of the insurance company who used to insure her father. James was the youngest director in the company and despised by most of his co-workers because of this. He tended to use ruthless tactics and use people to his own advantage. James loved the internet and social media outlets. He would post photos of himself and his wife on vacation in the Caribbean, staying in expensive five-star luxury resorts, drinking expensive wines, on fishing trips in the Pacific Ocean, off the coast of California with his in-laws. Professor Noble thought that James' life style reminded him a bit of his own. He needed to find out some more information, some secrets that would not be found on social media. Professor Noble decided that the best way for this would be to take a short trip to New York. He told Elizabeth of his plan and that, after all that had happened recently, they needed to have some time away. They had not had a proper holiday for two years and suggested that they went on an extended, albeit restricted, shopping trip and holiday to New York. He contacted the Centurion Card concierge at American Express and told them what he wanted. What he wanted was Upper Class flights with Virgin Atlantic on their new Airbus A350 as it had an improved Upper Class Suite more in line with Emirates Fist Class, which they had flown on to the Maldives, via Dubai, only a few years earlier. As they were having to cut costs, they ended up using Virgin Atlantic Air Miles, which they had collected over the years, in order to upgrade to Upper Class. The professor knew that the insurance office where James Hopkiss worked was in the Financial District of Manhattan. It was close to Battery Park where the ferry terminal is located and where you can get a ferry across to Liberty Island to the Statue of Liberty. It was also not far from the site of the Twin Towers of the World Trade Centre, which had been destroyed so publicly, in the worst terrorist attack on the United States, on September 11th 2001 – 911 as it has become known. He did not know where James Hopkiss lived and had contacted a private detective, Hannah Cozin, in New York. Hannah had been highly recommended to him by his friend, Linda Crossland, as she had solved the murder of Linda's husband before the police even arrived on the scene. Although the insurance office building was at the lower end of Manhattan, the professor asked the concierge of American Express to arrange for a hotel suite near to Central Park, as he preferred the open space there. There are several great hotels close to Central Park so the professor left it to the concierge to book one. The chosen hotel was The Plaza Hotel on the corner of Fifth Avenue an W59th Street. They could no longer afford to pay in full for a suite, instead they used the hotel points, which they had collected over the years. They also had the benefit of an upgrade, by using the American Express card. Not just any old suite but the Grand Penthouse Terrace Suite located on the penthouse level, 20th floor of the Plaza with amazing views of Central Park and the New York City skyline. It was all arranged. The flight was the VS45 from London Heathrow Airport, due to leave at 1:30pm in two days' time on the Airbus A350 with two suites booked in Upper Class and due to arrive at JFK airport in New York at 4:15pm on the same day. The timings were perfect, due to the five-hour time difference between London and New York. As part of the Upper Class experience a chauffeur driven limo was booked to take the professor and his wife from their home in Hampstead to Heathrow airport and also from JFK to their hotel.

Chapter Nine

The day of the flight had arrived and the chauffeur driven Mercedes S Class was parked outside the Hampstead house right on time. The chauffeur, Stefan, was smartly dressed in a dark grey suit as he went up to the gates at the entrance to the driveway and rang the buzzer. The gates opened and he drove to the front door. Stefan was in his early thirties, well-groomed with short brown hair and, introduced himself to the Nobles. Stefan had a slight eastern European accent as he introduced himself to Elizabeth, as it were she who opened the door. Stefan took the luggage from the house and put the large cases into the boot of the car. The professor kept his lap top case and pouch containing their tickets and passports with him in the car and Elizabeth kept her Chanel bag with her. The rush hour traffic and school traffic, which can be so bad in the morning and late afternoon in Hampstead and most of London, had finished. The journey to Heathrow was pleasant as Stefan negotiated the roadworks on the M4 motorway and entered into the tunnel at the entrance to the airport, this was a route that he had driven on so many occasions. Stefan guided the car to the Upper Class Drive-In area at the rear of Terminal 3. He stopped the car at the barrier and pressed the intercom to announce that he had arrived. He gave the name of the professor and Elizabeth to the person on the other end of the intercom, along with their flight number. The barrier rose swiftly and Stefan drove to the drop off point where the car was met by two very smartly dressed Virgin Atlantic staff members. The luggage was removed from the boot of the car and taken through to the reception area. There was a check-in desk and seating area, along with the customary large, scale-model of a Virgin Atlantic aeroplane. The professor and Elizabeth checked in and proceeded to the security area and Duty-Free section beyond. They perused the very busy Duty-Free shops where the professor bought a large bottle of Creed Aventus after shave and Elizabeth bought a large bottle of Chanel no.5 perfume. They left the Duty-Free area, with their purchases and proceeded to the

Virgin Atlantic Clubhouse, which is in a separate area of the airport, away from the hustle and bustle of the main terminal. They were greeted by the front desk staff who were immaculately dressed in their smart red uniforms and taken through to the Clubhouse. Inside the Clubhouse there was a large bar, several seating areas, a restaurant as well as a TV area with a huge screen, which dwarfed the size of even the professor's large home TV screen. There was a library area and also a hair and beauty section where treatments were available. There was also an open viewing area, approached via a lift, where aircraft operations could be viewed – this was of particular interest to the professor, due to having a private pilot's licence. The professor and Elizabeth decided that they would go to the restaurant where the professor ordered a burger and Elizabeth ordered Smoked Salmon and scrambled eggs, all of which arrived within a few minutes and was cooked to perfection. They had some coffee, after which Elizabeth went to the seating area to relax and the professor went up to the viewing gallery. It was a clear day and there were lots to see from the viewing gallery. There were so many different types of aircraft at the stands, including Boeing Dreamliners and triple sevens, as well as Airbus A350's and A330's all capable of transporting hundreds of passengers to all areas of the world – the professor felt like a child in a sweet shop.

The time in the Clubhouse passed very quickly and it was soon time to board the aeroplane. The gate was announced as gate 19 which was a ten-minute walk from the Clubhouse, even using the several travelators, to get to the gate. When they arrived at the gate the professor and his wife went through the additional security checks and straight on to the front section of the aeroplane where the Upper Class cabin was located. Each of the aeroplanes in the Virgin Atlantic fleet has its own name. The aeroplane which they were on today was G VEVE and was named 'Fearless Lady', it was named after Eve, the mother of the owner, Sir Richard Branson, as she had recently passed away. The Upper Class flight attendants were very smartly dressed in their bright red uniform, well-manicured nails and professionally tied up hair in bunches. The chief attendant welcomed the professor and his wife by name and introduced herself as

Miranda. She brought them champagne and the Upper Class amenity kit as well as the food menu for the flight. There was going to be a lunch and afternoon tea service on the flight. The flight time was announced by the first officer from the flight deck as being approximately seven hours and thirty minutes and there was no bad weather in the forecast – this was welcomed by Elizabeth, as she was a slightly nervous flyer. The captain of today's flight was Captain Skye, one of many female captains employed in the airline industry. Captain Skye had started her flying career much in the same way as the professor; learning in a small single engine Cessna, before progressing to the military and obtained her Commercial Licence, flying mainly short haul flights on A320's as first officer and then captain. She had worked for Virgin Atlantic for over five years and was now the captain of the A350. Having flown over 7,000 hours, she was a very experienced captain and proud of what she had achieved. The external cabin doors were closed and Captain Skye had finished her pre take off checks. The plane soon started to be pushed back on to the tarmac by the pushback tug, a small vehicle with tremendous strength, enough to push such a very heavy aircraft. There were a few other aeroplanes lining up in front of 'Fearless Lady' and there was a wait of about ten minutes before the large jet turned left on to the beginning of runway Two Seven Right, the northern runway, as it was to take off directly in to the west. It was a fine sunny day with only a thin layer of stratus clouds breaking the blue skies.

Captain Skye pushed the throttles forward together to full thrust, working the twin Rolls-Royce Trent XWB-97 jet engines as they are designed to be used. The aeroplane started to trundle forward along the runway until she built up the correct speed to lift off the tarmac and in to the air above the M25 motorway and the large reservoirs to the west of Heathrow. Soon the jet was above the clouds and on its way to JFK, New York. The service on the flight was superb and the food was great, just like some of the fine restaurants in which the professor and Elizabeth were used to eating. It was a day flight and not easy to have a full sleep but there was time to catch a short nap and watch a film. It seemed only a short while before the first officer was announcing that they would soon be starting the descent to JFK, where the weather was also dry and sunny, a beautiful day. After a smooth landing Captain Skye manoeuvred 'Fearless Lady' to the apron and stand at JFK's Terminal 4. A few minutes later the doors opened and the passengers were disembarked. The dreaded wait to get through passport control was fairly long but they used the Fast-Track system and by-passed most of the queues. They collected their luggage from the conveyor and were picked up by the chauffeur in a smart Town Car taking them to The Plaza at the southern end of Central Park.

Chapter Ten

They were met at the entrance to The Plaza hotel by John, who was to be their private butler for the course of their stay. John was an elderly gentleman who reminded the professor a bit of his father. John, or "Jack" as he wanted to be called, had kind blue eyes, was a bit overweight but not obese, and wore a distinctive butler uniform suit which fitted him well. Jack had been their private butler on their previous stay at the hotel. "Welcome back," he said to them before asking the usual polite questions about the flight and journey. "The weather forecast is good for your entire stay." He took them in the lift to the 20th floor and unlocked the door to the suite. Once inside the suite, Jack showed Professor Noble and Elizabeth around the suite and how to use the facilities. He explained that they had use of the chauffeur driven Rolls-Royce for the duration of their stay and then left them alone to explore the suite, saying that he would be back in thirty minutes to unpack their luggage. The first floor of the suite had a large living room, a dining room, a powder room and a King Bedroom with bathroom. There was an elegant staircase leading to the second floor where there was a main bedroom with a king bed, an en-suite bathroom with a large bath and walk in shower, there was also a large private terrace. There were luxury wood panelled wardrobes, the bathrooms had beautiful mosaic tiled floors and walls with a gilded floral motif and 24 carat gold plated fixtures. The views across Central Park were breath taking, but this was not the reason that they were in New York. The professor had work to do.

They ordered room service for dinner in their room. Jack brought their dinner on a silver trolley and set up the table on the terrace overlooking Central Park, on what was a warm, clear and starlit night in Manhattan. They discussed their plans for the following day. Elizabeth was going to do some light retail therapy on Fifth Avenue whilst the professor was going to meet with the private investigator with whom he had made contact with before they flew out to New York. They were both tired. It had been a long day and along with some jet lag they went to bed, to sleep, in one of the most comfortable King Size beds that they had ever slept in.

Chapter Eleven

The following morning the professor awoke early, it was five o'clock in the morning and he was jet lagged, Elizabeth was fast asleep and he decided to go for a run in Central Park to wake himself up. The hotel was just across from the park on the opposite side of W 59th Street with the nearest entrance being at the Grand Army Plaza at the corner of W 59th street and Fifth Avenue. Professor Noble had packed his running gear with him and changed in to this in the bathroom. He gave his sleeping wife a kiss and went on his run. Central Park can get extremely busy during the day, with this entrance being probably the busiest due to its proximity to the hotels. However, at five o'clock in the morning, it was less busy and mainly being used by likeminded joggers, enjoying the early morning sun before it got too hot. He ran down the narrow pathway that leads down to The Pond, past the iconic Lombard Lamp and in to one of the most photographed areas of New York. Although Central Park is approximately two and a half miles long and a half mile wide, the professor only wanted to do a short route today to freshen his mind and body after the flight. He chose to run in an anti-clockwise direction over Gapstow Bridge, past the Nature Sanctuary and The Waterfalls acknowledging the several other joggers in the park. He noticed that most of the other joggers had ear pods in and were listening to music or pod casts. He had spotted the Apple Store on the opposite side of Fifth Avenue from the hotel and made a mental note to go there and buy himself a set of Air Pods for his next run. He was clearly out of condition, sweating profusely, but soon arrived back at the Grand Army Plaza exit. There were more people around now with workers on their commute to work using the nearby Subway and Taxis. He returned to his room where Elizabeth was starting to wake up. He admired how beautiful she looked even first thing in the morning and realised how lucky he was to have her in his life. She also looked very sexy in her white silk La Perla night dress. Several thoughts were going through his mind but he was hot and sweaty after his run and needed to shower, a cold shower would probably be best, but that was not what he wanted. He undressed from his running gear and turned on the shower taps to get the temperature to a nice warm heat. He walked in to the shower cubicle, although cubicle was probably the wrong description, due to the fact that it was large enough for four or five people. He stood under the waterfall shower head and let the water run over his hair and down on to his body. He reached for the shower gel. He was using the shower gel provided by the hotel, it was from the Rose 31 collection of Le Labo and had a light rose scent, more woody than flowery and was a unisex product. It smelled sexy and made him feel a bit naughty, especially as the bottle came with a comment saying "for better results, have someone else apply it on you." The next thing he knew was that there was another pair of hands rubbing the gel over his body. Elizabeth had woken up and saw him in the shower. She had thought that, this morning in particular, her husband looked very sexy and fit for a man of his age and seeing him in the shower had turned her on. Elizabeth walked in to the bathroom and let her nightdress fall to the floor around her feet, she was naked. She also looked incredible for her age, and they both knew it. Their love making had reduced since the stress of her husband losing his work practice, to once a week instead of the two/three times a week that it had been. There was a time when they would make love all over the house but this was reduced to a quickie at the weekend. However, there was something about hotels that made them both relax and go wild. Elizabeth walked in to the shower cubicle and started to rub the gel in to her husband's back. Emerson turned around and Elizabeth rubbed the gel in to the front of his body, all over, paying particular attention to the lower abdomen area. Emerson then rubbed the gel on to his wife's body noticing how firm her breasts were and how erect her nipples were. They were both very turned on by what they were doing to each other. He turned Elizabeth around so that the back of her body was close to his front and she supported herself with her hands against the side of the shower cubicle. He entered her from behind and they made love in the shower as if they had just met, it was wild and the most amazing sex that they had had for some

33

time. They both came with strong orgasms, their bodies trembling in the aftermath. After rinsing in the warm water of the shower, they put on the robes provided by the hotel and cuddled for what seemed like ages.

Chapter Twelve

They ordered breakfast in their room from room service and within minutes there was a knock on the hotel suite door, it was Jack, their personal butler looking as smart as he had looked when they arrived the previous day. "Good morning," Jack said. "Where would you like the breakfast set up and served?" he asked. Emerson and Elizabeth both pointed to the terrace as a perfect place for breakfast; as it had been for the previous night's dinner with its views over Central Park. The table was set and the food was served. The sun was shining and it was a beautiful day with not a cloud in sight. The professor and his wife reconfirmed their plans for their separate day ahead. Elizabeth was wearing a beautiful creamy white Valentino shirt and Valentino blue denim jeans, which she had bought a few years earlier from Harrods in Knightsbridge along with a pair of white sandal shoes from Christian Louboutin, with their customary red soles. She also wore a classic black leather Chanel handbag with matching purse in which she kept her Black Centurion Amex Card. Emerson was wearing a smart pair of jeans with a white cotton Oxford style shirt, both from Ralph Lauren and a pair of Church's shoes. They were a great looking couple but today they were going their separate ways. It was ten o'clock in the morning and just the right time for the couple to make their way down to where the car was waiting for them. The car was a Rolls-Royce Phantom, just right for shopping in Fifth Avenue. It was the height of luxury with its sumptuous interior of hand-crafted wood and tanned leather, there were even stars in the ceiling and meticulous attention to detail right down to the electric footrests, champagne cooler and glasses. The chauffeur introduced himself to Elizabeth as Craig. He was smartly dressed in a classic grey chauffeur suit and hat. He opened the rear passenger door and Elizabeth stepped in. She kissed her husband on the cheek with a cheeky grin and smile, remembering their recent shower and whispered to him that there would be more to come later.

Chapter Thirteen

Empire State Detective Agency

The professor did not use the car as he was not going shopping with his wife, he was going to see a private detective, Hannah Cozin, his appointment was at eleven o'clock. The private detective agency was the Empire State Detective Agency based on the tenth floor of the iconic 1930's built, Empire State Building. The tall skyscraper was located on the west side of Fifth Avenue between 33rd Street to the south and 34th Street to the north with the entrance in Fifth Avenue. Emerson had checked the location on Google Maps and realised that it was only just over a mile from The Plaza Hotel, one road all of the way, Fifth Avenue. He decided that he would walk as it was such a lovely day. The walk along Fifth Avenue took just over 30 minutes. He stopped at the various cross walks and looked in some of the shop windows as he did not want to be too early for his appointment. The streets were busy with traffic and the pavements were busy with people shopping and sight-seeing. He stopped at an ATM machine close to the Empire State Building and took out enough cash for the meeting. He arrived at The Empire State Building ten minutes before eleven o'clock – perfect timing he thought. The doorman asked for his id. and showed the professor to the lift which would take him to the offices on the tenth floor. The lift door opened on the tenth floor and there was a long list of company names on a wall plaque. He found the room number for Empire State Detective Agency, which was shortened to E.S.D.A. and knocked on the part wood and part glass door. The glass was marked with the letters E.S.D.A, below the letters was a sign saying "incorporating Cozin Detective Agency." The waiting area was, in his opinion, very stereotypical of a private detective agency and reminded him of Philip Marlowe, a fictional private detective character in the Raymond Chandler books, which he read when he was younger. The door was opened by a young woman, in her early twenties. She had long straight black hair and a pale complexion, the red lipstick that she wore made her look scary. She was chewing gum and had a deep nasal New Jersey accent when she greeted the professor. Her name was Ava, apparently so named because her mother was a great fan of Ava Gardner, but the professor thought that Morticia, from The Addams family, would have been more appropriate. "Take a seat in the waiting area" Ava said to the professor. It was spoken with such a strong accent that the professor could only just understand what she had said. The waiting area was small, only about ten feet by ten, it was basic with a desk for Ava and had a computer screen and telephone. There was a door on the right side of the waiting area which had the name of the private detective with whom the professor had arranged the meeting, Hannah Cozin. There were two other doors from the waiting area, they were unmarked. The professor could not make out where they led but it appeared that they were leading to other offices and other detectives employed by Hannah, he was not completely wrong.

At precisely eleven o'clock Hannah Cozin's door was opened by a tall woman in her late thirties. She had long brown hair, tied in a bun at the top. She was dressed smartly with a dark two-piece trouser suit and white blouse. She introduced herself to the professor as Hannah, and invited him in to her office. Her accent was English. The room was not what he had expected, it was much larger than the waiting area, almost four times larger and much tidier. There was a large desk in front of a window, with some restricted views over the nearby streets. There was a leather Chesterton high back armchair behind the desk for Hannah and two more normal chairs for the clients, in front of the desk. There were three rows of four drawer filing cabinets by one wall, and a lower two drawer unit by their side. There was a laser printer on the lower drawer cabinet; some of the drawers were slightly open with the top of some of the paper files visible. There was also a wooden wall display cabinet with various whiskies and other

37

alcohol along with drinking glasses. On one wall there was the largest TV screen that the professor had ever seen, his TV in his Hampstead house was 75 inches but this was even larger. It had been set up as a CCTV monitoring system with boxes on the screen giving views of the waiting room, the lift area and corridor in the building they were in; as well as street level scenes, amongst others. On the desk there was another computer and keyboard as well as writing pads, pens and pencils. The computer was the most recent Apple iMac available and was linked wirelessly to the large TV monitor. The desk had drawers on either side of the central seating area. The professor could not see what was in the drawers, as they were closed, but wondered whether there was a gun. There was a coffee table on the far side of the room, a few more chairs and a coffee making machine. On the walls there were photos of Hannah Cozin receiving awards for excellency to her profession along with framed letters of appreciation from previous clients. There was also a photo of Hannah with a very handsome man, the professor thought that they were possibly married. Another photo was of Hannah with her father, Arthur Cozin, smartly dressed in his Metropolitan Police uniform. Most of Hannah's work came from recommendations and this was how the professor got her name, through Linda Crossland, one of his best friends who had used the services of E.S.D.A only a few years earlier.

The professor could tell as soon as he saw Hannah and the office that he had made the right choice. He sat in one of the client's chairs as the request of Hannah. The professor recognised her accent as being not just English, but from London, with a slight cockney twang, he liked it. He asked her where the accent was from but Hannah told him that her time is money and that she would talk to him on a personal level at the end of the meeting if he wanted, and also if she decided whether or not to take on his case. "Coffee, or something stronger?" Hannah asked the professor, pointing to the bottles of whisky on the wooden display cabinet. It was too early in the morning for the professor to partake in alcohol so he declined the latter and asked for a coffee. Hannah pressed one of the buttons on the telephone and the New Jersey accent of Ava sounded out, through the microphone. "Two coffees please Ava." Asked Hannah. A few moments later Ava entered the room and worked on the coffee machine to produce two hot and tasty Columbian Blend coffees. Hannah and the professor thanked Ava as they sipped the hot and strong coffee. "Hold all calls, please." Hannah ordered Ava and waited for Ava to leave the room. Ava closed the door behind her and Hannah and Professor Noble started their meeting.

They initially discussed the connection of Linda Crossland to both Hannah and the professor and the death of Linda's husband. Hannah remembered the case very well but would not discuss it with the professor as it was unethical. Hannah had already asked for a brief reason why the professor wanted to use her services when he had called her from England and now, she asked him for the full version. The professor told her everything he knew, which wasn't much. He told her the name of the insurance man, his company details and where he worked. That was all he really knew. "Leave it to me," Hannah said. "I will find out everything there is to know," she continued. She asked for a part-payment in advance and the professor handed her the cash which he had withdrawn only a few moments earlier from the nearby ATM. "I'll need a day and I will let you know of my progress." Hannah advised the professor. She stood by the window of her office with her back to the professor. She stared out looking at the people in the streets below. They all looked so small from the height where she was standing. She then told the professor her own story. "Thank you," replied Professor Noble and he exited the room.

Chapter Fourteen

Hannah Cozin

Hannah Cozin was born in Hackney in east London. Her father was Arthur Cozin, a high-ranking Detective Chief Inspector, working for the Metropolitan Police. Her mother, Hilda, was an NHS nurse. They lived in a large Victorian terraced house overlooking the vast open space of Victoria Park. Hannah had gone to the local school where she did well in Maths and English but she particularly liked the sciences. She spent a lot of time with her father discussing the type of work that he did, and she would try and help solve his cases. Hannah left school with good A level grades and went on to Oxford University, where she studied Criminal Justices and Computer Technology. She was very computer literate and she wanted to follow in her father's footsteps. She also wanted to have more knowledge of the workings of the computer system. It was a three-year course and she lived in student accommodation close to the campus. Hannah studied very complex areas around why crime happens, how to prevent crime, the workings of the criminal justice system and agencies such as police, courts, prison as well as sociology and psychology. She finished with a First-Class Honours Degree in both of her courses, of which she and her family were very proud.

During her studies Hannah had met a man, Matt Hewson. Matt was an American who had come to England to study Criminology at the same Oxford University as Hannah. He was a few years older than Hannah and they soon became friends, good friends. Matt was from East Hampton, Long Island, New York and came from a wealthy family. His parents wanted him to study law at one of the top American colleges such as Yale or Harvard but Matt had wanted to travel, and in particular travel to Europe. Although it was not what his parents wanted him to do, they were not going to prevent him from doing what he wanted and gave him a very healthy allowance for his travels. Matt went to the capital cities as well as beaches and rural areas around Europe but he mostly enjoyed his time in England and stayed in London as his base. He used the public transport system but would hire a car to go further afield. After several months of travelling, Matt decided that he wanted to study Criminal Law in the UK. His parents arranged for him to go to Oxford University, where he met Hannah. They spent every minute together and for the last year of their studies they shared a flat together in the centre of Oxford. Once they had graduated, Matt asked Hannah to go with him to New York to meet his parents. Matt had already met Hannah's parents and they all got on really well together. Hannah did not hesitate to go with Matt as she really liked him. Initially they stayed in Matt's parents' house which was a very large house close to the beach.

After a few months they decided that they wanted to live together, alone, and rented an apartment in West 65th Street in the Upper West Side area of Manhattan.

It was a smart two bedroomed apartment on the third floor of a seven-storey brick-built building between Broadway and Central Park. There was a resident concierge who would open the doors for the residence and arrange taxis if required.

Chapter Fifteen

Matt Hewson

Hannah reminisced about Matt and what happened to him. They had lived in their apartment in West 65th Street in the Upper West Side area of Manhattan for three months when Matt decided that he was going to propose to Hannah. He had gone to Tiffany's in Fifth Avenue and bought a sparkling flawless two carat bright white diamond ring, with excellent cut quality, it was not cheap, but worth every cent. He had not told Hannah where he was going, as it was to be a surprise. He was served by a senior assistant called Natalie, who told him that the ring was beautiful and must have been for a very special person. Matt agreed. Natalie went to a room at the back of the store and wrapped the ring in the classic Tiffany blue box.

It was late afternoon and warm, so he decided to walk the two-mile route home from Tiffany's. Matt did not see the two men who had been waiting at the entrance to Central Park – but they had seen Matt and decided to follow him from a distance. Matt took the scenic route through Central Park when he realised that he was being followed by the two men. He picked up his pace, but so did the two men. There were some people a few hundred yards away, but no one else in the immediate vicinity, when one of the men walked quickly past him and drew a gun. Matt recognised it as a Smith and Wesson hand gun. Matt stopped walking but the second man now stood behind him and held, what Matt assumed was another gun pushed in to his back.

"Hand over your wallet and phone and empty your pockets!" they demanded. Matt knew that he should not argue with the man but all he could think of was the ring and proposing to Hannah. He took out his wallet and phone and also the Tiffany box with the diamond ring. Matt was quite muscular and in good condition so it must have been a rush of blood that went to his head as he struggled with the two men. The gun from the man who was behind Matt shot a bullet into the upper part of Matt's back and directly in to his heart. Matt died immediately. The two men grabbed the items from Matt and ran. There was a pool of blood forming around Matt's body when a young woman saw the body and stopped. "Help! Help!" she shouted, and soon a crowd gathered. The young woman 911 and asked for the police; she told them where she was and what had happened.

Within minutes the police had arrived from their patrol at the northern end of Central Park. They created a barrier around the body and called for backup. Soon several police officers arrived from the 18th precinct in Midtown North, the 19th precinct was also nearby but were further away in Upper East Side, so it was the 18th who took the case. The lead detective was Lieutenant Krakowski, the grandson of a Polish immigrant, he may have had a Polish name but did not speak a word of the language. He understood it very well, as it was spoken in his house when he was growing up. Krakowski led a team of three detectives, Harper, Johns and Dawson; they took witness statements from the crowd which had now arrived at the scene. No one had seen the crime take place but several people had heard the shot being fired. One, an elderly man, had seen two men running away but could not describe them to the police as he was not wearing his spectacles. The id. of Matt had been taken during the robbery and the detectives did not know his identity. They knocked on doors in the nearby streets and avenues but no one recognised his photo, admittedly it was a photo taken of him lying dead on the ground, but still a photo.

A few hours had passed when Hannah started to be concerned as to where Matt was. He had been secretive about where he was going as it was going to be a surprise, but when she called his phone, it went straight to voicemail. Hannah was in her apartment and went in to the kitchen to make herself a cup of coffee. She turned the TV on and changed the channel to the local news channel. The presenter was talking about how a robbery had gone wrong in Central Park, someone had been shot dead. The detective asked for any witnesses to come forward. Hannah was not paying too much attention but when the detective on the news said that they did not know who had been shot and showed the photo of Matt, she recognised him immediately. She pushed the hold button on the remote control and stared at the screen. She was devastated and her entire body started to shake. She sat on the floor, curled up in to a ball, and cried. She was shrieking so loudly that she didn't hear her neighbour, Stella, knock on the door. After a few minutes of no reply and still hearing the shrieking in Hannah's apartment, Stella opened the door with the key which Hannah had given her to use in cases of emergency. This definitely sounded like an emergency. Stella found Hannah on the kitchen floor; the TV screen was still on hold with Matt's photo in full view. Stella comforted Hannah as best she could under the circumstances and eventually got Hannah to sit in a chair and gave her a glass of water to sip. Several more minutes passed until Hannah managed to compose herself. She thanked Stella for helping her and, with shaking hands, Hannah called the phone number at the bottom of the TV screen and was put through to Lieutenant Krakowski.

Lieutenant Krakowski asked Hannah to come to the precinct to identify the body. She was going to call Matt's parents but decided not to worry them just yet, in case it was not him; but Hannah knew that it was. The detective sent a patrol car to pick up Hannah from her apartment. Stella insisted that she went along to provide strength for Hannah, Hannah agreed. After a short drive, which seemed like miles to Hannah, they were escorted by a female police officer to a small room where a body of a man was lying on a metal table. Hannah recognised the clothes that the dead man was wearing as the clothes that Matt had put on that very morning, before going out on his mystery day. She recognised his face immediately and collapsed to the ground in tears, she started to shake. Stella and the police officer helped Hannah to her feet and found a chair for her to sit in, the police officer also arranged for a bottle of water. It took Hannah thirty minutes before she could speak, she was so devastated. When she spoke it was to ask the police officer to call Matt's parents and tell them where she was and what had happened to their son. Hannah filled in some forms and made a statement about where she was that day. Matt's parents soon arrived and

Stella left them with Hannah. The three people cried and cuddled in the police precinct. Matt's funeral was held a few days later. The service was in the local church close to his parents' house where hundreds of people attended, including Hannah's parents Hilda and Arthur, who had come over from England. It was a lovely service, under the circumstances; everyone who spoke had only good things to say about Matt. The service over-ran the time slot, there was another service waiting but the priest did not seem to mind. Matt's body was buried in the grounds of the church and Hannah was the first person to place flowers on top of his coffin.

Chapter Sixteen

A few weeks had passed and there were still no leads on who had robbed and murdered Matt. There was no history of similar attacks in the area either before or after Matt's attack, and still no witnesses. The CCTV cameras in Central Park had, for no apparent reason, stopped working on that day about half an hour before Matt was murdered. Was that just a coincidence? Hannah thought to herself.

Hannah's parents were still in New York when Hannah suggested to her father that they should try to find out what had happened to Matt. The police had not been able to progress the case further. Hannah's father was, after all, a Detective Chief Inspector with the Metropolitan Police force and Hannah was his protégé. Hannah introduced her father to Lieutenant Krakowski and told him that they would be looking in to the murder of her fiancé. Krakowski was not overly pleased with this news but as he had not been able to progress the case, he humoured them. Hannah had made some contacts in the computer world as part of her university studies, in England, and had kept in contact with them. They were now top-class computer hackers and knew every aspect of how to access even the most secure of computer systems. The main computer hacker went under the name of "Splinter". He had taken the name as a result of the speed in which he typed on the computer keyboard. "If the keyboard had been made of wood, then he would have got splinters in his fingers," was what he was told on many occasions, by his colleagues. The name Splinter was used ever since. Splinter become the world's most infamous hacker ever since he hacked in to US Government, NASA and the Federal Reserve, amongst others.

Hannah explained the situation to Splinter. Splinter and his team were more than happy to help her, especially as they had also known Matt. She told them the time and date of the murder and they were on the case. But it was not computers that broke the case, it was by talking to people. Hannah returned to the apartment where she lived with Matt, she was with her father. They were about to enter the lift when the resident concierge, George, approached them. George had been on vacation for a few days and this was the first time that he had seen Hannah since the murder. There had been an assistant concierge on duty the day of the murder. The deputy on duty whilst George was away was Jason, a former bodybuilder turned concierge. It was his first job but he was nowhere to be found since the day of the murder. George told Hannah that, when he returned to duty, he found a note for Matt with directions to Tiffany in Fifth Avenue. Hannah stood for a moment to take in the news that she had just heard. She thanked George for the information and asked him if he had told the police. He hadn't told them as when they came to interview the concierge, George was away and the assistant concierge did not tell that to the police. Hannah and her father did not go to the apartment but turned around and hailed a yellow taxi cab to take them to Tiffany. No words were spoken in the taxi. The journey was just under two miles and it took fifteen minutes as the traffic was light. When they arrived at Tiffany, Hannah and her father went to customer services and asked for the store manager. The manager at first refused to assist, stating data protection rules which prevented him from giving information to a third party without the consent of the person involved.

Once they had explained that Matt could not be there because he had been murdered, he looked in to their computer system. He could see that there had been many transactions on the day of Matt's murder but when Hannah showed him a photo of Matt that she had on her iPhone, he remembered him.

He remembered Matt because of the expensive engagement ring that he had purchased that day. He asked Hannah if she had received the item, but she had not. She began to cry and her father put his arm around her.

What they had was a time trail; they knew that Matt had left Tiffany at about 4pm and that he had walked back to their apartment through Central Park. That was all they needed, in order to start their investigations.

Chapter Seventeen

Splinter

Hannah contacted her friend Splinter and his team of computer geniuses. She had already given them the time and date of Matt's death, but now they had the location trail as well. Their fingers were typing so fast on their computer keyboards that it was a surprise that the keys had not worn out. Within seconds, Splinter and his team of hackers had accessed the entire CCTV system in Manhattan, specifically in the area around Tiffany at the date and time that Hannah had given to them. They saw Matt enter and exit the store. The next camera showed Matt walking along Fifth Avenue towards Central Park and they then saw two men at the entrance to Central Park. They watched as one of the men received a phone call and then they started to follow Matt.

The hackers utilised every working camera on the route but the cameras in Central Park had not been working that day. They had been turned off deliberately. They used the facial recognition software which Splinter had personally created. It was a far superior system of facial recognition than was available anywhere in the world and could recognise faces and features from only a small facial area. It could pull features from people wearing scarves and face coverings and from a much longer distance than was available on regular facial recognition systems. It was a system that the NYPD and FBI could only dream of having.

The system flagged up the two men as being known criminals, Finlan and Canio, each with a history of violent first-degree robberies and had both served time in jail. They had only been released a few months earlier. The facial recognition software was scanning all of the CCTV camera on the edge of Central Park and found the two men exiting the park on to Central Park

West, where they hailed a yellow taxi cab. The CCTV showed clearly the four digit number on the roof of the taxi cab, the taxi cab company and phone number were showing on the side doors. They made a note of these details but carried on following the taxi on CCTV. The taxi headed north and turned left on to W66th Street, right on to Broadway and followed the road for a few miles until the taxi turned left in to W131st Street and stopped outside a parking lot where the two men got out of the taxi. They watched as the two men walked in to the parking lot and a few minutes later they were seen driving out of the parking lot in a white Ford saloon. There was a third person in the car, the driver. The facial recognition software picked out his face clearly and the hackers scanned his face against the databases which they had also hacked in to. They were very surprised when the database matched the face with Dawson, one of the NYPD detectives on the case. Having got the names of the three men, Splinter accessed their phone records to see if they could find out who called them just before Matt left Tiffany's. It was easy for them to find out that the person who had called them was the assistant concierge, Jason, from the apartment building where Matt and Hannah lived.

Jason had called Finlan and given him Matt's description. He then called Detective Dawson to say that Matt Hewson was going to Tiffany's to buy an expensive engagement ring and that Finlan and Canio were following Matt. Finlan called Dawson to say that they were heading towards Central Park and asked Dawson to turn off the CCTV cameras, which he did. All of these conversations were recorded on the software created by Splinter. Splinter passed all of the CCTV footage, facial recognition results as well as the telephone recordings to Hannah, who thanked them profusely. Hannah discussed the findings with her father and wanted to take the evidence to Lieutenant Krakowski but her father stopped her, they did not know who else may be involved. Hannah's father had worked together with the NYPD in the past, solving crimes, and knew a high-ranking officer who had been recently promoted to Chief of Department, Chief Clark, he was of Irish descent and was a good friend of Hannah's father. They contacted Chief Clark and told him of the situation. They arranged a meeting in his office where they showed him all of the evidence which they had attained. Chief Clark was certain that Lieutenant Krakowski was not involved as he had worked with him on several cases over many years, he called Krakowski in to his office, with Hannah and her father's permission. Within minutes of their meeting, a patrol car had gone to Jason's private apartment. Jason confessed immediately to making the phone call, he was arrested.

Splinter had continued to trace the phone conversations, emails and text messages between Dawson, Finlan and Canio. He had picked up on a trail in the conversations which suggested that the three partners in crime were going to abscond with the takings from their robberies. Not only their most recent robbery and murder of Matt Hewson, but all of their robberies. They had booked a private jet from Newark airport to take them out of the country. Splinter had accessed the flight plan and passed the information to Hannah, who in turn, forwarded it to Lieutenant Krakowski. Dawson, Finlan and Canio' car had crossed George Washington Bridge and wase spotted on CCTV by Splinter. The cameras had recognised the number plate of their white Ford travelling on the Interstate 95 towards Newark airport. After a phone call was made by Lieutenant Krakowski, an NYPD Bell 412 EP helicopter lifted off from Floyd Bennett Field, Brooklyn. It was soon above the Interstate 95 and soon spotted the Ford. The pilot radioed to the nearby patrol cars and advised the location of the Ford, soon there were several police squad cars in pursuit. All other traffic had been stopped and the Ford was the only car on the road, with the exception of the police cars which were chasing it. The road ahead was blocked by police cars and the Ford was forced to take the exit on to a smaller road. Half a mile further along the road, the police were setting up a stinger spike trap and just as the Ford was approaching, the stinger was pushed on to the road. Dawson recognised the spike as he had used it himself on numerous occasions, but could not stop the car in time. All four of the tyres on the Ford burst and the car came to a stop. The car was immediately surrounded by several armed police officers. The three occupants were handcuffed, arrested and read their Miranda rights; the words were already familiar to them.

Following the successful arrests of the murderers of Matt Hewson, Hannah and her father discussed their futures and Hannah suggested that they should start up a detective agency together, in New York. It started off as The Cozin Detective Agency based in a small single office in Brooklyn where they solved many cases together. The more cases they solved, the bigger they became until they moved to their current office in the Empire State Building. They changed the name of the detective agency to ESDA soon after moving in to their new offices. They had solved cases for many rich and famous people including actors, politicians and even for a member of the British Royal Family and were now recognised as the number one detective agency in New York, and possibly the entire United States.

A few years later, Hannah's father retired and returned to the UK with his wife where they sold their large house in Hackney and bought a smaller two bedroomed flat in Islington. Hannah continued with the detective agency, she kept the contacts she had made in the police force and especially kept in contact with Splinter and his team.

Chapter Eighteen

James Hopkiss

After her meeting with Professor Noble, Hannah contacted Splinter and gave him the name and work details of James Hopkiss. Hopkiss was brought up in an expensive two-bedroom apartment in the upper west side of Manhattan with his parents. His parents were both wealthy stockbrokers working for the same firm in the Twin Towers. He was an only child and had always got his own way, there were no siblings vying for the attention of his parents. He was, however, not a nice person and had very few friends.

Hopkiss was at college, studying business studies, when he received a call from the local police department to say that both of his parents were killed in the terrorist attack on The Twin Towers; they had died instantly. The apartment had to be sold to pay death duties. After the death of his parents, he spent the next few years renting a small apartment close to where he worked. His parents had not believed in life insurance and, as a result of this, he changed his studies to insurance broking and made it his career to promote insurance products.

He now lived in East Hampton Village, in a sprawling ten-bedroom mansion, with his wife, Lorraine. The mansion had been given to them as a wedding present by Lorraine's father. They had one child, a young girl aged three and one on the way, due in two months' time. James met Lorraine whilst he was on a work trip to Los Angeles, arranging the insurance for her father's business. Lorraine's father was Harvey Holland, a self-made billionaire. He owned a chain of high-end retail units mainly in Rodeo Drive and received rent from the shop owners. He also insured these premises and it was that reason why James' company had been invited to meet with him. James had been staying in a suite at a five star hotel in Beverly Hills Hotel, set back from Santa Monica Boulevard. It was a business trip and the hotel was paid for by his company, including the food and drinks as well as room service and well-stocked mini bar. At least it was well stocked when he checked in, it was empty when he left.

The meeting with Harvey Holland was on the top floor of a thirty-storey office building in Downtown LA, the entire floor was owned by Harvey's company. James had made use of the Rolls-Royce provided by the hotel and arrived on time for his meeting. The views from the office were amazing, you could see the Pacific Ocean to one side and the sprawling hills beyond Pasadena on the other. There were photos on Harvey's desk of three very beautiful ladies. James assumed that one was Harvey's wife and the others were presumably his daughters. James asked Harvey about the photos and the identities were confirmed as he had thought. The lady holding Harvey's hand was his wife, Leigh. The younger ladies in the photo were indeed his daughters, Lorraine and Laurel. Lorraine was the elder of the two sisters and was a marketing director for a fashion company, she had a university degree in marketing. Laurel was more of a freeloader and had not held down a job since leaving high school, she had not progressed to university. Despite this, their father was extremely proud of them both and showed no favouritism. The meeting lasted two and a half hours and went very well for James. He had secured the contract for the ongoing insurance for the retail units in Rodeo Drive and other properties owned by Harvey Holland. Hopkiss could see the dollar signs in his eyes as he knew that the contracts would see him and his company a large and annually renewable commission. He would negotiate a pay rise and request an immediate further promotion, as soon as he returned to New York.

It was an annual contract but Harvey was a shrewd businessman and negotiated a clause in the contract to terminate for any reason. James was not over keen about the clause but had been selfishly looking at his personal commission, he made a mental note that he would try and re-negotiate the clause at the next renewal. James got on very well with Harvey and at the end of the meeting he was invited to an informal party the following evening, in Harvey's house in Malibu Beach, which he accepted. Harvey mentioned that Lorraine would be there and he would introduce them to each other. Harvey arranged for his chauffeur, Max, to pick James up from his hotel the following evening at around six thirty as the party was starting at around seven thirty; the traffic would be bad as it usually is in Los Angeles at that time of day. They said their goodbyes and James returned to his hotel.

Once back at his hotel, James celebrated his successful meeting by contacting a local escort agency and asked for them to send their best two young ladies to meet him in his room, that same evening. The two stunning ladies, both in their early twenties, one a blonde and one brunette, arrived at 8pm as arranged and stayed through until the next morning. After the girls had left, James arranged for room service to bring him breakfast. The breakfast consisted of pancakes with maple syrup, scrambled eggs and bacon as well as toast and coffee. He had used a lot of energy the night before and needed to regain his strength. After breakfast James rented a poolside cabana at the roof top swimming pool and enjoyed the beautiful sunny day. He ordered a signature cocktail and lay back in the plush chaise lounge. He relaxed and enjoyed the panoramic views of the Los Angeles and Century City skylines whilst his mind took him back to the last evening. He wished that he had asked the two beautiful escort girls to spend the rest of today with him but he would save that thought for another time as he was looking forward to meeting Lorraine at the party later that evening. He went for a short swim in the pool and admired the beauty of the other occupants in and around the pool. After his swim he dried himself and went to the roof top restaurant, where he took a light meal. The tuna salad was delicious and he washed this down with a bottle of Dom Perignon Brut 2010. The heat of the sun was still strong as he went back to his suite. He showered and washed his hair in the luxury shower cubicle, cleaned his teeth and added some whitener – he wanted to impress. "Informal" was the word that Harvey had used when he invited James to the party, and it was a beach house in Malibu Beach. James had packed for all occasions; he was an experienced traveller and knew exactly what he would wear. He had unpacked all of his clothes when he arrived at the hotel. The formal shirts and trousers were hanging in the wardrobe whilst his t-shirts and shorts were neatly folded and placed in the many drawers in the suite. It was going to be a warm evening so he decided to wear a pair of beige coloured shorts which stopped just above his knees, with a short sleeve blue formal Oxford shirt along with a pair of canvass espadrilles, all from the latest Ralph Lauren range. He looked at himself in the full-length mirror and thought that he looked good.

He took another bottle of Dom Perignon Brut 2010, this time from the bar in his suite. He thought that after the deal that he had secured yesterday, it was the least that the company should do. He took the lift and went down to the hotel lobby.

Chapter Nineteen

At precisely six thirty, Max arrived in the forecourt of James's hotel, in a brand new Aston Martin DBX, the first SUV made by the iconic British sports car manufacturer. It had black paintwork and a dark red interior. Max opened the rear door and James stepped in to the smell of luxury leather. The distance from the hotel to Malibu was over twenty five miles and took them just over an hour. Max knew a few short cuts to avoid the permanent rush hour traffic of Los Angeles. Instead of driving along Santa Monica Boulevard he took Wilshere, across the I 405, on to San Vicente, past Brentwood Country Club and turned north on to the Pacific Coast Highway. They were driving on the PCH for a few miles. Out of the window, James noticed Gladstone's restaurant on the beach, just past the junction with Sunset Boulevard, and then Moonshadows and Dukes restaurants. They looked good and he made a mental note to go there at another time. Max slowed the car down to a stop and James assumed that they were nearly at Harvey Holland's beach house. Max pressed a button on the dashboard of the Aston Martin and a gate in front of an inauspicious looking house on the opposite side of the road started to slide open. It was seven thirty, right on time. Inside the gates, Max drove the Aston Martin into the garage and parked next to a Bentley SUV and a Tesla Model X. There was further parking in front of the house for several more cars. Max got out of the car and opened the door for James, James stepped out.

The road side front of the beach house was a bland, white painted façade, nothing special thought James. The front door was opened by a butler and wow! Harvey had bought the beach house only two years earlier but had since spent several million dollars in refurbishing it. The interior of the beach house was extremely impressive; it was arranged over three floors with a lift between all floors. The entrance was huge and opened on to an even larger reception room with a terrace overlooking the calm blue Pacific Ocean. There were steps leading down from the terrace directly on to the soft yellow sand on Malibu Beach.

It was such a beautiful clear evening that you could see Santa Catalina Island in the distance as well as the airplanes turning on to their final approach, over the Pacific Ocean, to LAX. "I could get used to this life," James thought to himself.

There were a few people already in the house and James recognised a few of them from his meeting with Harvey the day before. Harvey came over to James. "Welcome to my home. I would like to introduce you to my wife, Leigh." He said smiling at his wife. Leigh was in her late fifties, she had short dark hair to her shoulder and was wearing a smart pair of shorts and a cropped shirt,. She looked extremely good for her age and James could see why Harvey kept a photo of his wife in his office, she was beautiful. James looked at Leigh and thought that if this was Lorraine's mother then how beautiful must Lorraine be? He didn't have to wait long to find out as he handed the bottle of Dom Perignon to Harvey. Lorraine walked in to the room; she was only a few years younger than James. She had long black hair, much longer than her mother's, and a beautiful face. She looked stunning in her red satin weave strappy back bodycon mini dress. The dress was low and backless, apart from the straps, and clung to her model like body. It stopped a few inches above her knees, revealing a very sexy pair of legs as well as a great cleavage. "Wow!" thought James, for the second time in a few minutes.

"This is my daughter Lorraine," Harvey said, introducing his daughter to James. "Enjoy the party." A waiter came over and poured two glasses of champagne for Lorraine and James. There were canapes and buffet food laid out on the tables in most of the rooms. Lorraine offered a guided tour of the house and James readily accepted. The house was very impressive and so was Lorraine. She was proud of her parents and what they had achieved but she was not the sort of person to sit back and accept charity from them. Lorraine was her own person and had a high-powered job as a marketing director for a fashion company which had offices and shops in Los Angeles, New York and London. James could again see dollar signs both for his future and also the commission he would receive, if he could get Lorraine's fashion company as a client.

During their conversations Lorraine and James realised that they had a lot in common and chatted for the whole evening. The champagne was flowing, their glasses were being constantly topped up and they helped themselves to the buffet food, throughout the evening. Most of the time they were standing on the terrace overlooking the Pacific Ocean and looking up to the stars. James was besotted by Lorraine's beauty and at the back of his mind he saw the money that her family had; he used the opportunity to seduce her. Once the party was over Max took James back to his hotel, but not before James had made arrangements to see Lorraine the following day, she agreed. When he returned to the hotel, James went to the Club Bar and had a drink of scotch whisky. He called his office and left a message to say that his trip to Los Angeles was going very well and that he would need a few more days there. He then called the escort agency.

Chapter Twenty

James had arranged to meet Lorraine at Gladstone's Bar and Restaurant, which he had noticed on his way to the beach house the previous day, for lunch. He requested an Uber and arrived a few minutes before Lorraine, who arrived in her Tesla. They sat at a table overlooking the Pacific Ocean and, with the sound of the waves in the background, they ordered lunch. James had the Lobster whilst Lorraine had the Coconut Shrimp. They talked as if they had known each other for a lifetime, it had only been one day.

"I've extended my stay as I would like to spend more time with you," he told her. "If that is OK with you?" he asked. Lorraine called her work and took the next few days off, too. "That sounds great," she replied. After lunch they drove Lorraine's Tesla north along PCH to Santa Barbara where they looked around the shops and walked on the beach and pier. They did the usual touristy things which James had not done before, but as Lorraine was a local girl she had, but she didn't mind seeing them again. They went to Venice Beach, looked around the cheap stores and watched the local entertainers as well as people on Segways and e-scooters, people smoking weed. They drove down to Laguna Beach and stopped at the road side Milk Shake hut overlooking the ocean, before spending more time walking on the beach. Lorraine and James went to see the Hollywood sign and then to the hand and foot prints of famous actors at Grauman's Chinese Theatre. After these few days together, they were in love and knew that they wanted to be together.

James asked Lorraine to move to Manhattan with him and, although one of her company's offices was in New York, she had never been there. Lorraine made the necessary phone calls and it was agreed that she could transfer to the New York office. Within a few months they had married, it was a beautiful ceremony one which they would never forget. It took place in Los Angeles and the party was at the beach house, where they first met. Lorraine's father bought a beautiful ten bedroomed mansion in East Hampton Village, as a wedding present. It was one of the largest single residential lots in nearly ten acres of land with a large direct ocean front. James knew that with the wealth of Lorraine's family, he was made for life - but it was not enough for him. James loved to party and loved talking about himself. He would go out after work to the local bar and drink with some of the few colleagues who he could still call his friends, those who he hadn't trodden on in order to get where he was today. He also liked to chat up women in the bars. He was very confident and despite the fact that he was married, he was not faithful to his wife and had had several one-night stands and affairs. Before they got married, James had an affair with Lorraine's sister, Laurel. On the morning of his wedding day, he slept with one of the bridesmaids. James and Lorraine had been married for five years and had a beautiful daughter but during the pregnancy he had another affair. Lorraine was pregnant again and during this time he had hired two beautiful escorts to meet him in a Manhattan hotel, close to his work. He had done this on several occasions and where they would have amazing sex all night, at a cost of thousands of dollars.

The cost was not important to him as he had a well-paid job and had also married in to money. James would tell Lorraine that he had a late client and would be staying in a local hotel. Lorraine had got used to these "late" client appointments and although she was not overly convinced, she had accepted this as a reasonable excuse.

Chapter Twenty One

Hannah had listened to the professor and had made copious notes. The meeting had lasted over two hours and the professor had told her what seemed to be his whole life story. Hannah knew, through her experience, which parts were relevant to the case and which were not. Hannah initially wrote the notes onto sheets of A4 paper and placed them in a paper folder, she would write the notes on to her computer later. At the end of the meeting Hannah told the professor to wait for a couple of days and she would report back to him with her findings. Hannah counted the money which the Professor had given her, once she had counted it she put it in to an envelope. She wrote his name on the envelope, opened a large safe and put it on the top shelf.

The professor had told Hannah where James worked and that was where she would start. She looked on the insurance company's web site to find the personnel and found James immediately. She called Splinter. The information on the company web site about James was a very glowing praise of his career so far. It included how he had obtained many high-net-worth companies as his clients, including that of his father-in-law, Harvey Holland, in Los Angeles. Hannah thought that his rise in the company seemed all too good to be true and started her research into James. She found his home address and saw that it was in East Hampton and not far from where Matt's family lived. Hannah knew the area well and knew that the property in that area was not cheap, especially one with such a large beach frontage. She found out that James was married to Lorraine and that Lorraine used to work in marketing but had stopped in order to raise their child, and that she was pregnant again. She also found out that Lorraine's father, Harvey Holland, was one of the richest men in the country, this was going to be very useful information to her case.

She drove to see the mansion where James and his family lived. She parked her car discretely, so as not to be seen, and waited to see him leave so that she could follow him. The old-fashioned detective way. She didn't have to wait long before a chauffeur driven black Mercedes S Class saloon pulled out of the long driveway with James sitting smugly in the back, talking on his mobile phone. Hannah took photos of the car and then went back to the house where she used her long telephoto lens on her Canon EOS 1D camera to take photos of the house and Lorraine. Lorraine was still standing by the front door, child in arms and waving goodbye to James. What a loving family she thought. Hannah got back in to her car and drove quickly so that she could catch up with the Mercedes. Once she caught it up she kept her distance, so that she was not spotted by the driver. Hannah assumed that he would have been trained to spot if he was being followed and did not want to show her hand just yet.

Whilst she was driving, Hannah called Splinter from her hands-free mobile phone to find out if he had any updates for her about James. Splinter had been very busy since he had put the phone down from Hannah after the professor had left her office. He had hacked in to James' mobile phone and both his private and personal emails. He had listened to voicemails left on James' phone and ascertained who James had called. The information was very revealing. One of the calls that James had made was to a local escort agency which specialised in arranging for high class ladies to visit men, and women, in hotels. James had called the agency on several different occasions. The voicemail on his phone was the most telling. It was confirmation of a booking for two ladies to visit James, although that was not the name that he had used when he called the agency. Although he was a regular client, he did not see why the agency need to know his true identity. The meeting was set to take place that evening at 7pm in an exclusive five-star hotel, in his "usual suite". Later that day, Hannah took a taxi and arrived at the hotel at 5pm, she waited in the reception area. It was not long before James arrived, he was in a smart suit and it seemed that he had come straight from his office to his "late" client appointment. James did not notice Hannah as he walked past her and checked in at the reception. He took the lift to the top floor of the twenty-three-storey building where his suite was located. The suite was over 1,200 square feet and had a large bedroom with super king size bed, perfect for his intentions. It was addressed as his "usual room" by the staff, when he booked. Hannah had got close to the reception when James checked in and found out in which suite he was staying. At precisely 7pm two of the most beautiful young ladies entered the hotel, they went straight to the lift and pressed the 23rd floor button. The ladies were in their early twenties, one was blonde and one brunette. They were tall at around five foot ten and were dressed in expensive short dresses, showing their long legs, just what James had requested. They knocked on the door and James let them in.

Hannah remained in the reception as she did not want to interrupt the meeting too soon. She used the next hour to check her notes and have a couple of coffees, it could be a long night. After a while, Hannah took the lift to the 23rd floor and waited in the side corridor, close to James' suite. At around 10pm James made a call to room service and asked for three house special mixed fish and meat boards as well as some more champagne, to be brought to the room. The room service waiter arrived with a food trolley; this was her chance. He knocked on the door. "Room service," he announced. James opened the door and let the waiter in. "Put the trolley in the dining area," he told the waiter, with an abrupt voice. James handed the waiter a tip and walked away, turning his back on the waiter. He didn't see Hannah slip in to the room. Hannah had already looked on the hotel's web site and found a floor plan of the suite. She knew that there were two bathrooms in the suite and that one of these was immediately by the entrance door to the suite, whilst the other was en-suite to the bedroom. Hannah sneaked in to the bathroom closest to the entrance and waited. She could hear lots of talking and giggling in the dining area in the suite, James and his two lady friends were eating and drinking the food and champagne which had been brought in to the room. After the food was eaten, James spread lines of cocaine on to the table and, using a rolled up hundred dollar bill, snorted it in to both nostrils. The two ladies joined in. "It could be a long wait," Hannah thought to herself. She had done this type of work on many occasions in her profession as a private detective, catching cheating spouses. This was no different to the others except that it was in a posh suite in

63

a posh hotel. She knew that the secret was in waiting for the right time to make her move. It was now after 11pm and the talking had stopped, James and his two lady friends had moved in to the bedroom. "At last," she thought. Hannah waited until she could hear some noise from the bedroom and moved quietly out of the bathroom. She opened the entrance door from the suite to the corridor, so that she could make a quick escape if needed. She had learned this from experience, when she had nearly been caught during a previous job.

The noise from the bedroom suggested that the occupants were very much interested in each other; that was just what Hannah had been waiting for. Moans and groans of pleasure were filling the room. She reached for her Canon camera and tip toed in to the bedroom, she did not need the telephoto lens this time. She had already adjusted the settings on the camera for a dim light scenario and also to make sure that the flash did not come on. What she saw when she opened the bedroom door resembled the set of a blue movie. James and the two ladies were all on the huge super king size bed, their bodies were entwined and, along with the moans of delight emanating from them, it was an extremely sexy sight and one which Hannah would never forget.

Hannah had witnessed many extra marital affairs but usually with one man and one woman, man with man or woman with woman – this was the first threesome that she had witnessed. She was not there to comment on what she saw but to report back to her client, she was however very turned on by what she saw. She felt butterflies in her stomach and a pleasant sensation between her legs. Hannah stood inside the door to the large bedroom, making sure that she could not be seen. She started to take photos, lots and lots of photos. Some of the photos she would keep for her own pleasure. James did not see Hannah as he had his head elsewhere. Having gathered sufficient evidence Hannah quietly left the bedroom and walked to the door. On the way to the door, she saw some of the food left on the plates in the dining room. She took a few slices of beef, as she had not eaten for ages; she was very hungry.

Chapter Twenty Two

Elizabeth Noble

Elizabeth was extremely distraught by what Charlotte Mobbs had personally done to her husband. She had been extremely supportive of her husband since the decision had been made forcing him to close his clinic. Elizabeth did her best to make him feel good and knew that, although their financial situation was deteriorating, that there were many more people in the world much worse off than they were. One way in which Elizabeth supported her husband was to always look as sexy as possible and one thing that she did not cut back on was her beauty. She had cut back on many of the expensive trips to the beauty salon and hairdresser and would no longer buy the latest fashion items. She had trained as a professional make-up artist in her younger days and knew exactly what type of make up to use. She had applied small amounts of foundation and just a bit of rouge to her almost perfect skin. She used an eyebrow pencil to plump up her eyebrows and just a bit of gel to make them set. A lip pencil was used to apply red colour to her beautiful lips, not too overpowering, just right. She had blow-dried her shoulder length to perfection. She looked amazing. They had decided, before the trip to New York, that they would go shopping but not buy as many things as they would normally have bought. Elizabeth arrived in Fifth Avenue in the hotel's private Rolls Royce with Craig the chauffeur at the wheel. Craig had told her that he would be her chauffeur and guide for the entire day and that he would wait in the car whilst she was in the shops. She was spoiled for choice, there were so many shops selling brands that she usually wore. She started in Bergdorf Goodman, with its museum quality window displays and eight floors of retail house in-store boutiques. Then on to Victoria's Secret, Louis Vuitton and Gucci, where she browsed the latest designs. She was very tempted by what she saw but restricted herself to a few purchases in Victoria's Secret, only.

Then on to Dolce and Gabbana, Armani, Valentino, Versace and finally, to Saks Fifth Avenue for Chanel and Alexander McQueen. There were so many stores, it was an A-Z of fashion and she felt like she was a child at Christmas but without the same spending power that she was used to having. She would normally buy several items in each of these shops, but due to their cutting back on expensive purchases, she restricted her purchasing to only a few items. She would leave the jewellery stores for another day. Once finished, Craig returned her to the hotel. He had already called ahead to the hotel where Jack was waiting at the entrance, to assist with the shopping bags. Professor Noble and Elizabeth had stayed in the same hotel on many occasions in the past and had met Jack before. Jack was surprised that there were so few shopping bags this time, but he made no comment to the guests, he was too professional for this. Once inside the hotel suite, Elizabeth started to open her shopping bags. She had bought the latest Chanel bag and admired the quality of the leather and finish.

She would normally have bought at least two other bags but didn't think that it was the right thing to do; at least not until everything had been sorted out with her husband's work situation. Her best buys were the underwear from Victoria's Secret and the very sexy lingerie from La Perla, to complement what she already owned. Elizabeth couldn't wait for her husband to get back from his meeting with the private detective to show these off to him.

She called her husband's mobile and it went to voicemail. He was still in his meeting so she left him a message and sent him a text to call her when he was on his way back. About thirty minutes later the professor emerged from his meeting with Hannah and saw the missed call, voicemail and text from Elizabeth. He called Elizabeth to say that he had just finished his meeting with the private detective and was on his way back, Elizabeth asked Jack to ask Craig to take the car and pick him up. She went to the bathroom and had a shower in the huge shower in which she and her husband had made love that morning. She let the water from the shower run all over her body and touched herself; she stopped after a few minutes as she had other plans in mind, which involved her husband. After her shower she dried her firm body and put on the sexy underwear and lingerie which she had just bought, she covered up with the hotel's dressing gown robe. A few minutes later, her husband walked in to the room and couldn't believe his eyes. Elizabeth looked absolutely stunning as she let her robe fall to the floor. She pulled her husband towards her and started to undress him in a slow and determined way. The professor let her do her magic with him. He was soon naked and they made love on the bed, passionately.

Chapter Twenty Three

It was early in the morning, the day after she had sneaked in to James' hotel room, when Hannah went to her office in the Empire State Building. She had hardly slept as she had so much information to give to the professor. This was what she liked about her job, not just catching people in the act of cheating, but knowing that the client could use the information that she had found and knowing that she had earned her fee. She was not the cheapest detective agency in town but she was the best, and she felt that the professor had definitely got what he was paying for. She took the SD card from the side of her Canon camera and inserted it in to the slot at the side of her Apple iMac computer. The photos that she had taken in the hotel room the night before were of an amazing quality, considering that she had not used the flash on the camera.

Hannah had taken over one hundred photos. She created a folder on the screen and called it "Professor", and copied the photos in to the folder. She then made five copies of the photos onto five memory sticks; she had a plan. She also printed the photos on the colour laser printer in her office and put the paper copies in to the paper folder on her desk. It was nine o'clock in the morning as she made a call to the professor. "Please come to my office, I have some interesting news for you," she said to the professor. An appointment was set for eleven and the professor arrived a few minutes early. It was Ava who again greeted the professor when he arrived. He sat in the same chair in the waiting area in which he had sat in on his previous meeting. Ava was wearing the same scary lipstick as she had at the last time he was in the office. At exactly eleven o'clock Hannah opened the door of her office. "Come in," she said with a wide smile and invited the professor in. "Have a seat," she continued. The professor sat down, intrigued and not knowing what to expect. Hannah sat at her desk and opened the folder on her computer screen. In a few seconds she had cast the photographs from the folder on to the huge TV monitor on the wall of her office. The photos were displayed on the TV monitor, in full colour. Professor Noble and Hannah could clearly see the faces, as well as the many other naked areas of flesh, of James and the two ladies that he was with. A broad smile came to the professor's face.

Hannah gave the professor one of the memory sticks with the photos and placed one memory stick in her safe. She still had three memory sticks left; she re-named the files on the remaining memory sticks. The professor thanked Hannah profusely and they discussed the next stage of his plans for James. He had not finished with Hannah's services just yet and he knew exactly what he wanted her to do. It was the same plan that Hannah had already started to put in motion. Hannah was ready to complete the job for the professor the following day and started to make the necessary arrangements.

Chapter Twenty Four

There were still three days left of their trip. Professor Noble called the American Express Centurion concierge and asked them to arrange for two tickets to the following day's matinee performance of The Phantom of The Opera at The Majestic Theatre in W44th St. It was their favourite play and one which they had seen on several occasions in Her Majesty's Theatre in London's West End. The tickets were arranged; they were centre orchestra seats, six rows from the front, the best seats in the house. The professor confirmed the timings with Hannah and the final arrangements were set in place. "Relax," she said to the professor. "Enjoy the show, I'll let you know once it I done," she continued. The performance was to start at one o'clock. The professor and Elizabeth arrived in the chauffeur driven Rolls-Royce, provided by the hotel, with Craig at the wheel. They arrived at twelve thirty and collected their tickets from the box office and had a drink of champagne in the bar before taking their seats. The theatre was full and there was a buzz of excitement in the audience, in anticipation of the show. The lights dimmed and at exactly one o'clock, the show began. The performance was sensational but the professor could not concentrate as he had other things on his mind.

At the exact moment at the end of Act One, when "All I Ask of You" was finishing. The Phantom shouted "Go" and the chandelier above the stage dropped down to the shrieks of the cast and audience – this was an iconic moment in the play. It was also the exact moment when Hannah knocked on the door of James' and Lorraine's mansion in East Hampton. She handed a small brown envelope addressed to Lorraine Hopkiss, consisting of a memory stick. The memory stick contained the photos of James with the two ladies in the hotel bedroom. There was a brief further message in the envelope simply stating the date, location and time of when the photos were taken. It was also the exact moment when a colleague of Hannah arrived in the office of Harvey, James' father-in-law, in Los Angeles, with the same style envelope, addressed to Harvey Holland, containing another memory stick with the same photos and message. And it was also the exact moment when another colleague of Hannah arrived in James' office in New York, with the same style envelope, addressed to James Hopkiss, containing yet another memory stick, with the same photos and message. The delivery of the envelopes was carried out with almost military precision, and Hannah was proud of her team.

The chandelier had fallen, it was the end of Act One. The lights came on in the auditorium to a massive round of applause from the excited audience. The professor turned on his mobile phone. There was a short message from Hannah simply saying "Job done." The professor showed the message to Elizabeth and they smiled at each other, they both knew exactly what was meant by the message. The lights soon dimmed for the start of Act Two, the professor was more relaxed now and they both enjoyed the rest of the show. Once the show had finished, the professor and Elizabeth went back stage to meet the cast and crew. Craig was waiting in the Rolls-Royce outside the theatre and when they finally came out of the theatre, he took them back to the hotel.

Chapter Twenty Five

Lorraine Hopkiss

Lorraine opened the envelope and saw the memory stick, with her name on the file. She was curious as to its content and put the stick in to her Apple iMac computer. When she saw the contents she stood still, her initial reaction was one of shock and horror. She felt her heavily pregnant stomach and after a few moments of thought she became furious. Lorraine picked up a pair of sharp scissors and went in to James' large walk-in wardrobe. She cut up his tailor-made suits and shirts into shreds and put them in black bags, before throwing the bags out of the window. She found photos of the two of them when they were on vacation and happy. She took the photos out of their frames and cut a hole where James' face had been. Lorraine threw away the gifts which he had sent her as they no longer had any meaning. She called her father; he answered immediately as he knew exactly why she was calling.

After Lorraine told her father about the memory stick, he told her that he had received the same photos on a memory stick with his name on the file. He told Lorraine that he would arrange to have the locks changed on the gates and all of the doors in her mansion. "I'll arrange for a car to collect you and your daughter to take you to East Hampton Airport, my private jet will fly you to Los Angeles and you can stay with us until we can sort this out," he told her.

The private locksmith company, which was owned by Lorraine's father, was already on the way and turned up at the mansion within thirty minutes. There was a team of eight people, due to the number of locks which were to be changed. Initially, it was to make the house "James' proof", replacing the locks like for like, the instructions were also to upgrade the security in general as the intention was for Lorraine to be living there later with her children, if she wanted. It was a large property and would take several hours to change the locks but the company was owned by her father and Lorraine knew that they could be trusted.

A car arrived, as arranged, and picked up Lorraine and her young daughter, along with a few cases containing their clothes, as well as some toys for the child. It was only a fifteen minute drive to East Hampton airport where a Cessna Citation Latitude was waiting on the tarmac, fully fuelled for the near 3,000 mile flight to Santa Monica Municipal Airport. The airport was much smaller than LAX, the main international airport of Los Angeles, and approximately seven miles to the north. It was much easier to exit and enter than LAX and was where Harvey Holland kept another of his private jets.

There were two pilots and a flight attendant on the Cessna Citation Latitude, ready and waiting for their passengers. Lorraine and her daughter climbed the few steps up to enter the cabin where they were greeted by Michael. Michael was a highly professional flight attendant, employed by Lorraine's father and known to Lorraine, as she had flown with him before. Michael showed the passengers to their seats.

Although the Citation Latitude could take up to nine passengers, this one was customised with only six luxury chairs, to give more space to the passengers. The pilots had already finished their pre-flight checks and filed their flight plan. The plane was fuelled and ready to go. Within minutes of their passengers embarking, they were ready to depart from runway Two Eight in a westerly direction for the five-hour long flight to Santa Monica Airport. As soon as the plane took off, Lorraine called James. "I want a divorce. Don't bother going home as I've changed the locks and destroyed your clothes. I don't care where you go, you can go and live with your whores!" she shouted and disconnected the call.

Chapter Twenty Six

The flight was smooth. Flying at an altitude of 45,000 feet most of the way meant that there was little air resistance and virtually no turbulence. Soon the Citation started its descent in to Santa Monica Municipal Airport and landed smoothly on runway Two One, before taxiing into a private hangar, where Max, her father's chauffeur, was waiting with a shiny new Mercedes S Class saloon. Within a few minutes after landing, Lorraine and her young daughter disembarked from the plane, thanked the pilots, waved goodbye to Michael and got in the car. Max placed their small amount of luggage in to the huge boot of the Mercedes.

It was fifteen miles to her parent's beach house in Malibu and the traffic was surprisingly light. It took only 45 minutes to get there from Santa Monica Municipal Airport, this time Max did not need to take any short cuts. The interstate 10 was close to the airport and within a few minutes the car was close to Santa Monica pier where it joined with the CA1 north, on to the Pacific Coast Highway. They soon arrived at the beach house where Harvey and Leigh held out their arms to Lorraine; Lorraine ran to them, trying her best to hold back the tears. Lorraine went to her old bedroom and lay on the bed. She was exhausted and fell asleep, whilst her daughter ran around the beautiful house staring at the endless views of the Pacific Ocean.

After she woke up, Lorraine went to her parents and discussed the situation. She told them that she was going to get divorced and told them what she had done to James' clothes and photos in the house in East Hampton, before she left. She knew that the house was secure and also knew that she and her daughter were safe with her parents. It was getting dark and dinner was served, but Lorraine was not hungry.

Having confirmed with Lorraine in an earlier conversation that there would be no reconciliation with James, Harvey had already contacted his lawyers. He had initiated the clause in the contract between his company and James' company to terminate their contract, with immediate effect. Harvey had also contacted his previous insurance company who were only too keen to reinstate the insurance policies on the entire portfolio of his properties.

Chapter Twenty Seven

James was in a meeting with a potential new client in a large meeting room when he was interrupted by his assistant, saying that a small package had arrived for him with "Urgent, Private and Confidential" written on the front. James excused himself from the meeting saying that he would be back in a few minutes. He went in to his office and closed the door. He opened the envelope with curiosity and saw the memory stick. He sat at his desk and placed the memory stick in to his Apple iMac computer. He opened the file with his name on it and the large pictures showed on his screen. James sat back in his chair and put his hands on his head in horror; not at the photos which were on his screen, but at the thought that he had been caught. He did not know what to do. He started to phone Lorraine but stopped just before he pressed the dial button. He did not know whether she knew, maybe this was meant for his eyes only and was just a warning, or maybe it was blackmail. There was no note in the envelope, he would have to wait and act as if nothing was wrong.

James' secretary knocked once on the door and entered his office, she saw that his face had turned a very pale colour. "Are you OK?" she asked him. "I'm fine," he snapped back as he brushed past her and went back in to the meeting room to continue the meeting with his new client. The meeting lasted over an hour but his mind was not in the room. The potential client could tell this and they excused themselves from the meeting, never to return. He had lost their potential business. James returned to his office and a few more minutes passed before he was again looking at the photos. He was not sure who had taken them, or even how they had been taken and made a note to contact the hotel to discuss their security arrangements. He actually admired the quality of the photos; the content of the photos sent his mind back to the previous evening, it seemed such a long time ago. His mobile phone rang, it was Lorraine. "Hi darling" James said nervously, as if nothing was wrong. He did not know whether Lorraine had the same photos, but it was not long before he found out.

Lorraine screamed at him down the phone and asked for a divorce. She told him that she had received a memory stick with the photos, she also told him about changing the locks and what she had done to his clothes. She ended the call but James heard in the background that she was on a plane. He did not know where she was going but he did not have to wait long to find out.

The phone on James' desk rang. It was the CEO and founder of the company, Carla Golding. "Come to my office, I need to speak with you," she said to James. Carla had set up the company over twenty years ago, starting as a small insurance broker firm mainly insuring cars and homes in New York State, and had expanded to the current multi-national company with offices worldwide.

Carla Golding was a ruthless business woman and had seen the potential in James when he first started to work in her company. So much so, that she had personally promoted him after sealing the contract the multi-millionaire, Harvey Holland, in Los Angeles. She had just received an email from Harvey Holland's lawyer stating that the contract for the insurance of all of the properties owned by Harvey's company, as well as his and his family's personal properties, was being terminated with immediate effect.

She had also received a personally addressed email from Harvey Holland, stating the reason for the termination along with an attachment containing a selection of several of the photos taken from the memory stick which had been personally delivered to Harvey. Carla Golding felt sick, she knew what it felt like to be cheated on as her first husband had cheated on her. She knew what she had to do; this was her company and she did not want its previously impeccable name brought in to disrepute. James was still in shock and was sitting by his desk. Carla walked over to James' office. "My office, now!" She said with a harsh tone in her voice, one which James had not heard before.

Chapter Twenty Eight

There was a lot of whispering going on in the corridors of Carla Golding's insurance company's office and people were looking at James, not knowing what was going on. "What was in the envelope?" the staff were asking each other and speculating as James followed behind Carla along the corridor to Carla's office. James entered Carla's office. Her office was a lot bigger than his and had far better views; you could see the Empire State Building, looming tall through the large windows. On the walls were photos of her husband and family along with photos of the original office where it all started and the many offices around the world, which it now owned. There were accolades of "Best CEO", "Best Business", best this and that, James lost count.

It was too much of a coincidence to be asked in to Carla's office just moments after receiving the memory stick. He assumed that she must have been notified of its existence. He was right. "Shut the door and sit down" Carla Golding snapped. He did as he was told. Carla got straight to the point. She told him that she had received an email from Harvey Holland, terminating their contract and asked James if he knew why that might be. He said that he did not know. Carla then showed him the email and photos received from Harvey Holland; then he understood. James assumed that Lorraine had sent a copy of the photos to her father. He was wrong, but he now understood why Harvey Holland had terminated the contract. James had cheated on Harvey's daughter.

The contract had been worth millions of dollars in commission and renewals and this was now over. So was James. He was accused of bringing the name of the company into disrepute. It was deemed to be gross misconduct as was written in the terms of his own contract with his employer, the insurance company. He knew that the punishment was instant dismissal.

Carla fired James with immediate effect. She also told him that there would be no severance pay and that he would need to pay back the percentage of commission, which he had already received in advance, for that year. Two burly security guards arrived at the door to Carla's office and entered the room at the exact time that Carla had asked them to. They had a box with James' personal possessions in it and escorted James to the lift.

The two security guards and James entered the lift, not a word was spoken as they descended to the ground floor. James took the box from the security guards and left the building. He knew that word in the insurance world would spread like wildfire and that he would be unemployable. His wife had changed the locks on their mansion, he was homeless. He was ruined. Word did spread around the insurance world and it spread very quickly. It was less than an hour after James was marched out of the insurance company's building in New York that the news of his demise was received by the insurance company in London, where Professor Noble's daughter, Judith, worked. Judith smiled and sent a text to her father confirming James' dismissal. "James Hopkiss fired!" was all that she wrote, along with a smiley face. The professor and Elizabeth received the text from Judith and smiled at each other; they knew that the first part of their mission for revenge had been a success.

Revenge was sweet, and they were going to celebrate.

Chapter Twenty Nine

Professor Noble and Elizabeth spent the next day, their last in New York, shopping. The professor bought a set of air pods, which he had promised to buy for himself, from the Apple store. They went jewellery shopping in Tiffany's before having lunch in Katz's Deli on E Houston Street, taken there by Craig in the hotel's Rolls-Royce. They had plenty of time as their flight was not leaving JFK until 9pm that evening. They discussed all of the events that had occurred whilst they were in New York over classic pastrami on rye sandwiches; looking at the photos on the walls of the famous people who had frequented Katz's Deli, in the past. They also re-enacted the famous scene from "When Harry met Sally", which was filmed there. It went un-noticed by the other people in the restaurant, as it happened all the time.

Whilst they were out, Jack, their hotel butler was packing their luggage. They had to purchase a further small suitcase in order to fit in the items that Elizabeth had bought whilst she was in New York. They arrived at JFK airport two hours before the flight was due to leave. Passport control was quiet for that time; they breezed through and went straight past the duty-free shops to Virgin Atlantic's Clubhouse above the boarding gates in concourse A. They checked that the flight was on-time and relaxed, had a few drinks and a bite to eat before they were called to board the flight. It was a night flight and Elizabeth slept on the smooth flight to London. There were so many thoughts going through the professor's mind that he could not sleep. He usually had trouble sleeping on airplanes anyway, so it was not a surprise to him. He was so impressed with the results from Hannah's detective agency. He thought that it was a shame that she could not help him with the rest of his tasks, or maybe she could.

The flight arrived early at Heathrow Terminal 3 and they were soon through passport control and in to the Virgin Limo. The timing of the flight was perfect as they were on the tail end of the London rush hour traffic and soon arrived back to their house in Hampstead. When they opened the door to their house there was a waiting committee comprising of all four of their children, glasses of champagne in hand and two more full glasses for the professor and Elizabeth. Professor Noble liked a glass or two of champagne and joined in the celebrations, but whilst he was drinking, he was thinking that his revenge was not finished yet and he would not be able to celebrate fully until it was. Their children had prepared a lovely lunch for them, mainly courtesy of Jackie and Steven's Michelin star La JaSte restaurant. They sat around the large table in the dining room whilst Elizabeth and the professor related the story of what had happened in New York. The professor also discussed the plans he had in mind for Charlotte Mobbs.

Chapter Thirty

A few weeks had elapsed since their successful trip to New York and the professor had begun to look in to the life style of Charlotte Mobbs. The final written words in the note which was left to him from Clementine Follows, were firmly implanted in his mind.

"TAKE DOWN CHARLOTTE MOBBS BEFORE SHE RUINS MORE PEOPLE'S LIVES, SHE IS CROOKED".

He already knew that Charlotte Mobbs lived in a large house and owned a new Mercedes C Class convertible, which she had recently bought; but should not have been able to afford. He looked at the time on his wristwatch and contacted Hannah Cozins in New York, knowing that she would be at work. After a few more compliments about her recent work for him, the professor gave Hannah as much information as he could about Charlotte Mobbs. He asked Hannah if she would be able to research Charlotte Mobbs for him. Once the conversation had finished, Hannah walked out of her office and past Eva in reception, smiling at her on the way. Eva was still scary looking; it was one of the many things that Hannah liked about her. Hannah continued walking and opened one of the doors on the opposite side of the reception, ignoring the "Private" sign on the door. Apart from the "Private" sign there were no other markings on the door. It was one of the doors which Professor Noble had seen when he was in the waiting area. He did not know who or what was in there. Hannah opened the door and was looking at Splinter and his team. They were in an office just as large as hers but there were no trophies, photos or filing cabinets in this room, just computers and more computers, monitors and more monitors. The windows had been darkened and there was very little natural light in the room. They did not pay Hannah any rent for their room but assisted her whenever she wanted help, at no cost. It was an arrangement which suited them all. Hannah gave the details of Charlotte Mobbs to Splinter and walked out of the room. She did not need to say anything else; she knew that they were the best at what they did and that is why she used them.

The team comprised of Splinter, the most feared computer hacker in the world. His real name was Danno and he was extremely intelligent with an IQ in excess of 180, which put him in the exceptionally gifted category. He was tall and slim, had dark blond hair which was long and straggled, he was clean shaven but with a few fluffy bits of hair on his chin. Danno was assisted by his close friend Markie and three other computer hackers, Kaza, also blonde, very pretty with shoulder length hair, Lucia and Ninja. Markie was just as smart as Danno, if not smarter. They would constantly argue as to who was the best hacker and have regular competitions; they were both extremely competitive. Lucia and Ninja were identical twins who would usually play games by pretending to be the other person – it could be fun to watch, they were both tall with long dark hair and bodies to die for. They all had similar IQ's and were all as good as each other with their computer skills. The five had met at Oxford University, studying computer science and programming and that is where they also met Hannah.

They were always competing against each other, trying to prove who was best. They soon realised that, instead of competing against each other, it was more productive to pool their amazing skills into one unit and that they would be much stronger as a team. Danno, Markie and their team were responsible for some of the most high-profile computer hacks in the world. As well as hacking in to the US Government, NASA, the Federal Reserve and even The Kremlin, it was also rumoured that they had hacked in to the latest US Presidential election and changed a few votes. This was never proven, and one which was never spoken about by the team. It was a sort of moral code not to boast about what they did, as they would most likely be arrested. They had also accessed the personal computers of both the Russian and Chinese presidents, inserting ransomware on to their computers for which they were paid millions in Bitcoin for the release. The team had never been caught, and had no intention of being caught now. They had mellowed slightly since they joined with Hannah, but they had skills which were now being used for helping people. They were, however, not a charity and knew how to charge for their services. The rent-free arrangement that they had with Hannah suited them, just fine.

Chapter Thirty One

Danno, Markie and the team started researching the private life of Charlotte Mobbs. Professor Noble had already searched the usual social media pages and found out basic information such as her date of birth, the school she went to, and who her friends were. Danno and his team would search deeper than that. They hacked in to all of the major UK banks and found her bank details. They hacked in to the mobile phone networks in the UK and found out her phone number as well as the type of phone she was using. They even found out that she had two mobile phone accounts, on different networks. Charlotte Mobbs had recently purchased the latest iPhone from the Apple Store at Westfield Shopping Centre in West London, she had paid cash. She had also recently bought her Mercedes C Class Convertible, paid for by a cheque, not from her main bank account but from a Swiss bank account with the name Missy Mobbs. Missy was the name of one of her cats. She had opened a Swiss bank account in that name, and was clearly hiding something. Her main UK bank account had the usual entries, her monthly salary, council tax bill, phone bill, other utilities along with a mortgage payment and a few low payments for credit card bills. The team ascertained that she had recently bought her house for over one million pounds and only had a mortgage of a quarter of that, presumably for tax reasons. Her salary was not enough to cover the cost of the house purchase and there was no public record of where the balance of the money had come from. They started to look in to the Swiss bank account in the name of Missy Mobbs and, despite the security of the Swiss bank being the strongest in the world, it was only a matter of moments before Ninja had accessed the account details in full. She high-fived her twin sister in recognition of her computer skills.

The entries on the account were far more interesting than the UK bank account, the balance was several millions of pounds. The account had been open for over five years and there were lots of income entries all on different dates. The income amounts ranged from £10,000 to £100,000. The only references against the income were names; no two names were the same. There was no pattern to the income which had started as soon as the account had been opened and no obvious explanation. There were payments out, made to an un-named account in the same Swiss bank, the same account each time. The payments were for exactly forty percent of each payment received, and went out on the same day as the money came in. There were only a few expense items, including the car purchase and a few withdrawals for cash, large amounts of cash, again on the same day as income was received in to her account. The team had found this out all within two hours of Hannah entering their office. They relayed this information, along with a list of the names on the bank entries, to Hannah. Hannah then emailed it to Professor Noble.

Chapter Thirty Two

The List

When the professor saw the information, he was shocked. He didn't know what to make of it and not sure what he should do first. He looked at the long list of names paying money into Charlotte Mobbs' Swiss bank account. He kept staring at the names on the list. Everest, Smythe, Gupta, Fenton, Fisher, Barron - the list went on and on, there were over fifty names on the list. There was something familiar about them. Initially he could not work it out, then something in his brain clicked. He turned on his computer and accessed the General Medical Council web site. He searched for the medical register where it has a list of doctors in the United Kingdom, showing their registration status, training and other useful information - what he found astonished him. All of the names on the list of income entries in to Charlotte Mobbs' Swiss bank account were on that list, it could not be a coincidence. He looked at the first name on the list, Everest. Professor John Everest was a neurologist surgeon and had been practising for over thirty years. Professor Noble searched his history and found that Professor Everest had an unblemished career, as did all of the other names on the list. What was he missing?

He recognised another of the names on the list as a surgeon who he had worked with several years ago, Doctor Paul Barron. He searched for Doctor Barron on his computer and saw that he had recently retired. Professor Nobler scrolled through the long list of contacts on his phone and found that he still had the surgery phone number for Doctor Barron. Professor Noble got through to the surgery, knowing that Doctor Barron had retired. He knew the assistant who had answered the telephone and he introduced himself. He reminisced with the assistant and told her that he was an old friend of the doctor and asked for his mobile phone number. After putting the professor on hold for a few moments, she found the mobile phone number of Doctor Barron and gave it to Professor Noble. He called the number immediately and, after a few rings, Doctor Barron answered. Professor Noble introduced himself and they started to talk about old times. Doctor Barron lived in St John's Wood which was only a few miles away from Hampstead. It was another affluent area in a north west London suburb and they agreed to meet up the next day for lunch. Lunch was at The Ivy Café in St John's Wood High Street. Professor Noble had booked the table for two and they met on time at the restaurant where they were taken to a quiet table at the back of the restaurant. Professor Noble had taken his digital voice activated dictation machine and turned it on when they sat at the table, to record the conversation. Doctor Barron was older than Professor Noble by a few years and was now retired. He had a dishevelled look about him; his hair was grey and untidy; he was wearing a jacket and tie but the jacket was stained. It was clear to Professor Noble that Doctor Barron had hit hard times. Lunch comprised of the Ivy Burger and Shepherd's Pie, two of The Ivy's specialities and was washed down with a fine red wine, a very pleasant Cotes-Du-Rhone. The two professors talked for ages, mainly about their respective careers as well as their personal lives. Towards the end of the main course Professor Noble decided to make a bold statement to Doctor Barron. "I can't believe the cheek of Charlotte Mobbs." he said to Doctor Barron. Doctor Barron stopped his fork just as it was about to enter his mouth with some lamb from the shepherd pie on it. The meat fell back on to the plate. "What do you mean?" the doctor asked, but was clearly startled by the statement. Professor Noble called Doctor Barron's bluff as he thought that he knew where the conversation was headed. "How much did you pay her?" he asked. He already knew the answer as it was on her Swiss bank account statement entry - £20,000. Doctor Barron stared at the professor. "I don't know what you are talking about," he replied but soon realised that the professor knew and there was no point denying it. "I paid that bitch £20,000 in to a Swiss bank account. How did you know?" he asked the professor. Professor Noble did not answer. "Why did you pay her? Why did you pay Charlotte Mobbs? What did she have on you?" he asked. "I made a mistake during a minor surgery and there was a medical negligence claim against me," he replied. "I was investigated by Charlotte Mobbs, James Hopkiss from the insurers, Clementine Follows, an accountant. There was one other person involved, but they did not show their face during the meetings," he continued. "The investigation didn't go well and I was about to be struck off the medical register. I couldn't afford to lose my job as I had many expenses and was in over my head with a gambling debt," he continued. "Mobbs could see that I was upset and took me to one side separately, after the meeting. She told me that there was another way forward. She told me that for a one-off payment of £20,000 she would, in return, recommend that I would be given a warning only. I had no choice but to agree and made the payment to her Swiss bank account. A few days later I received a letter from Mobbs with a warning and fine, but kept my job." Professor Noble told him not to worry, he would not tell anyone about this but may need his assistance in the future. Doctor Barron seemed almost relieved that he had been able to tell his story. They finished the rest of their lunches and went their separate ways.

Professor Noble went through the list of payees on Mobbs' Swiss bank account and met up with most of the doctors and surgeons on the list. Some had passed away, some were still practising, and some had retired. He started with the retired doctors as they were the easiest to meet up with, their stories were the same as Doctor Barron's story. A mistake during surgery, followed by a medical negligence claim and an investigation. The payments ranged from £10,000 to £100,000. The names of the investigators were always the same, Charlotte Mobbs, Clementine Follows, James Hopkiss and one other male - none of them could remember the name of the other person, it was as if he did not want to be known. They were all was given the option to carry on practising with a written warning, rather than being struck off. Now that he had this information, the professor had to be very careful. It was possible, but unlikely, that one of the doctors would report back to Charlotte Mobbs and warn her about him. Professor Noble had a few more lunch and coffee meetings with the doctors and surgeons from the list, who were still practising. He had more than enough information to proceed with the next stage of his revenge against the system and the people who had worked against him, specifically Charlotte Mobbs. He needed to find out the name of the mystery fourth person in the meetings with the other surgeons. There were only three people in the room during his investigation. Maybe this was why he wasn't offered the same get out payment, not that he would have taken it as it was unethical and against all that he believed in.

Chapter Thirty Three

Professor Noble could not sleep that night, there were so many thoughts going through his head. The following morning, he decided to take an early morning run through Hampstead Heath. It was a beautiful summer morning in London; bright blue sky no clouds and quite warm but not too hot. Hampstead Heath is a large open space in the north west suburbs of London and covers around 800 acres including several ponds and heathland areas as well as paths and cafes. One of the entrances to the heath was close to the end of his road. The professor dressed in his running clothes and put his recently purchased Air Pods in his ears; listening to classical music was his way of concentrating his mind. His run took him from Kenwood House, a 17th century manor in the middle of the park, past several ponds and down to the southern point in Parliament Hill to the bandstand. He didn't notice that he was being followed, and had been since he left his house.

There were several other early morning runners, some running slower and some faster than he was and some running the other way around the heath. He thought that he saw some one that he recognised running towards him, but it was just his imagination. He arrived at a view point area in the heath where he sat on a bench to admire the breath-taking views of the London skyline. He had been sitting on the bench for only a few moments when the person who had been following him, ran up to him. The person was wearing a hoodie and the professor could not see their face. He could not even tell whether it was a man or woman. "Are you Professor Noble?" the person in the hoodie asked him, using a disguised voice. The professor nodded in surprise. The hoodied person handed him an envelope, before running off. He opened the envelope with curiosity and also with caution. Inside the envelope was a memory stick with his name written on one side. He looked around but the hoodied person was nowhere in sight, they had disappeared in to the wooded areas in Hampstead Heath. The professor got up from the bench and continued his run home. He showered, washed his hair and changed in to a smart pair of navy blue jeans and a white cotton short-sleeve shirt. After his shower he went to his Apple iMac computer and inserted the memory stick in to the usb slot. He opened the file on the memory stick and saw a familiar face appear on the screen. It was the face of Doctor Harris, his former surgical assistant from his Harley Street Clinic. Doctor Harris had left a video message for him in a whispered voice. It was clear that she did not want to be heard by whoever was near her. "Meet me at twelve o'clock on Saturday at Lord's Cricket Ground by the entrance to the museum, behind the pavilion. I have some important information which you need to see," the message said. The message did not say why she needed to see him but that he should come alone. She was clearly scared. Saturday was two days away and the professor was extremely curious. He called the number he had for Doctor Harris from when she worked with him but the number was unobtainable. He would have to wait.

Chapter Thirty Four

Saturday came, it was a warm and sunny day, no clouds and a beautiful day to watch a game of cricket, but that was not why he was going to Lord's that day. Professor Noble told Elizabeth what had happened and where he was going, he put his digital dictating machine into his trouser pocket. He had also sent a message to Hannah when he received the message from Doctor Harris. He had asked Hannah if her team of computer experts could hack in to the security system at Lord's cricket ground on Saturday and keep an eye on him. It was a few days away and he knew that it would be an easy job for Hannah and her team. Hannah got his message; it was as good as done. It was only a few miles from the professor's house in Hampstead to St John's Wood and he decided to drive there himself, rather than take public transport. Traffic was light, it was a weekend, and there was none of the usual weekday morning rush hour traffic. He parked his Tesla in St John's Wood Road, right outside the cricket ground. There was a charity cricket match being played and there was a small entrance fee to pay. There were many people dressed in fancy dress as the theme to the day was animals, in line with the charity. Not everyone was dressed up but there were many people dressed in animal suits including rabbits, pandas, leopards, frogs and even a giraffe, amongst others. It was going to be a fun day. He walked the short distance from the W.G Grace Memorial Gates entrance, adjacent to the Lords Tavern pub in St John's Wood Road, to the entrance to the museum. He was fifteen minutes early which gave him time to have a quick look around. He knew Doctor Harris but he wanted to see if he could recognise anyone else. There were a few people milling around but no one that he recognised. He saw the figure of a man with his back to him, by the Tavern stand. The man looked suspicious at first but had clearly been waiting for someone as, after a few moments, he walked away to greet his friend. It was warm and the professor bought himself an ice cream from the shop inside the ground and ate it. He ate it too

93

quickly as it gave him a stomach pain and temporary brain freeze and he regretted his choice.

Twelve noon came and went; Doctor Harris had not turned up for the appointment which she had arranged. The professor was worried but had no way of contacting her. It was nearly 7 am in New York and already Splinter and his team were busy in their office scanning the CCTV cameras in St Johns Wood. They had taken control of the cameras inside the cricket ground with ease. The street cameras were a little more difficult to access but they managed this too, within a few minutes. They had full control. They had seen the professor park and leave his car in St John's Wood Road. They watched him enter the cricket ground through the W.G. Grace Memorial Gates adjacent to the Lords Tavern Public House. They watched him wait, eat his ice cream and look at his watch on several occasions. They later watched him leave the cricket ground to go to back his car.

Chapter Thirty Five

Doctor Helen Harris

At precisely eleven o'clock, Doctor Helen Harris left her apartment in Cambridge Terrace, in the Outer Circle of The Regent's Park. She lived alone in a beautiful two bedroomed apartment on the second floor of the Grade 1 Listed building designed by John Nash which was built in 1825. The open space of The Regent's Park could just about be seen through the trees on the opposite side of the road. As it was such a lovely day Doctor Harris decided that she would walk the one and a half miles from her apartment to Lords Cricket Ground, through The Regent's Park, to meet with Professor Noble. She was really looking forward to seeing the professor; she thought of him as her mentor and also looked up to him like a father figure. She had transferred to working with Professor Clement Tomkins, but had not enjoyed the work she did as much as when she was with Professor Noble. She did not like Professor Tomkins.

Doctor Harris wanted to look good, which was not difficult as she was so attractive. She wore light make up and a pink shade of lipstick. She had put on a pretty floral dress which came to just below her knees and revealed a lovely pair of legs. She knew that the professor had always seen her as a surgeon and she was always in her surgeon gown or suit, but she wanted to impress him. Her hair was tied at the back with a pink ribbon. She changed her mind at the last minute and put on a pair of light weight jeans, a white blouse and trainers, to make the walk more comfortable, she still looked stunning. She also wore a Mulberry clutch bag in which she put her phone, purse and another memory stick with the information for the professor. She also had a sealed envelope with the professor's name on it.

Doctor Harris had had a few relationships but none were serious enough to consider settling down with or marrying. She had a very successful career ahead of her and was concentrating on this. "My time will come to meet the right man," she would tell herself often. She checked herself in the mirror in the hall by her front door, made a few slight adjustments to her clothing and hair, she looked good. Doctor Harris took the lift to the ground floor, she smiled and said good morning to the resident porter, Dave, sitting behind his desk and watching a small TV monitor. "I'm going for a walk around The Regent's Park" she told Dave. "It's such a lovely day, I won't be too long". She opened her clutch bag and handed the sealed envelope addressed to Professor Noble to Dave. "Please give this to Professor Noble and no-one else" she said, "and make sure that you ask for identification". Dave looked at her with a curious expression but nodded and put the envelope into his desk drawer.

Doctor Harris waited for the traffic to clear and crossed over to the opposite side of the Outer Circle, where she entered into The Regent's Park. She looked around to see if she was being followed, but couldn't see anything suspicious. She did not notice a man smoking a cigarette, lurking in the bushes, on the opposite side of the road. She was worried because she knew that the information which she had on the memory stick was incriminating to one particular person. She knew that this person would do anything to stop the information being leaked. She stayed to the main paths, only stopping to sit on one of the many benches to take a rest and admire the beauty of The Regent's Park. She looked around, was she paranoid or did she see someone lurking in the bushes?

Some people in the park were sunbathing and picnicking, whilst others were playing softball and cricket with temporary pitches, using clothes for bases and boundaries. She continued her walk along the side of the boating lake. There were some people on the rowing boats and adult pedalos on the lake, with other people paddling, close to the side, as well as children playing and splashing on the water's edge. There was no one else around her, although she did see a man turn his back on her as she walked past him, Doctor Harris did not pay much attention to him. She had reached the outer circle on the opposite side of the park by Hanover Gate, close to the London Central Mosque.

96

There was not far left to walk to Lord's Cricket Ground, when a man came up to her. He was wearing a dark mask and a cap, with only his eyes visible. She recognised something about the man in the mask, was it his eyes? She stared at him. "I know you. What are you doing? Why are you wearing a mask? she asked. No words were spoken but there was a struggle, Doctor Harris pulled at the mask and revealed the face behind the mask. She was right, she did know who it was. The man grabbed Doctor Harris by the arm. He pulled out a six-inch serrated hunting knife from his pocket and stabbed her several times in the stomach and chest before she even had a chance to scream or call for help. The man dragged her body to a slightly wooded section of the road, opened her clutch bag, took the memory stick out and ran off into the distance, there were no witnesses.

Doctor Harris died within seconds of the first stab entering her body. A few minutes after the attack, the body of Doctor Harris was found behind bushes close in the London Central Mosque in Hanover Gate, The Regent's Park. There was blood all over her white blouse. She had been so close to Lord's Cricket Ground and her meeting with Professor Noble, another few minutes and she would have been there. The professor was oblivious to all of this as he waited outside the museum entrance in Lord's Cricket Ground.

It wasn't long before Doctor Harris' body was found by a couple of young American tourists, walking to The Regent's Park from their hotel on the corner of St Johns Wood Road and Park Road. They were on their way to see the home of the American ambassador, Winfield House, which is on the Outer Circle of The Regent's Park and backs onto the open space of the park. They called 999 and within minutes there were several police cars and ambulances arriving at the scene, with their sirens blaring. The police cordoned off the area where the body of Doctor Harris lay, still and lifeless.

Chapter Thirty Six

Professor Noble sat in his car, outside Lord's cricket ground in St Johns Wood Road and wondered why there was so much traffic for a Saturday lunchtime, it was clearly not because of the cricket match. Several police cars and ambulances raced past his parked car. The noise of the sirens from the emergency services was very loud, something must have happened. He wondered whether it had anything to do with the fact that Doctor Harris had not turned up to meet him, as arranged. He hoped not. He sent a text to Hannah in New York asking if they knew what was happening. Hannah replied saying what they had seen so far and that her colleagues were looking in to an incident on the CCTV cameras around London Central Mosque and The Regent's Park.

The CCTV cameras were very helpful. Splinter and his team could see the scene and a body. They had already received a photo of Doctor Harris from the professor and could see immediately that it was her blood-stained body lying there, motionless. They relayed this information to the professor in a text message, which the professor received immediately. He was speechless and shocked at the news. He had really liked Doctor Harris both as a colleague and friend. Professor Noble could not move his car as the traffic was now gridlocked. He opened the driver's door and put on the security system in the car. He walked the short distance along St John's Wood Road to the London Central Mosque, where he could see the cordoned off area at Hanover Gate and a large crowd gathering. He carried on walking to the scene but was stopped by a police officer on duty.

Splinter and his team started to search the CCTV in the area and reverse traced Doctor Harris' movements from when she left her apartment to the moment that she was murdered, close to the London Central Mosque. They scoured the CCTV images and saw that a man was following her discretely, concealing himself in the bushes and not following the open paths or spaces. The man did not look up and they could not see his face, he clearly knew where the CCTV cameras were and did not look at them.

He was wearing a plain track suit and trainers, like a normal jogger in the park and blended in well with the surroundings. They saw the moment that the knifeman put on his mask and they also witnessed the murder of Doctor Harris. The facial recognition software which they had created could not find a match to the face of the mystery man as he had not looked up at all. They traced the mystery man back to the moment where he was hiding close to Doctor Harris' apartment, in Cambridge Terrace. They could tell by his movements and by his demeanour that he was not a young man. He had a slightly rounded figure and did not seem to be very healthy. They noticed that he was walking with a slight shuffle, or a limp. He had been waiting on the opposite side of the road from Doctor Harris' apartment and they could see him smoking a cigarette. They watched him stubbing out the cigarette, and several others previously, whilst he had been waiting for Doctor Harris to emerge from her apartment. They followed the cameras back in time to see where he came from. The mystery man could be seen entering in to The Regent's Park Outer Circle from Park Square but lost him in Marylebone Road, where the CCTV cameras were not working. Before that, the trail stopped. There was no visibility of him anywhere, they did not know who the mystery man was. Splinter and his team were annoyed with themselves; this was not like them and they did not like to fail. They reported their findings back to Hannah.

Chapter Thirty Seven

Arthur Cozin

Hannah called her father, Arthur Cozin, on his mobile phone, in London. She told him what Splinter and his team had witnessed and asked for his assistance. He was only too happy to assist. Arthur Cozin had retired from being a detective in the Metropolitan Police force but had helped Hannah set up her private detective agency in New York, and still kept in contact with his colleagues in the Met. Arthur and Hilda Cozin had sold their large family house in Islington and now lived in a two bedroomed flat in Islington. Arthur did not drive anymore, due to ill health, and relied very much on the London transport system. As soon as he finished the conversation with his daughter, he put on some sensible walking shoes and went to the nearest Underground Station, Angel. He waited on the platform for a couple of minutes before a blast of air entered the station platform, preceding the arrival of the northbound Northern Line train. He waited for a few passengers to exit the train and then entered the carriage, he was only going for one stop and stood by the door. The next station was King's Cross & St Pancras where he got out of the Northern Line train and walked through several passageways and up staircases, to the Metropolitan Line platform. He was only on the westbound Metropolitan Line train for two stops and exited at Great Portland Street Station as it was the nearest station to where he needed to be. He walked up the steps to street level, but had to stop a couple of times to get his breath. He was not as young as he used to be, he thought to himself. He was on Marylebone Road where the traffic on the dual carriageway was constant and noisy. He waited for the traffic lights to turn red before he crossed over the road and was soon by the Park Road entrance to The Regent's Park. He walked the short distance to Cambridge Terrace. He called Hannah to let her know that he had arrived. She already knew this as she had been in Splinter's office and they had tracked him all the way from the moment he left his flat in Islington.

There were several marked and unmarked police cars outside Cambridge Terrace and numerous police officers both in uniform and plain clothes. Arthur Cozin recognised one of the detectives as someone who had worked in his department just before he retired, Christine Acton, known to everyone as Chrissy. Detective Inspector Chrissy Acton was in charge of the investigation in to the murder of Doctor Harris. Chrissy had, in his mind, always been going places and it was no surprise to Arthur that she was in charge. Arthur looked at Chrissy, she was about the same age and height as his daughter but that was where the similarity ended. Chrissy had short cropped blond hair, rather boy-like, and a face with strong features suggesting that you would not want to get on the wrong side of her. She was wearing a pair of smart dark jeans and white blouse. Chrissy was five foot nine inches tall and had a tough character, she had been brought up in Mile End, in the east end of London, where there were many gangs and drug dealers. She had always managed to stay out of trouble. She had an elderly mother to look after and her father had died when she was only nine. She had attended the local school and got herself a Saturday job in the local supermarket on Mile End Road, at the age of fourteen. Chrissy was a good student and knew that an education would keep her out of trouble. At sixteen she went to a careers event in the local Town Hall and that is where she met Arthur Cozin, he was explaining the pros and cons of working in the police force to anyone who would listen. Arthur had seen that she had a lot of potential and was not surprised when Chrissy signed the forms to join the police. She studied hard and sailed through the police training in Hendon, north west London. She soon became a detective and joined the team headed by the then Detective Chief Inspector, Arthur Cozin.

When Arthur Cozin retired, his place was taken by Detective Inspector Tony Pallett, a man twenty year's younger than Arthur and one who had progressed through the ranks quicker than expected. Tony Pallett was soon promoted to Detective Chief

Inspector and then to Detective Superintendent, one of the youngest in the Metropolitan Police, and the country. Chrissy Acton now headed her own team of detectives and was based at Police HQ in New Scotland Yard on Victoria Embankment close to Westminster Bridge and the Houses of Parliament. She had worked with Detective Chief Inspector Cozin at the previous New Scotland Yard building, but it had since been sold for development. She now answered directly to the recently promoted Detective Superintendent Tony Pallett. Arthur Cozin went to the police officer who was standing by the marked police car and asked to speak with Chrissy Acton.

Chapter Thirty Eight

It had been several years since Arthur Cozin had worked with, or even seen, Chrissy Acton but as far as he was concerned, she had not changed, and that was good because she was a very good detective. Chrissy recognised her former boss immediately and greeted him with a warm smile and a hug. "Hi old timer, how are you? Long time no see. What are you doing here?" she asked him, curious as to what he was doing there and what he wanted. "I was just out for a walk in the park when I saw the police cars and then you," he told her. Arthur Cozin did not want to tell her the main reason he was there. She did not believe him, and he knew it, but she did not let on.

He asked her what was happening and she told him what he already knew. "Someone who lived in this apartment building had just been stabbed to death, on the other side of The Regent's Park," she told him. "We are going in to her apartment to see if there was anything there which might explain why she had been murdered. Would you like to come with me, you never know what your experienced eye might find?" She asked him. He was after all one of the best detectives she had worked with and he may be able to help. Arthur Cozin pretended to be thinking about what to do, and then agreed.

They walked up to the resident porter and explained what had happened, he was shocked by the news. The porter held spare keys to all of the apartments. He went to a locked room and came back with the spare key to Doctor Harris' apartment. The flat was on the second floor and Arthur Cozin did not fancy walking up two flights of stairs. The lift was old and small, just enough for the two of them, it was slow but did not take long to reach the second floor. They exited the lift and Chrissy opened the door to the apartment. It was a very clean and tidy apartment, there was no sign of a disturbance and it was clear that the apartment had not been searched. The beds were made in beautiful Egyptian cotton sheets, with many plumped up cushions on top of the bed. Arthur had never understood this, as you had to take the cushions off when you went to bed, but it did look good. The furniture was expensive and the kitchen goods were top range.

It was a very nice apartment and the views from the front were amazing, the open space of The Regent's Park was there in all of its glory, just above the tree line. Chrissy looked around for any clues but there were no obvious ones. She found what she assumed to be Doctor Harris' Apple Mac Book lap top computer on a table in the reception room. The computer was password protected. She did not even attempt to guess the password and put the computer in to a clear plastic evidence bag so that the tech experts could try and open it, back at New Scotland Yard. Whilst she was doing this, Arthur Cozin was secretly video recording the apartment on his iPhone and transmitting live via Facetime to Hannah in New York, just as Hannah had asked him to do.

After a good look around, Detective Inspector Chrissy Acton and Arthur Cozin left the apartment and agreed to keep in touch with the investigation. Arthur Cozin walked across the road and called Hannah on his iPhone. Hannah told him where the mystery man had been hiding and that he had been smoking. Arthur went to the area and, sure enough, there were four fresh cigarette butts on the floor. Arthur took a clean plastic bag from his pocket and placed it around his hand, as he did not want to cross contaminate the evidence by transferring his DNA on to the cigarette butts.

He had seen this happen so many times in his career and knew that it could make or break a case if you do it the wrong way. He picked up the cigarette butts, turned the bag inside out and sealed it with the cigarette butts inside.

Chapter Thirty Nine

Detective Inspector Chrissy Acton

In Chrissy Acton's office, on her desk, was a photo of her family. A smart looking husband and two small children, a boy and a girl aged five and seven, taken on a family holiday two years earlier in Portugal. They all looked very happy as a family but that was then and not the case now. Chrissy was having problems with her marriage due to her working over eighty hours per week and being on call 24/7. Her husband, Pete, had asked her on many occasions to reduce her work load, but to no avail. She was a workaholic; they had tried but could not sort out their differences and they had separated. Chrissy had moved out of their family home and was staying in the Park Plaza, Westminster Bridge Hotel. Her children were staying with their father in the family home. The hotel was on the opposite side of the River Thames and a pleasant half mile walk across Westminster Bridge to her office, in New Scotland Yard. Her room was an upgraded studio room at the front of the tenth floor and had amazing views of Big Ben and the River Thames.

Chrissy Acton returned from Cambridge Terrace, with her team of detectives, to Police HQ. The security to get in to the building was immense as there had been several recent, unsuccessful terrorist attempts trying to cause damage to the building. Having passed through the security scanners, she took the lift to the fourth floor, where her office was located. There were glass doors and a glass screen between her office and the open plan floor area where the other detectives had their desks. Her office was fairly small; there was enough room for her desk and a filing cabinet. On her desk was a computer screen and keyboard. Despite the size of the office, there were amazing views over the River Thames towards Westminster Bridge. The London Eye was on the opposite side of the river, next to the former County Hall building. Chrissy would stay in the office on New Year's Eve and watch the fantastic firework display right in front of the building, she had a front row seat. She looked out of her office window and took a deep breath as she walked out of her office to her team of detectives.

The contents which they had removed from Doctor Harris' apartment, including the computer, were in evidence bags on the desk of one of the other detectives, Detective Sergeant Harry Bond. His colleagues nicknamed him James and he had got used to this. Detective Sergeant Bond fancied himself as a bit of a computer wizard, but he could not get past the password protection of the computer. The computer would have to be sent to the police tech lab to be opened. The other members of her team were detectives Pearce and Cross, both in their mid-forties. Despite being older than Chrissy, they were both happy to be working with her as they knew how good she was and how well they worked as a team.

Chrissy had arranged for a magnetic board to be cleared and then placed at one end of the room. A photo of Doctor Harris had been put on the board and kept in place by four small magnets, one in each corner of the photo, with her name below. Next to the photo of Doctor Harris was a photo of the apartment block and a large map of The Regent's Park. It had been marked with a red marker pen, clearly showing the area where Doctor Harris had entered the Park and also where she had been brutally murdered. The photo of her dead body was on the board, also on the board was a photo of Arthur Cozin. She knew it was not a coincidence that he just happened to be passing at the exact moment that they were investigating a murder. She doubted that he would have had anything to do with the murder, but he had been there at exactly the same time and she wanted to know why. Coffee was brought to her by the new Detective Constable, Andi Lester, who had only recently started working with Chrissy's team after being transferred from Thames Valley division. Andi was a slender thirty year old woman who had a pretty, slim face with lovely hazel-coloured eyes, brown hair to just below her shoulders and well-manicured nails. She had a great figure, which she kept hidden by the loose blouses and trousers that she wore to work. Andi was a very sexy lady and one that many men, including the detectives in the office that they were now in, had tried to chat up - but to no avail. Andi was not interested in men anymore, not after several bad relationships, including the most recent one - an affair with her married cousin. She was far more into women these days.

Chrissy liked the look of Andi and sometimes fantasised about what it would be like to have sex with her. Chrissy had always been straight and had only had a few sexual partners before she married Pete, they were all males. There was something about Andi that turned her on, she was indeed a very sexy woman. Andi had just finished a relationship herself and fancied Chrissy. Although she did not let Chrissy know, everyone else seemed to know – it was not a well-kept secret. Chrissy put her thoughts to one side for a moment, this was not the time to be fantasising. She had seen so many nice and horrible things in her line of work that she had learned to compartmentalise her thoughts. It was something that she could do easily and it was a very good asset for the job she did. "You two, go back to The Regent's Park with photos of Doctor Harris and interview as many people in the park as you can, to see if someone had witnessed the murder, or even to confirm the route which the doctor had taken," Detective Inspector Chrissy Acton instructed detectives Pearce and Cross. "Detective Constable Lester and I will go and interview the resident porter at the apartment where Doctor Harris lived. Detective Sergeant Bond, you check the CCTV in the areas around The Regent's Park," she continued.

Chapter Forty

Arthur Cozin had put the cigarette butts in the plastic bag and returned home. He called his good friend and former colleague, Stuart Barnes, an expert in DNA and had often assisted Detective Chief Inspector Cozin when the police DNA team could not get results. Stuart Barnes worked for a large company with an office in The Shard, close to London Bridge on the south side of the River Thames. The Shard became the tallest building in the European Union when it was built, at just over 1,000 feet in height and seventy two storeys. The building can be seen from miles away and became an iconic building very quickly since it was finished in 2012. There are twenty six floors of offices, three restaurants, the five-star Shangri-La Hotels and Resorts, residential apartments and the UK's highest viewing gallery, The View from The Shard. The offices where Stuart Barnes was based had 9,000 square feet, it was on the twenty second floor and had views all over the north, east and west of London and beyond. The two men arranged to meet in The Aqua Restaurant on the 31st floor. They had not seen each other for a few years, not since Arthur Cozin had retired. Neither of them had changed much, perhaps a few pounds heavier in weight, they recognised each other immediately.

They sat at the pre-booked table, close to one of the large windows. They were creatures of habit and ordered a glass of whisky, before ordering a light meal of sea bass, they had eaten there before many times. They glared through the glass and amazed at the views across London's west end, spotting land marks and pointing, like excited children. They could see Wembley Stadium to the north west, The Houses of Parliament to the west and Canary Wharf to the east. They could see the twists and turns of the River Thames and airplanes turning on to the approach to land at Heathrow. You could spend all day there just looking out of the windows but that was not why they were there. After talking niceties, they got down to talk about the real reason that they were there. Arthur Cozin gave the plastic bag with the cigarette butts to Stuart Barnes to test for DNA.

"I'll have the results for you tomorrow" Stuart told Arthur as they ate their delicious sea bass. After a long catch-up chat, they left the restaurant. Stuart went to his office a few floors down in The Shard whilst Arthur took the London Underground, Northern Line from London Bridge Station, the few stops to Angel and back to his apartment in Islington.

Chapter Forty One

Professor Noble, having been turned away from The Regent's Park by the police cordon, called Hannah. Hannah gave him as much information as she felt he needed to know at this stage. She told the professor where Doctor Harris lived and that it was only a short distance away on the opposite side of The Regent's Park. There was so much traffic that the professor decided to wait a while and walk across The Regent's Park to Cambridge Terrace, in the Outer Circle. He did not realise that he was actually following the exact reverse route which Doctor Harris had walked only a short while ago. The professor soon reached Cambridge Terrace and went to the main entrance door where the resident porter was sitting behind his desk. The porter was not used to all of the attention that he was receiving.. He asked the professor who he was and why he was there. When the professor told him his name the porter looked surprised. He remembered what Doctor Harris had said when she had left and asked the professor for identification. The professor produced his driving licence and the porter handed him the sealed envelope with his name on it. It was now the professor's turn to look surprised, he was not expecting this. He looked at the envelope but did not open it. Instead he thanked the porter, put the envelope in his pocket and walked out of the building.

A minute later, Chrissy Acton and Andi Lester returned and parked their unmarked black Audi A3 in the slip road in front of the apartment building, a place usually restricted for residents only. They did not see the professor leave the building. There was a sign saying that illegally parked cars would be towed away and the owners face a heavy fine, but they were the police and this did not apply to them as they were on official business. The professor returned across The Regent's Park and back to his car. He drove home to where Elizabeth was waiting, she had seen the news and was worried about the safety of her husband. He went in to his study and turned on his Apple iMac computer. He then put the memory stick in to the USB reader slot and waited a few moments for the information to appear on the large screen in front of him. The screen lit up with figures and dates, along with names, many names. He recognised some of the names on the list, they were the same names as he had come across when he found the Swiss bank account names. Only this time there were more names and dates. He could not believe what he was seeing, but it explained a lot of things and he could understand why Doctor Harris had been scared, and for which she was ultimately murdered.

The professor also knew that the information which he had received could put him and his family in danger, if the person mentioned on the screen in front of him knew that he had a copy. Doctor Harris had already been murdered for this information. He would have to be very careful what he did with the information and who he shared it with. He knew that one person he could trust was Hannah Cozin. He pressed a few icons on the computer screen in front of him and sent the contents of the memory stick by email to Hannah, she received it immediately. He called Hannah and told her that he wanted to go to the police with the memory stick but Hannah told him not to go just yet. She needed to check to make sure that no-one in the police was involved. She did not want to put the professor in any more danger than he already was. The professor showed the contents of the memory stick to Elizabeth and they both sat staring in disbelief at the information on the monitor. Now all they needed was a plan, and some assistance.

Chapter Forty Two

Cambridge Terrace, The Regent's Park

Detective Inspector Chrissy Acton and Detective Constable Andi Lester walked in to the building and acknowledged the porter, showing him their id's, as they walked past him to the lift. The lift arrived and the gates opened. Andi pressed the lift button to the second floor where Doctor Harris' flat was located. The lift was slow and also very small. There was a moment when the two police officers' arms brushed close to each other and touched, albeit slightly. Chrissy wondered whether it was just an accidental touch, but she felt a shiver go down her spine and her body tingled. She felt her face flush slightly and hoped that Detective Constable Lester had not noticed, but she had. Their eyes made contact for just a moment longer than usual and they gave a knowing smile at each other, no words were spoken. They were both professionals and knew that this was not the time or place to proceed with whatever had just happened in the lift. Chrissy and Andi both knew that there was chemistry between them but needed to concentrate on the reason that they were in the building.

The door to the flat was marked with blue police tape for a crime scene and a notice saying not to enter unless with police authority. When they went in to the flat it was clear that something was not right. They noticed a few changes, very small changes and so small that they would probably not be noticed by a civilian. Some of the drawers and cupboard doors in the kitchen had been opened and closed slightly, but not fully closed. When Chrissy had left the flat earlier, she had personally closed the drawers and doors. It was also apparent that someone had searched the bedrooms as the bed coverings had been moved slightly. They looked around the flat but there was no one there. They had a further quick look to see if there was anything that they had missed the first time and then they walked down the two flights of wide stairs to the entrance lobby.

"Has anyone else had been to the flat today?" Chrissy asked the porter. "I have not seen anyone, but I did take a thirty minute break earlier and my desk was un-manned during that time," he replied. Chrissy asked to see the CCTV footage of the time when he was not there, he duly obliged. The black and white pictures on the screen were grainy and unclear but they could see a man enter the building a few minutes after the porter had left his desk. The man had been very deliberate in trying to avoid the CCTV cameras, as if he knew exactly where they were located. He had his back to the camera and wore a cap on his head which was lowered over the top of his face so when he did turn around, they could not see his face. He was wearing gloves.

They could tell that the person on the screen was male. He had a slightly rounded figure and he shuffled a bit when he walked. They watched him get in the lift to the second floor and break in to Doctor Harris' flat. The mystery man must have been watching the building for some time as he knew the exact time that the porter went on a break and for how long the area was unattended. About fifteen minutes later he emerged from the flat and took the lift down to the ground floor and out to the street. "I will need a copy of that recording," DI Acton said to the porter. The porter nodded and went away for a few moments before coming back with a memory stick in his hand. "All yours," he said to the Detective.

Chrissy called the forensic department and asked them to re-check the stairs, lift and apartment for fingerprints, but she knew that they would not find anything, as the mystery man was wearing gloves.

Chapter Forty Three

Charlotte Mobbs

Charlotte Mobbs worked from home and was sitting at the mahogany desk in her home office in her large house in Mill Hill. It was a large square room with matching mahogany wood display cabinets and shelves attached to two walls. There was a photograph of her and her previous partner and another photo of her cats on the shelves, along with a copy of her Oxford University degree in medicine and psychology.

She was researching her next unfortunate victim when her phone flashed with a notification from Sky News. The news was about a female doctor being brutally stabbed to death in The Regent's Park. She knew that Doctor Harris had accumulated information about her and her associate and had instructed her associate to "deal" with the situation. She smiled as she knew that the situation had been dealt with and was turned on by this news and decided to stop her research for a few hours. She went upstairs to her bedroom where she opened a drawer which was full of vibrators. She decided to use her favourite rabbit style vibrator. She went in to her shower, turned the water on and pleasured herself, she came immediately and with such intensity that her whole body shook. She sat on the bed and dried herself. After a few moments she dressed in to a tight fitting, pink swimsuit which was very unflattering. Her shoulder length hair was tied up in a small pony tail at the back of her head. She picked out a small Chanel bag from her walk-in wardrobe and put her Chanel glasses and the latest Apple iPhone inside. She walked down the stairs to her spacious kitchen where she opened the freezer compartment of the large double door American fridge/freezer. She reached for a bottle of unopened limited edition, individually numbered, Absolut Crystal Pinstripe Black Bottle Vodka. There were only 800 bottles made; each bottle had cost her well over £5,000, she owned ten of them. They were for special occasions and this was definitely one of those special occasions.

She poured a small amount of the rare vodka in to a shot glass and drank it down in one throw of the glass. She then poured another three shots and tipped each one in to a glass tumbler. She usually took ice from the ice bucket section of the freezer department, but this time she did not. The vodka was cold enough. She walked towards the glass doors at the rear of the kitchen, opened them and walked in to the garden, holding her Chanel bag in one hand and the tumbler with vodka in the other. It was a glorious sunny and warm day as she walked to the swimming pool in her large garden and sat on one of the six sun loungers, beneath a cantilevered parasol.

She put her Chanel bag and glass tumbler on the table beside her, took out the Chanel sunglasses from the bag and placed them on the top of her head. As soon as she sat down, her phone rang. She recognised the name and answered immediately. There were no pleasantries spoken. "Have you heard the news about Doctor Harris?" asked the person at the other end of the phone.

The voice was not its usual calm style and she could tell that there was something not quite right, she was right. The person on the other end of the phone told her that there was a missing memory stick but that he would find it and that she should not worry. The conversation ended abruptly, it was always a short conversation when they spoke and this was no different. Charlotte Mobbs had become a very cold and nasty person as she had made more and more money and manipulated more and more people's lives. She finished her vodka and decided that it was too hot in the garden; she went back inside to her home office and continued her research.

Chapter Forty Four

Charlotte Mobbs' research was in to a surgeon who, similarly to all of the other surgeons that she had investigated, had made an error whilst carrying out surgery. The surgeon, Professor Diane Clifton, was well qualified and well established as an ophthalmologist and had her clinic in the same building as Professor Noble, in Harley Street. A routine operation for laser surgery, which Professor Clifton had carried out hundreds of times, had gone wrong. The patient was a famous tv presenter; he had been left permanently blind in one eye and was suing the clinic for millions. In addition to researching the facts of the case Charlotte Mobbs did what she always did before visiting the clinic. She looked in to the personal information of her next potential victim. She looked in to the records kept about the number of operations that Professor Clifton had carried out in her career, there were thousands. She knew what the average cost was for each of the operations and did a quick calculation as to the future potential income of the professor, as well as searching Companies House for any company accounts. Charlotte Mobbs then researched the professor's private life. She looked on social media and saw that Professor Clifton had a good life style. Lots of luxury holidays, an expensive car and lots of socialising. She also had a young family. She was, in Charlotte Mobbs opinion, a perfect victim.

The following day Charlotte Mobbs took a taxi from her home in Mill Hill and met up with her colleagues for the new investigation. Her former colleague, Clementine Follows, was now deceased and had been replaced with a young boy, Franklin Mack. Franklin was fresh out of accountancy school and had started with the investigation team only six weeks earlier. It was to be his first time working with Charlotte Mobbs. The insurance company was the same company who had insured Professor Noble. James Hopkiss was no longer employed by the company and they had sent another representative, Clare Court. Clare had worked in the same office as James Hopkiss and was glad that he had been so publicly dismissed. He had attempted to seduce her on several occasions; each time she declined him, the nastier he became towards her. James had become angry when Clare declined his advances and she was not sure what he was capable of... but he was gone and she was now doing his job.

Clare had heard about Charlotte Mobbs' reputation but this would be her first time working together with her. Charlotte Mobbs had arranged to meet with Clare and Franklin half an hour before the meeting, in a café around the corner from the clinic, so that they could go through their research.

At precisely nine o'clock in the morning the three investigators went to the clinic in Harley Street to their meeting with Professor Clifton. Professor Clifton had cancelled any operations that day and sent her staff home so that they would have the office to themselves. The phones were transferred to an answer service. During the investigation, Franklin was looking through the previous three years of accounts and a projected cash flow forecast for the next year. The annual income had been in excess of one million pounds and the profits of just under half a million. The investigation had slowly progressed until lunchtime, when Charlotte Mobbs announced to Professor Clifton that they had nearly finished. There was a knock on the door and a man stepped in to the clinic, it was Professor Clement Tomkins from the open-heart surgery clinic in the same building. Charlotte Mobbs saw him and looked surprised, she advised Professor Tomkins that it was a private meeting and that he should leave. He scowled at her but did as he was told.

Clare Court and Franklin Mack had been writing down copious notes during the meeting. The meeting was over and Charlotte Mobbs told them to go to the café where they had met before the meeting and that she would follow them shortly. Clare and Franklin left the office, Charlotte Mobbs went to the window and made sure that they had also left the building. Mobbs allowed a few minutes to pass before she went out of the office and into the communal area of the building. She waited for a few moments before she re-entered the surgery and spoke with Professor Clifton. Mobbs told Professor Clifton that, based on the evidence that she and her team of investigators had collected,

117

it was not looking good. She reminded Professor Clifton about the unfortunate situation concerning Professor Noble two years earlier, whose clinic had been in the same building, and that he was forced to close his clinic because of a similar situation. Mobbs explained to Professor Clifton that the professional indemnity insurers will pay out the financial damages to the patient, but that it will be virtually impossible for her to obtain insurance going forward. She explained that the insurance premium would be so high that it would not be affordable, and that no other insurance company would insure her.

She also told Professor Clifton that she would more than likely be struck off the list of surgeons and would not be able to carry on her practice, or her luxury lifestyle. Charlotte Mobbs lowered her voice, which startled the professor. "There is another alternative solution," she said to the professor. "In order to make the investigation go away, I can recommend that the insurance company settle the claim. The file will be closed and there will be no further investigation," she continued. "I will advise the insurers to carry on insuring you with only a small rise in premium. There will, of course, be a written warning and a fine. The cost to make this happen will be a one-off payment to me of £100,000. You have five minutes to consider the offer, or the offer will be withdrawn," Mobbs continued.

Professor Clifton's initial reaction to this was one of outrage but soon realised the horror of the alternative. She agreed to the payment. Mobbs gave her the details of her Swiss bank account and how to make payment, she left the building passing Professor Tomkins in the waiting area, giving him a smile as she passed him. Mobbs went to the café and sat at the table with Clare Court and Franklin Mack. She took her iPhone out of her bag and opened the app for her Swiss bank account. She saw that there had been a deposit within the past five minutes for the equivalent of £100,000. She thanked Clare and Franklin for their assistance and told them that she would make her report to them shortly. She had a quick cappuccino, two Danish pastries and left to go back to her home office. Mobbs then hailed a black taxi and sat back noticing the lack of noise in the electric motored taxi. She re-opened the Swiss bank app on her iPhone and transferred the equivalent of £40,000 to her associate.

Chapter Forty Five

Detective Inspector Chrissy Acton and Detective Andi Lester left Doctor Harris' flat with the copy of the CCTV recording. Before returning to New Scotland Yard police HQ, they decided to go and see Arthur Cozin in his flat in Islington. They did not discuss their moment in the lift. Arthur knew that Chrissy was on her way to him as Hannah had asked Splinter to keep an eye on any development. Splinter had been tracking Chrissy's car and phone conversations, it was one of the many things that he could do in his sleep, if required. Chrissy and Andi arrived at the duplex penthouse apartment on the top two floors of a recently converted former warehouse just off Upper Street, Islington. They pressed the Entryphone doorbell at the communal entrance and waited. Arthur Cozin's voice answered the Entryphone and he invited them in. The lift in this building was much larger than the lift in Cambridge Terrace, with plenty of room for more than two people. Chrissy and Andi looked at the size of the lift and smiled at each other, each knowing exactly what the other person was thinking. The lift opened straight in to the penthouse flat, where Arthur and Hilda Cozin were waiting inside. A quick guided tour showed the open plan accommodation of just over 1,000 square feet and there was a roof terrace of 500 square feet. There were views over other surrounding flats and rooftops. From the terrace, you could see The Shard where Arthur had had his meeting with Stuart Barnes earlier. Hilda offered cups of tea to the detectives and left them to talk on the roof terrace, where they looked at the views before sitting at the table and chairs provided. Tea was soon served with an old-school tea pot, vintage bone china tea cups and saucers, and a plate full of assorted biscuits.

After a few moments the polite conversation soon turned to business. Chrissy did all of the talking to begin with, she knew how Arthur's mind worked, having worked with him on several cases together. Arthur had spoken with Hannah only a few minutes before Chrissy had arrived, they decided that it would be OK to share some of the basic information with Chrissy. Chrissy asked Arthur again what he was doing in The Regent's Park and how he just happened to be at the crime scene at the exact same moment that she was there. Chrissy was not expecting a full answer and was surprised when Arthur told her that he had not been just passing but had been asked to go there by his daughter, Hannah.

He explained that Hannah was a private detective, working in New York, and told her of the connection between Hannah and Professor Noble. He told Chrissy that Doctor Harris was on her way to meet Professor Noble at Lord's, but was killed on the way to the meeting. He also told Chrissy that Doctor Harris had some information for the professor. He did not know what it was, but it must have been important as she was murdered for it. Andi was writing the information down in her note book, every word. Arthur did not mention about the cigarette butts or his meeting with a DNA expert. Tea was finished, and so was the questioning. The two detectives returned to New Scotland Yard police HQ, where Chrissy convened a meeting with the rest of the detective team. She wanted to be updated on the progress.

Detective Sergeant Bond had sent Doctor Harris' laptop computer to the tech lab to be opened and was waiting for news. Detectives Pearce and Cross had returned empty handed from The Regent's Park. There had been no witnesses and no clues to be found at the site where Doctor Harris' body had been found. Chrissy wrote a name on the white board, with a blue marker pen, "Mystery Man" along with the time line of when the mystery man was seen entering Doctor Harris' flat. She had found a photograph of Professor Emerson Noble online. She printed it out, attaching it to the board next to his name, along with a large question mark.

It was late in the day and Chrissy suggested to her team that they go home and come back with some fresh ideas in the morning. "I will be looking in to Professor Emerson Noble tomorrow," she told her colleagues. She asked Detective Lester to remain behind as there was something that she wanted to run by her. The male colleagues gave knowing glances to each other and left the office. Once the male colleagues had left, Chrissy asked Andi to come in to her office. Chrissy was standing behind her desk. Andi walked past her and looked through the darkened double-glazed window down to the streets below. It was twilight and the street lights were lighting up. The traffic was solid in the London rush hour. The offices and shops were closing and there were hundreds of people on the streets. Office workers were making their way to the bus stops and Westminster Tube station. Tourists were crossing both ways over Westminster Bridge to the London Eye on the south bank and the Houses of Parliament and London's West End on the north, with its many theatres, restaurants and pubs. Chrissy walked towards Andi and stood behind her, breathing on Andi's neck. Andi did not move, she wanted to wait to see what Chrissy was going to do. It had been obvious to them both, earlier that day, that there was a sexual connection when they were in the lift going to Doctor Harris' flat. On that occasion it was inappropriate as they were at a potential crime scene and looking for clues. Now, they were off duty. Chrissy pressed the front of her body gently in to Andi's back. She put her arms around Andi, cupping her breasts and gently massaged them until she could hear Andi moaning with pleasure. She kissed the back of Andi's exposed neck, above her shirt collar, and could feel Andi's nipples stiffening in the bra concealed by the cotton blouse. Andi turned around slowly and they kissed, passionately. This was the first time that Chrissy had kissed another woman. The kiss seemed to last for ages, such was the passion, but it was only a short kiss. No words were spoken as they took the lift to the ground floor and hailed a taxi. The taxi took them the short distance across Westminster Bridge to the Park Plaza Westminster Bridge Hotel, where Chrissy was living. They took the lift to the tenth floor and entered the upgraded studio room. Chrissy and Andi explored each other's bodies and made love for hours before they fell asleep, cuddling up in the comfortable but dishevelled bed.

Chapter Forty Six

It was late morning when Stuart Barnes received the DNA results from the cigarette butts which Arthur Cozin had left with him to be tested. He called Arthur to let him know the name of the mystery man. Arthur thanked Stuart and pressed the red button on his phone to end the call. He immediately called Hannah to let her know the news. It was early morning in New York when Hannah saw her father's name light up on her iPhone but she was already in her office discussing her latest case with Splinter and his team. It was about a politician who had been caught with his fingers in the till, embezzling from a charity and also suspected by his wife of having an affair. She put that aside for a few moments as her father's news was to take priority.

Splinter took control as soon as he had the name of the person whose DNA had been found on the cigarette butts. Danno split his team into groups to do their specialist tasks – they all knew exactly what was needed and what to do. Danno and Markie brought up photos of the mystery man on to the large monitor on the wall in front of them. They had found all of his personal information of family, friends as well as schools, colleges and work places from when he was born until today. There was a long list, including the masonic lodge to which the mystery man belonged. Lucia and Ninja looked in to the finances of the mystery man, whilst Kaz looked in to his phone records. What they found was compelling and they could see exactly why this person could be wanting to kill Doctor Harris.

The mystery man had a bank account at the same Swiss bank as Charlotte Mobbs and there were transactions in to the mystery man's account on the exact same days as money was paid in to Mobbs' cat's account. Each transaction was a transfer from Mobbs' account for exactly forty percent of the money received by Mobbs, including the latest payment of £40,000 within the past 24 hours. There was also a cash withdrawal, representing ten percent of the total amount, taken out of this account on the same day as the money arrived in to the account. This information, along with the information on the memory stick information received from Professor Noble, was enough information to have the mystery man questioned, but they were not the police and the police did not have this information. Kaz discovered from the phone records that the mystery man had Charlotte Mobbs' number stored in his phone, and every number that he had called was still in the system. There were a few voice messages and text messages between them as well. All of the calls, voicemails and texts messages were downloaded by Kaz in to their system and a big picture of the entire scam was falling in to place. Kaz re-accessed Mobbs' phone records and cross referenced the calls and messages to see if there were any other patterns or calls made at the same time. There were. Every time money was paid in to Mobbs' Swiss bank account, there was a phone call trail between Mobbs and the mystery man as well as a call from the mystery man to another mobile phone number. It would take only a matter of moments before Kaz found out who this was, she was that good. Danno called Hannah in to his team's office and updated her with the information which they had found. Hannah recognised the names of the people who Splinter and his team had uncovered, including who they suspected was the ring leader. He was a member of the same masonic lodge as the mystery man, Hannah passed this information to her father.

Chapter Forty Seven

Chrissy and Andi woke early to the bright sunlight shining through the hotel suite window. Andi got out of bed and walked naked to the window, and gazed across the River Thames towards the Houses of Parliament and Big Ben. Chrissy admired the perfect curves of Andi's naked body before she ordered room service for breakfast to be delivered in one hour. She got out of bed and stood next to Andi, they kissed and held hands and looked across the river together. They had lots to do at work but before that they took a shower together, kissing as they rubbed shower gel on to each other's bodies. After the shower they dressed just as breakfast arrived, perfect timing. Breakfast was made up of toast, coffee and orange juice as well as scrambled eggs and bacon. They discussed the day ahead whilst having breakfast but it was decided that Andi would go home and change in to fresh clothes so that no one in the office would suspect that she had spent the night with Chrissy and not been home. They also agreed not to mention the previous night when they met at the office, but thought that it might be a good idea for Andi to bring some spare clothes, just in case. After they had finished breakfast, Andi ordered an Uber to take her to her rented flat in Westbourne Terrace, Paddington. Andi kissed Chrissy goodbye and went downstairs to the hotel lobby, the Uber arrived within minutes. The route to Westbourne Terrace took her over Westminster Bridge, across the River Thames, with Big Ben on her left, along Birdcage walk to Buckingham Palace and then Hyde Park Corner to Park Lane. The expensive hotels and properties were on the right and the open space of Hyde Park on the left. The whole journey had only taken twenty minutes. The traffic was light as rush hour was only just starting. Andi was dropped off outside the long terrace of Victorian houses. There were no full houses left, some were hotels but most of the houses had been converted in to flats. Andi's rented flat was a one bedroomed flat on the fourth floor, there was no lift. She did not mind this; she saw it as extra exercise as she ran up the four flights of stairs to her flat. Once inside her flat Andi reflected on the night she had spent with Chrissy, she smiled to herself.

Andi changed in to fresh clothes comprising a pair of smart tailored blue suit trousers and a loose fitting white, slightly see-through blouse. Her bra could be seen through the blouse material but was concealed when she put on her blue suit jacket. She applied a small amount of make up to her already pretty face and within a half hour Andi walked down the four flights of stairs to the street door and turned left along Westbourne Terrace, walking to Paddington Station where she took the Tube to Westminster Station. When Andi arrived at New Scotland Yard the team were all there, including Chrissy. They all greeted each other and discussed their plan for the day ahead. Nothing was mentioned about the previous night. Doctor Harris' computer was back, it had been opened by the tech experts. They had carried out a deep search in to the computer but there was nothing of interest. Detective Inspector Chrissy Acton reported to her immediate boss, Detective Superintendent Tony Pallett with an update on the case. There had been no new information but Detective Superintendent Tony Pallett had insisted on regular updates, more than usual and one that Chrissy did not understand. The meeting only lasted a few minutes.

After the meeting had finished, DI Chrissy Acton and Detective Constable Andi Lester went to the car pool and took an Audi A4 to go to Professor Noble's house in The Bishop's Avenue. It was about seven miles from Victoria Embankment to the professor's house and was going to take over half an hour to get there. En-route to the professor's house they chatted about the previous night and what they had experienced with each other. They decided that they would like to see each other again, that evening. They soon arrived at the professor's house and looked at each other with shock as they saw the size of the house. The front security gates were locked. Chrissy pressed the button to lower the side window of the Audi. She pushed the intercom button on the brick pillar by the gates to the house, and announced their arrival. There were a few moments of silence before the gates started to open, first the right gate and then the left gate until there was enough space for the car to enter the driveway. Chrissy parked the car next to Elizabeth's Tesla and they walked to the front door where Professor Noble greeted them with a smile.

Chrissy and Andi introduced themselves and produced their warrant cards as id. The professor invited them in. He had already been updated by Hannah with the latest information. Hannah had advised him what he should and should not say to the police, at this stage. He had done nothing wrong but Hannah wanted to proceed carefully, especially with what she had just found out. The professor showed the detectives in to the large drawing room where the they looked at the famous art work hanging on the walls, was that a Faberge Egg in the display cabinet, surely not? There were French doors opening on to a large patio in the rear garden. The professor gestured to the detectives to follow him to the table in the garden where cups, saucers and plates were waiting. It was a lovely sunny day and they sat at the table, enjoying the view of the garden. Elizabeth served tea and biscuits.

Detective Inspector Chrissy Acton explained why they had come to see the professor. She told him that his name had come up in their enquiries and that they knew that Doctor Harris had been on her way to meet with the professor, when she had been murdered. Professor Noble confirmed that a meeting had been arranged at the request of Doctor Harris but that he did not know the reason for the meeting. He explained that he had really liked Doctor Helen Harris and that she used to work with him but he had not seen her for a few years, not since he had retired and closed his clinic. Chrissy and Andi looked at each other, had the professor given them a clue as to what was going on, without him realising? They pressed the professor for more information but he stuck to Hannah's game plan and only told the police officers what he thought that they needed to hear. He did not mention the memory sticks and they did not ask. He told Chrissy that Doctor Harris had some information for him but did not know what it was, it must have been important as she was killed for it. Chrissy asked a few more questions related to Doctor Harris, before the two detectives departed.

Once back in the car and on the road, away from the house, the two detectives spoke about the meeting and how they both felt that the professor knew more than he had told them. They also wanted to look in to the reason the professor had closed his clinic. He had told them that it was due to his retiring, they would soon find out.

Chapter Forty Eight

Back at New Scotland Yard police HQ, the board was filling with information. The photo of Doctor Harris now had a line joined to the photo of Professor Noble as well as to the mystery man. There was a further line between Professor Noble and his Clinic. "I want to know if there is a connection. Doctor Harris used to work for Professor Noble, his clinic had closed and she went to work for Professor Tomkins, in the same building," DI Acton addressed the room. A photo of Professor Tomkins was located from the internet and placed on to the board. "Could he be the mystery man and, if so, why?" she asked. There were still too many questions and not enough answers.

Detectives Pearce and Cross began to look in to the reason why Professor Noble closed his clinic, was it purely to retire early? All they could find were exemplary testimonials many from famous sports stars, including Kyle Scott, the captain of the England men's football team. There was one bad review from a Mr Kirk King. It was written at about the same time as Professor Noble closed his clinic, surely not a coincidence. "Detectives Pearce and Cross, find the address where Mr King is living and pay him a visit to see why he had given a bad review to the professor," DI Acton instructed.

It was mid-afternoon when the detectives arrived at Mr King's house. It was in a rural location just outside Chesham, an old market town in Buckinghamshire. His house was about 25 miles away from New Scotland Yard and they had taken the same Audi which Chrissy and Andi had used earlier. He lived in a beautiful Victorian detached cottage, with a thatched roof. it was so pretty; it was like a picture. Detective Pearce had phoned ahead to make sure that Mr King would be at home as they wanted to see him and ask a few questions. Mr King was curious as to why the police wanted to speak with him and he opened the door as soon as they arrived. Kirk King was in his mid-forties with thinning light brown hair and brown eyes. He was not a tall person and the detectives noticed that he walked with a slight limp in one leg. Could he be the mystery man? They sat around the table in the dining room; Detective Cross took the lead in asking the questions. It was purely a routine line of questioning and concentrated on why Mr King had given a bad review of Professor Noble. It soon became clear to the detectives that there had been a problem with a surgical operation performed by Professor Noble. Mr King was a roofing contractor and, following a mistake during surgery, he had been unable to work for nine months. He had sued the professor and the claim had been successful. He had received compensation but he was still not walking properly. He felt bitter and posted a bad review of Professor Noble on-line, trying to tarnish the professor's high-profile career. He was pleased when he had heard that the professor had closed his clinic. Back in New Scotland Yard, Chrissy and Andi had looked in to the reason why Professor Noble had had to close his clinic. It was not due to his retirement but as a direct result of him being sued by Mr Kirk King for medical negligence and the subsequent refusal of the insurers to continue to insure the professor. Detectives Pearce and Cross returned to the office and shared their findings with the rest of the team. They now knew why the professor had closed his clinic, but what did this have to do with the killing of Doctor Harris?

Chapter Forty Nine

It was the day of Doctor Harris' funeral, she was being cremated at the crematorium in Hoop Lane, Golders Green, in the north west London suburb. The location was chosen especially because Marc Bolan from T-Rex was cremated there; his music was a favourite of Doctor Harris. His life had also been taken too soon in a car crash at the age of 30. It was another lovely sunny day and there was a good turnout of people, as is usual when someone so young and popular dies before their time. The car park was full and even parking a car in the road was difficult. Doctor Harris had not been married and had no children but her parents and brother were at the funeral. Professor Noble was there, with his wife and their children. The professor had employed Doctor Harris but was also a personal friend. Professor Tomkins was also there as he was Doctor Harris' most recent employer. There were several of Doctor Harris' work colleagues, relatives and friends, as well as members from the Royal College of Surgeons. People were gathering in the waiting area outside the West Chapel, everyone was wearing black clothes out of respect. Doctor Harris' coffin arrived in a hearse and was taken in to the West Chapel, followed by her immediate family members. The coffin was put on to a table in front of a curtained-off area at the rear of the chapel. There were over one hundred people in attendance, the seats in the aisles in the West Chapel were full and there were many people standing, in the aisles as well as at the rear of the chapel. The service was tearful with many eulogies spoken of how kind Doctor Harris was and how she was taken away too soon with so much more to offer. Professor Noble gave one of the eulogies, it was a very emotional speech. At the end of the service the coffin was moved behind the curtains to a medley of T-Rex and Marc Bolan music, there were no dry eyes in the room.

After the ceremony, the mourners walked solemnly through to the memorial gardens where flowers had been laid out in memory of Doctor Harris. Doctor Harris' parents made a point of speaking to Professor Noble and thanked him for the kind words he had spoken during his eulogy. Her father had also been a doctor and it was he who had introduced their daughter, Helen, to work with Professor Noble. They had known each other for a long time. Professor Tomkins was also involved in the conversation.

The mourners started to leave, albeit slowly. Some walked around the memorial gardens, admiring the ornamental trees and flowering shrubs. There were also many other people wandering around, with memories of their own loved ones. Professor Noble and Elizabeth said their goodbyes to Doctor Harris' parents and talked to Professor Tomkins for a few more minutes before they also left.

Detective Inspector Acton and Detective Lester were also amongst the mourners, looking out for any sign of people at the funeral who they thought should not have been there. They did not see anyone who looked out of place, so they left.

Chapter Fifty

Professor Karen Moore

Detective Inspector Chrissy Acton had made many contacts during her training and subsequently as a successful detective. One of those contacts was Professor Karen Moore. Professor Moore was in her mid-forties and her hair was starting to grey, slightly. She was on the board of directors of the Royal College of Surgeons, based at their main office in Lincoln's Inn Fields, near Holborn in central London. Chrissy called Professor Moore and told her that they were investigating the death of Doctor Harris and wanted to find information on the reason why Professor Noble had closed his clinic. They agreed to meet at her office later that day.

They arrived at the Grade ll Listed building with its large porticos and stucco fronted elevations and parked on the opposite side of the road, close to the open space of Lincoln's Inn Fields. Professor Moore's office was on the fourth floor. She was expecting Chrissy and hugged her when she arrived with Detective Andi Lester. Andi looked at the hug. She could see that it was not a sexual hug but that of a hug of friends, who had not seen each other for some time. Andi was not a jealous person but things between her and Chrissy had just started and at that moment she wanted Chrissy all to herself. Chrissy gave her card with her phone number and email address to the professor; it was an official visit. Professor Moore's office was not overly large but was tidy. There were a few tables and chairs as well as an antique desk with a matching chair with leather padding. An old-fashioned computer monitor was on the desk, it must have been at least twenty years old. The walls were panelled and the room was fairly dark as a result of this. There were photos of family as well as diplomas, adorning the walls. The office was at the front of the building and there was a window which overlooked the open space of Lincolns Inn Fields below. Professor Moore poured three cups of coffee from the dispenser, which was located on one of the tables near the window and passed two of the cups to the police detectives.

She sat down at her desk and typed away on the computer keyboard, whilst Andi and Chrissy sat on the opposite side of the desk. Andi took out her notebook and started to make notes of the conversation. She noticed that the computer was not password protected, which she thought was strange but did not mention it.

An electronic copy of the file relating to Professor Noble soon appeared on the screen in front of her. The notes were copious and dated back to when the professor first qualified in the medical profession. The file showed a virtually exemplary career, as would be expected of someone with the experience of professor Noble, with the exception of two complaints. One of the complaints was nearly thirty years earlier and the most recent was that of Kirk King. The notes relating to the complaint made by Mr King referred to the meeting held at his office with Charlotte Mobbs, Clementine Moore and James Hopkiss. This was the first time that Professor Karen Moore had looked at the file. She reviewed the notes on the screen and made curious questioning and humming noises. The noises she made were loud enough to get the attention of the police detectives. Detective Inspector Chrissy Acton asked what Professor Moore had found in the notes to make that reaction. Professor Moore turned the computer monitor around so that the police detectives could see the information on the screen. The notes showed an almost exemplary record over the thirty plus years in which Professor Noble had been in the medical profession. It showed the complaint made by Mr King along with the review by Charlotte Mobbs and her team. It also showed a copy of the decision made by Mobbs and the subsequent refusal of the insurance company to re-insure the professor. When questioned by the police detectives, Professor Moore said that the punishment given to Professor Noble seemed to be extremely unfair, and unusual for the complaint made, especially with no challenge to the decision allowed. "This is not normal practice and, as far as I am aware, it should not have happened," she told the detectives. She told them that she would be looking in to the actions of Charlotte Mobbs personally, as it seemed that Mobbs had let power go to her head and did not reflect the role of her job. Detective Constable Lester looked at Professor Moore and wrote the exact words in her note book, followed by an exclamation mark. The police detectives thanked Professor Moore and asked for a copy of the file notes. The professor pressed a few buttons on the keyboard and the printer on the table on the opposite side of the room sprang to life. The printer was as old as the computer and whirred away, slowly printing the notes on to several sheets of A4 paper.

The professor also emailed a copy to Chrissy using the details on the card which Chrissy had given to her at the beginning of the meeting. They said goodbye to the professor and got to their car just as a traffic warden was about to issue it with a parking ticket. They showed their police warrant id cards, opened the doors to the car, smiled and drove off. Chrissy and Andi headed back to New Scotland Yard with the information which they had just received from Professor Moore. They could now add a few more photos and lines to the board. Clementine Moore, James Hopkiss and the Insurance Company along with a photo of Charlotte Mobbs. There was also a photo of Professor Karen Moore. Most of the lines on the board were pointing to Professor Noble. Did he kill Doctor Harris? Had Doctor Harris found out something about him and was she the reason why Professor Noble had received such a harsh punishment? This opened up a whole new line of enquiries for the team and they were pleased with their work so far.

Detective Superintendent Tony Pallett looked through the internal glass divider from his office to see the progress being made. His face looked surprised when he saw the new photos.

Chapter Fifty One

The following day a masonic lodge meeting was taking place in one of the lodge rooms on the first floor of Freemasons' Hall in Great Queen Street, close to Covent Garden and Holborn in London. Freemasons' Hall is an Art Deco stone faced Grade ll Listed building and home to the United Grand Lodge of England. The room was fairly large and rectangular in shape and had an east to west orientation. There were three rows of seats to each side and an altar in the centre of the room. The floor was arranged in black and white squares. The room could hold over a hundred people and, on this occasion, there were around eighty people in the room, all dressed in their masonic regalia. The Worshipful Master of the lodge, sitting in a large carved wooden chair on the east end of the room, was Detective Superintendent Tony Pallett. He was surrounded on either side by the secretary and treasurer of the lodge. On the opposite west side of the lodge was the Senior Warden, Professor Clement Tomkins.

Business of the day was discussed, including the treasurer's report and minutes of the previous meeting along with the receiving of a new candidate into membership. During the meeting there was no free discussion between members but once the meeting was over the free talking would begin. The lodge meeting had lasted about ninety minutes and it was now lunchtime. Detective Superintendent Pallett and Professor Tomkins had pre-booked a table for lunch after the meeting, this was something that they had done for several years. There was nothing in common between the two men with the exception of belonging to the same lodge.

Pallett was young, energetic, intimidating and rising quickly in his career as a police officer. Tomkins was overweight, unfit and nearing the end of his career as a surgeon. Both men were wearing suits; Pallett's suit was an expensive tailored suit and had a perfect fit whilst Tomkins's suit was poorly fitting and had clearly seen better days. The two men walked along Great Queen Street, towards Covent Garden. Tomkins was shuffling along trying to keep up with Pallett until they reached The Ivy Market Grill in Henrietta Street, where they had reserved a table. The restaurant was full but they had already booked and were shown to their table by Gail, the front of house manager. The reservation was for three people, the third person was already at the table, it was Charlotte Mobbs. Mobbs had already ordered herself a double vodka and ice. She had nearly finished it when the two men arrived; it was not the expensive vodka that she had at her house, but still a nice Grey Goose vodka. Detective Superintendent Pallett and Professor Tomkins sat down at the table with Charlotte Mobbs. Mobbs acknowledged the two men but carried on drinking. Gail brought menus to the table, mentioned the daily specials and asked the two men what they would like to drink. Two scotch whiskies were ordered. Detective Superintendent Pallett looked around the room to see if he recognised anyone or if they were being watched. Once he was sure that there was no-one he knew he lowered his voice and started the conversation. "Which one of you two was careless?" he asked them. "Your name, Charlotte, has come up in the investigation into the murder of Doctor Harris" he added. Mobbs' looked shocked. As far as she was concerned, she had been careful. It was Professor Tomkins who had killed Doctor Harris and not her. "This could go one of two ways" he told her. "I can either make it go away or make your life very difficult." "Make it go away" Mobbs replied. "If I go down for this, I will tell everyone about our arrangement," she continued. "I will also tell everyone that it was Professor Tomkins who had killed Doctor Harris and not me." The two men were suddenly not very hungry and waved away the waitress who had come to the table to take their orders for lunch. They discussed their arrangements and decided that the best thing was for Pallett to make this line of enquiry go away. They were making too much money and did not want it to stop. "In order to protect you both further, I want a larger share of the money," he announced. He already had a large amount of cash in his home safe but was getting greedy. "I started this; it was my idea" interrupted Professor Tomkins. "I came across Charlotte Mobbs many years earlier as she was starting her career and worked out that there was a way to make money.

137

I could also see the benefit of having a policeman like you, Pallett, on our side, in case we were ever investigated by the police." Professor Tomkins was a good doctor and surgeon but was not overly street wise. He had asked his contact at the Lodge, Tony Pallett, how best to proceed with a person in Charlotte Mobbs' position. Pallett at the time had not yet been promoted to Superintendent but could see a use for the situation to help himself financially. Tomkins saw it as a way to protect himself against disciplinary proceedings, if the situation ever occurred. It had been decided that the three should work together. Mobbs would let Tomkins know about her next investigation, Tomkins and Mobbs would then look in to the private life of the person to be investigated to see if they were vulnerable in any way. Pallett would be their protection from any police investigation. Mobbs would get paid by her victims and pay a percentage to Tomkins, who would then pay Pallett. A perfect arrangement. Everything was going well and had been for several years, until Doctor Harris had started to work for Professor Tomkins after Professor Noble had closed his clinic.

It was at the insistence of Professor Tomkins that Charlotte Mobbs had not offered Professor Noble the option of a money payment. He wanted Professor Noble to be struck off and his surgery closed down. Tomkins despised Professor Noble for being the perfect person. He was jealous of him and wanted him to be ruined; it was the perfect opportunity. Doctor Harris had found out what Tomkins was doing and confronted him, she had to be silenced. They argued about the way she was silenced and agreed that Detective Superintendent Pallett would divert the investigation away from Mobbs, to save his own career. They also decided to put on hold any more jobs until the current situation had subsided.

They did not notice the security cameras in the restaurant. All of the nearby cameras had been re-directed and were pointing at their table, most of the cameras had listening devices attached. The cameras were being controlled by Splinter and his team in New York, the entire conversation had been recorded.

138

Chapter Fifty Two

In the offices of Hannah Cozin's detective agency, in The Empire State Building, Splinter and his team had been extremely busy. They had taken control of the entire CCTV network in England, through a back door loophole which they had created with their own software. The main users could still use the system and had no idea that someone else was also using it. They had hacked in to the cameras in the unmarked police cars used by the detective team investigating the killing of Doctor Harris. They knew about the intimacy between Chrissy and Andi, but drew the line in watching any of the sexual activity in their hotel room, despite having control of the hotel's security system. They saw and heard the interviews between the detectives and Professor Noble at the professor's house and they had just seen and heard the conversations during the meeting between Detective Superintendent Pallett, Professor Tomkins and Charlotte Mobbs. They now had all of the information they needed in order to proceed to help the police with their investigation. Until now they had not been sure who they could trust in the police. It had been obvious to them that someone high up in the police was involved, they had now found out who it was. This also meant that they knew who they could trust.

Splinter emailed the information to Hannah, including the video and audio recordings from the meeting between Mobbs, Pallett and Tomkins. Hannah emailed it all to her father in London with a message for him to call her, they needed to discuss how to handle the information. Hannah had not spoken with her father for a few days as she had been busy working with other investigation cases of her own in New York. The time difference of five hours between London and New York meant that when Arthur Cozin received the email from his daughter it was already early evening in London. The sun had set for the day and it was starting to get chilly. Arthur and Hilda were sitting in their lounge having a glass of red wine when Hannah Facetimed her father using her Apple iMac, the picture was extremely clear. After the initial pleasantries were over, they discussed the latest situation in the case.

Arthur Cozin knew Detective Superintendent Tony Pallett very well. He had not liked him or his tactics, when they worked together, but he did not realise that Pallett was capable of this. They would have to be very careful and clever in devising a way to put a stop to the situation. After the Facetime conversation, Arthur Cozin called Detective Inspector Chrissy Acton. Chrissy's mobile phone rang several times and went to voicemail. Arthur left a message for Chrissy to call him and he then called Professor Noble.

Chrissy and Andi had been in the office most of the day and were desperate to hold and touch each other, but resisted. After work they went back to Chrissy's hotel for a drink in the bar and then took the lift to her room on the tenth floor. Chrissy had heard her phone ring but could not answer it as she was in her hotel room, making love to Andi. Chrissy and Andi's love making lasted for several hours until the early hours of the morning, when they fell asleep.

Chapter Fifty Three

Detective Superintendent Pallett arrived in his office much earlier than usual that day. He wanted to be sure that no-one was there so that he could have a good look at the crime board in the main office. He looked at the photos and names which had been recently added. He took a photograph of the board with his phone and sent it to Charlotte Mobbs and Professor Tomkins. He also sent a copy of the notes which had been sent by Professor Moore to Detective Inspector Acton. Mobbs and Tomkins were both surprised to see the name of Professor Karen Moore on the board. Professor Tomkins had been a surgeon for a long time and knew that Professor Moore was on the board of directors of the Royal College of Surgeons. Tomkins looked at the file notes relating to Professor Noble. He knew that the punishment which Noble had received looked extremely suspicious, but until now no-one was looking at it.

Professor Tomkins had seen Professor Karen Moore at various seminars, but they had never met close up, or even spoken with each other. Tomkins decided that he had to go and see Professor Moore and went that morning to Lincoln's Inn Field but did not go in to the Head Office of the Royal College of Surgeons.

He waited outside for a few minutes, waiting for her to arrive. Professor Moore arrived at her place of work wearing a smart dark grey trouser suit and white shirt, along with matching white shoes and hang bag. Her hair had been recently coiffured, she looked like a very important person. Tomkins waited for thirty minutes before he phoned the professor's office. He put on a fake voice and gave the fake name of Detective Johnson. He explained that he was working with Detective Inspector Chrissy Acton on the case and that he had some more questions relating to the murder of Doctor Harris. He told Professor Moore that she needed to be careful as there was someone working in her office who wanted to harm her. He asked her to be discreet, not to speak with anyone else, and come to meet him in the café in Gate

Street, a narrow cul de sac just off the north west corner of Lincoln's Inn Field, in fifteen minutes. Ten minutes later Tomkins saw Professor Moore exit the building, still looking very important, but this time he could tell that she was clearly agitated by something. She was looking around to see if she was being followed. Professor Moore crossed over the road and entered the gate at the southern end of the open space of Lincoln's Inn Fields, towards the bandstand in the centre.

She walked straight past the bandstand to the north side of the open space. It looked lovely at this time of year, she thought to herself. She turned left on to the north side of Lincoln's Inn Fields and then right in to Gate Street. She had noticed an elderly man shuffling along nearby, was he following her? She walked a bit faster, looking around but the man had disappeared. As she arrived in Gate Street, Tomkins called to her and told her that she was being followed and to come with him in to New Turnstile, a very narrow passageway leading to High Holborn. Tomkins checked to make sure that the passageway was empty when he pulled out his six-inch serrated hunting knife and thrust it in to the body of Professor Moore, six times.

Professor Moore had been caught by surprise and did not even have time to scream but collapsed on to the floor. Blood was spilling on to the ground, all around her lifeless body, she was dead within seconds of hitting the ground. It was the first thrust of the knife which killed her.

Tomkins walked away quickly, not looking up as he did not want to be recognised by the many CCTV cameras in the area. He had already seen where the cameras were located. He disappeared in to the distance before the first passer-by arrived on the scene. He could hear the screams of the people behind him, when the body was discovered and a crowd of people was now surrounding the lifeless body of Professor Karen Moore. The first person at the scene was a young student, Carly Matthews, on her way to the Queen Mary University of London, School of Law. Carly called 999 and reported the incident to the operator.

Tomkins went back to the Royal College of Surgeon's building. He used a fake police id., which he had been given

142

some months earlier, by Detective Superintendent Tony Pallett. He walked in to Professor Moore's office. Tomkins knew that his connection with Detective Superintendent Tony Pallett would come in useful. He had a good look around the office and turned on the computer. He seemed to know that the computer was not password protected and searched the recent opened files. He soon found the file relating to Professor Noble and made a few subtle changes. He did not email the file as he did not want to leave a date and time trail. Instead, he printed the file on the slow printer on the opposite side of the room. Once the file had printed, he grabbed the papers and left the building. When he got back to his own office, Tomkins scanned the amended the papers and emailed them to Detective Superintendent Tony Pallet. Pallett then replaced the original files with the amended ones.

Chapter Fifty Four

After breakfast in the hotel room, Chrissy called Arthur Cozin, apologising for not having taken his call the previous evening. Arthur told Chrissy that he wanted to see her but did not say any more than that over the phone. An appointment was made for later that morning. Chrissy and Andi arrived at their office together, raising knowing smiles, nudges and winks from their colleagues. Chrissy ignored these and updated the team with the call from her former boss, Arthur Cozin. She left with Andi, raising even more smiles, to go to Arthur Cozin's apartment in Islington. There was more traffic than usual and it was apparent that there had been an incident near Holborn. Chrissy radioed her team in the office; they had been told that there had been a stabbing near Lincoln's Inn Fields.

As they were only a few hundred yards away from the area, Chrissy turned on the screeching siren and blue lights on their un-marked police car, they soon arrived at the crime scene. Chrissy showed her police warrant id card to the police officer controlling the crowd, the area had already been cordoned off with a blue tape. Chrissy and Andi lifted the tape and went to see the lifeless body of Professor Karen Moore. They recognised the body immediately as being that of the person who they had only recently interviewed; this was clearly not a coincidence. The knife wounds looked similar to those which they had seen on the lifeless body of Doctor Harris in The Regent's Park. They had a serial killer on their hands. Chrissy called Arthur Cozin and told him that they would have to delay their meeting. She told him the reason why and made arrangements to meet up with him, the following day.

Chrissy assumed control of the investigation as it was clearly linked to the case which she was already working on. The local police officers were asking the people in the crowd if they had seen anything, but no-one had. Tomkins was very good at blending in to the background and not being seen. An ambulance arrived and took the professor's body away to the morgue.

Chrissy asked to be updated as soon as there was any news, but she already knew the modus operandi. Chrissy and Andi went to the Royal College of Surgeon's building on the opposite side of Lincoln's Inn Fields and went to the reception. They were told about a telephone call which was put through to Professor Moore and that she had left the building soon after the call, looking nervous. There was no phone number left and the name given by the caller was fictitious, saying that he was a police officer. There was no CCTV available and no further leads. Chrissy knew that the cases were connected and was determined more than ever, to find the murderer. The detectives went back to New Scotland Yard and re-visited the crime board. A red cross was added to Professor Karen Moore's photo to notify that she was deceased. "What are we not seeing, what are we missing?" Chrissy asked herself.

That afternoon the preliminary findings came back from the coroner, confirming what Chrissy had already known. Professor Karen Moore had indeed been killed with a six-inch serrated hunting knife. There were six stab wounds but she was dead after the first stab as it had gone straight in to her heart. The knife markings were an exact match to the knife used to kill Doctor Harris in The Regent's Park.

Chapter Fifty Five

The following morning Detective Inspector Chrissy Acton went to see her former boss, Arthur Cozin. Andi had a previous arrangement, which she had not discussed with Chrissy, but meant that she was not available to go with Chrissy to the meeting. Chrissy went by herself to the apartment in Islington. When she got to Arthur's apartment, Chrissy was surprised to see that Professor Noble was also there. It was warm and sunny and the three sat around the table on the roof terrace. Hilda brought a pot of tea and some biscuits and left the others to talk on the terrace. "Why is Professor Noble here?" Chrissy asked, "what is going on, what aren't you telling me, Arthur?"

Arthur Cozin explained to Chrissy what Splinter's team had found out using their state-of-the-art equipment, monitoring and recording CCTV cameras, in and around London, without anyone knowing. He showed her the CCTV video and audio footage of the meeting in The Ivy Market Grill restaurant in Covent Garden between Charlotte Mobbs, Professor Tomkins and Detective Superintendent Tony Pallett. Chrissy was shocked by the revelation. She did not like her boss, but did not realise that he was capable of doing this. The CCTV information that they had received from Splinter could not be used as evidence as it had been procured illegally. Chrissy would have to be very careful how she handled the situation but was more shocked by the further information that she was about to receive. Professor Noble was equally as shocked by the revelation that it was his supposed friend, Professor Tomkins, who had been responsible for killing his good friend, Doctor Harris. He could not believe that someone who he had thought of as a friend for so many years could do something like that to him, as well as be a killer.

Splinter had looked in to the personal life of Tony Pallett. Pallett had a cousin a few years younger than himself. His cousin was also in the police force and had recently moved from Thames Valley Police to the Metropolitan Police, her name was Andi Lester. It was the superintendent who had requested Andi's transfer. Splinter and his team had monitored Andi's calls, she had contacted her superintendent cousin on several occasions, always after an important meeting or update. They had monitored a phone call between the two soon after Chrissy and Andi had interviewed Professor Karen Moore. Andi had told the superintendent that the computer in Professor Moore's office was not password protected, Pallett relayed the information to Tomkins. Chrissy was speechless, she had shared her bed and body with Andi and had no idea that she was a traitor to both her and the department. Chrissy was determined to find out why Andi was doing this; there must be a reason. It was decided at the meeting on the roof terrace that Chrissy could not let Andi know that she knew about her relationship to the superintendent. Chrissy would have to continue as if nothing had changed. She would have to continue to make love to her and be with her, she would have to be a good actor.

The meeting continued and they planned what they had to do to catch the killer and his accomplices, at least Chrissy now knew who the killer was and who they were dealing with.

Chapter Fifty Six

Doctor Kayleigh Hughes

Charlotte Mobbs was checking her Swiss bank account details using her online mobile phone app, it showed a very healthy balance. There was more money in the account than she would ever need for the rest of her life; but she was not happy with this. She was a greedy person and did not like the fact that she had to give so much of the money away to her accomplices. Tomkins was a murderer and Pallett was a nasty person, why should they benefit from her hard work? Mobbs decided that she would not tell the others about her next investigation, she would keep all of the money herself. If that was successful, and why shouldn't it be, then she would keep going on that basis. It wasn't long before her next investigation.

Doctor Kayleigh Hughes was a young GP doctor in a modern NHS doctor's surgery in Barnet, an outer suburb to the north of London. It was her first practice since qualifying from her five-year medical school, two-year foundation training, and three years of GP training. Doctor Hughes came from a medical family, both her father and her uncle were doctors, her father had recently retired but her uncle still had his practice in Harley Street. Her family were so proud when she qualified and even more proud when she started her first job as a General Practitioner doctor. The surgery comprised of three GP's, including Doctor Hughes, a nurse and a receptionist. Doctor Hughes had been with the surgery for two years and had built up a good reputation amongst her colleagues and patients.

It was her long-term goal to have her own surgery, or take charge of where she was now. Unfortunately, Doctor Hughes had misdiagnosed a patient a few months earlier. She had seen a patient who was complaining of constant headaches and, instead of recommending further investigations, she initially prescribed the patient with pain killing tablets and told the patient to come back in a week's time, if the pain was still there.

The patient, Peter Kempster, was a middle-aged man in generally good health with the exception of slightly raised blood pressure and the occasional gout, both of which were being medicated. The day after seeing his doctor, Peter Kempster did not feel well and his wife called 999 for an ambulance. The ambulance arrived at their house within minutes and, after making a few preliminary checks, they strapped Peter Kempster to a stretcher and in to the back if the ambulance. His wife went in to the ambulance with him. The journey to the hospital was only fifteen minutes with sirens blaring and blue lights flashing. However, Peter Kempster suffered a seizure and was pronounced dead in the ambulance. His wife was screaming and crying by his side. The sirens and blue lights stopped. The ambulance slowed down to normal traffic speed. The investigation in to the death was instigated by the complaints made by Mrs Kempster, the surgery was being sued for a million pounds. The investigation took place at the surgery, the investigator was Charlotte Mobbs and her team comprising a representative of the insurance company and an accountant. Mobbs had not worked with this team before. Charlotte Mobbs was investigating not only Doctor Hughes, but the entire practice. Mobbs had carried out so many investigations that she knew exactly what to look for and what to say. To Mobbs it was a game, but to the people she investigated, it was their careers, and their lives.

A room in the surgery was set aside for the investigation, which took all day. The accountant had requested a business plan and previous year's accounts from the doctors. Files were strewn across the desk and Mobbs was giving a really hard time to the doctors. The business plan and accounts showed good figures and Mobbs knew that she was on to a winner. As the meeting was ending, Mobbs took Doctor Hughes to one side and gave her the news. "Based on the evidence, the surgery would be OK, there would be a disciplinary fine and the insurers would cover the claim, less the excess amount payable by the surgery," Mobbs told her. "However, there is not such good news for you, Doctor Hughes. You will be struck off the medical register," she continued. In her research, Mobbs had looked in to Doctor Hughes' bank accounts and savings. She calculated Doctor Hughes' earnings and loss of her potential income over the rest of her career. She wrote a figure on a piece of paper which she handed to Doctor Hughes. "There is an alternative way in which you can keep your career and stay on at the surgery, with only one month suspension and no detrimental comments in your file. It will cost you £20,000," Mobbs announced. "But I will need an answer immediately or the offer will be withdrawn." Mobbs continued. Doctor Hughes quickly assessed the situation and reluctantly accepted the offer, transferring the money to Mobbs' Swiss Bank account, immediately. Mobbs was not sharing this money with anyone, it was all hers. Mobbs told Doctor Hughes that she should not tell anyone about this arrangement or things could get bad and her decision could be reversed.

Chapter Fifty Seven

Detective Andi Lester

Detective Andi Lester had not told Chrissy where she was going that morning for a good reason, she had been requested to a private meeting with her cousin, Detective Superintendent Tony Pallett. They met at Pallett's family home in Muswell Hill, north London. It was a red brick fronted late Victorian terraced house arranged over three floors. It had been extended at the rear to create a large kitchen/reception area looking onto a tidy, but small, garden. There was a large three-seater sofa on one side of the room, two smaller sofas on the opposite side of the room and a large TV screen on the wall. There was a coffee table in the middle. The house was nicely decorated and modernised, this was the work of Pallett's wife, Mandy, as he was too busy at work to worry about the house.

Andi took an Uber from her flat and arrived at precisely ten o'clock in the morning as requested by her cousin. Pallett opened the door and invited her in, they kissed politely on the cheek. Andi was wearing a floral dress which showed off her figure nicely, and a small matching light pink shoulder bag. She was a very attractive person and she knew how to show it. Andi was flirting with her cousin but he had seen it all before and was not interested, not this time anyway. Andi remembered that it had been only a year ago when Pallett had been at an unofficial after work party in a central London hotel, celebrating his latest promotion. He had seen Andi on the opposite side of the room, their eyes had met across the busy room and Andi had walked over to Pallett. Andi had been wearing a short length cream coloured mini dress and looked stunning. Pallett had offered Andi a drink, and then another and another. The party had finished but they were still chatting, their faces were getting extremely close to each other. They kissed. Pallett had put his hand up Andi's short dress and felt her skimpy white panties, which had been getting moister with every touch. Pallett had given Andi the spare key to his hotel room; they had gone to the room separately and had amazing hard sex for several hours. Andi did not see the hidden camera high up on the wall, above the bedroom door. Pallett had set the camera up earlier when he checked in, just in case. He had clearly done this before. Andi Lester stayed the night but the following morning Tony Pallett's mood had changed. He told Andi that it was a one-off and that he did not want to continue the affair as he did not want to ruin his career, or his marriage. Andi was devastated but had understood. They had an understanding with each other that this was not to be discussed and that if she wanted to keep her job then she would do everything that he wanted of her. He was using his high-ranking position in the police force to blackmail her. This was one of those times.

Mandy Pallett was away on business for a few days and Tony Pallett had the house to himself, until later that day. Pallett showed Andi through to the kitchen area and offered her a drink. It was too early for her, but Pallett poured himself a glass of scotch whisky. Pallett sat on one end of the three-seater sofa and Andi sat at the other end, her floral dress riding up slightly to reveal the bare flesh above her knees, her legs were slightly parted. Pallett had already been updated by Chrissy and had seen the investigation board in the office, with the names and photos of the current suspects. He wanted to ask Andi questions about how the investigation was going, but more importantly, he suggested to Andi that she should divert the attention away from Mobbs and Tomkins. Andi knew what the consequences would be if she did not do what he wanted. Pallett gave her the names of several criminals currently under investigation in other unsolved knife crimes in London and the suburbs. He told Andi that one of them could easily be framed for the murders of Doctor Harris and Professor Moore. Pallett was very convincing, there was something about him and Andi was under his spell. She was about to accept the names without questioning him, until he went and ruined everything.

Pallett shuffled across the sofa to Andi and put his hand on her bare leg above her knee. Andi flinched and moved her leg away slightly but Pallett was not going to accept this. No-one refused him, ever! He moved closer to Andi and put one arm across her chest so that she could not move, whilst he put his other hand back onto her leg. He moved his hand further up her leg and under the base hem line of her dress. Andi slapped Pallett around the face. He was not expecting this and moved back, slightly startled. Andi got up from the sofa, picked up her shoulder bag and started to run to the front door. Pallett was bigger, faster and stronger than Andi and was soon pulling her back before she could reach the front door. "You bitch!" he shouted, "Get back here and let me fuck you, you know you want it!" Andi reached in to her shoulder bag, took out a small canister of pepper spray and sprayed it in to her cousin's face. "Fuck you, you bastard!" she shouted back at him as she opened the front door and ran to the pavement in front of the house. As she got to the pavement a taxi pulled up and a middle-aged woman got out of the car. It was Mrs Pallett, home earlier than expected from her business meetings. Mrs Pallett was a very attractive lady in her late thirties. She was 5'9" tall, had light brown hair just below her shoulders, and had a great figure. No one knew why her husband felt that he had to cheat on her. Mrs Pallett had seen Andi running out of the house and called her over. She put her arms around Andi and looked to see her husband at the front door. He was holding his face which was red from the pepper spray.

Mrs Pallett got back in to the taxi and told Andi to get in with her, telling the taxi driver to drive off. The taxi drove off, taking Andi back to her flat in Westbourne Terrace. During the taxi ride Mandy Pallett told Andi that everything would be OK, and not to worry. After dropping Andi at her flat, the taxi continued and took Mrs Pallett to the Hyatt Regency, London Churchill Hotel, in Portman Square, where she booked into a suite. She liked this hotel due to its proximity to Oxford Street and it was where she used to go for breakfast after a late night out dancing, eating and drinking at La Valbonne, in London's Soho.

Chapter Fifty Eight

Chrissy had finished her meeting with Arthur and was driving back to New Scotland Yard, trying to make sense of all the information which she had just received, when her phone rang, it was Andi. "I need to meet with you, Chrissy, there's something I have to tell you," Andi said with a quivering voice. Chrissy could tell by Andi's voice that something was not quite right but Andi would not say over the phone what was wrong. They agreed to meet in the Hyde Café, in The Royal Lancaster Hotel, as it was only a short walk from Andi's flat. Andi changed out of her floral dress and in to a pair of smart blue denim jeans with a white blouse and walked the seven-minute walk along Westbourne Terrace, to The Royal Lancaster Hotel. Chrissy had not been too far away when Andi had called her and got to the hotel café first. She had found a table in a corner, so that no-one would be able to hear their conversation.

Chrissy had only just found out that Andi and Tony Pallett were related, was that why Andi wanted to speak with her, or was it related to the case? She would soon find out. Chrissy stood up and gave Andi a hug and a kiss, she did not want to let on that she knew about Andi being related to her boss and working for him, behind her back. They both sat down. The table was arranged so that they were sitting at a right angle and not opposite each other. The waiter came over and they ordered coffee and Danish pastries. There was an awkward silence before the conversation started. It was Andi who started, she was clearly enraged. She told Chrissy the whole story, from being related to Detective Superintendent Pallett, to having sex with him at his promotion celebration right up to date where she told Chrissy that he had been blackmailing her to spy on Chrissy and the investigation. She admitted telling Pallett that Professor Karen Moore's computer was not password protected, but that was all that she had done. Andi also told Chrissy that she had just been to his house and that he had given her a list of names of suspects to divert the investigation. She told Chrissy that Pallett had tried

154

to sexually assault her and that she managed to pepper spray him and escape, just as his wife arrived. Perfect timing.

Andi was clearly upset and tried to apologise to Chrissy. She told Chrissy that she knew that she had harmed their relationship. She was in a no-win situation as Pallett was the senior officer and, as well as blackmailing her, she could not refuse a direct order from her superior officer. Chrissy had mixed emotions. She did not tell Andi that she already knew about the relationship, that would not have helped the situation. Chrissy was relieved that Andi had the courage to tell her and knew that Andi was now one hundred percent on her side. Chrissy was upset and angry when Andi had told her about Pallett trying to force himself on her. She saw the funny side when she heard that Mrs Pallett had arrived at the exact moment that Andi had run out of the house, after spraying him in the face with the pepper spray.

The coffee and cakes arrived at a perfect moment in the conversation. They stopped talking and watched as the coffee was poured in to their cups from a glass cafetiere. Andi was eating her apricot pastry but some of the pastry had flaked on to the edge of her lips, Chrissy lifted her hand and gently wiped the crumbs aside. Andi gently grasped Chrissy's hand and held it tightly. Chrissy knew that things would be good between them and was relieved that she did not have to pretend, next time they made love. Chrissy told Andi about her meeting with Arthur Cozin and Professor Noble and the input from Splinter. She did not mention that Splinter had told her about Andi being related to the superintendent. As far as she knew, Andi had not given Pallett any important information about the case that he did not already know, they would be able to use that to their advantage.

After they had finished their coffee and their Danish pastries, Chrissy drove Andi to New Scotland Yard. There was a message waiting for Chrissy when she got there, it was to call Detective Superintendent Tony Pallett. She called her boss and he told her that, due to unforeseen family issues, he would be taking a few days off and she was in charge. He still wanted Chrissy to keep him informed of any updates. He knew that he did not have any control over Andi anymore.

Chapter Fifty Nine

Doctor Hughes had told Charlotte Mobbs that she would not tell anyone about their arrangement. It was, however, clear to her colleagues at the practice that Doctor Hughes did not seem to be the same warm and friendly person that she used to be, before the meeting with investigators. Doctor Hughes shrugged off the attention of her colleagues as she had someone else that she knew who may be able to help her. She had recently purchased a two bedroomed flat in a recently built block close to the surgery and also close to her parents' house in Hadley Wood. After work Doctor Hughes went home to change and then went to see her parents. She had already told them of her misdiagnosis and the follow up investigation. She had not, however, told them the reason why she had not been disbarred. When she arrived at her parents' house, she saw a car in the driveway which she did not recognise. It was a classic 1950 Jaguar XK120 roadster in British Racing Green. It was her uncle's.

Her mother and father greeted her and cuddled her in the entrance hallway. They went through to the large reception room and she saw someone else already in the room, sitting in a double seater sofa, it was her uncle, Professor Clement Tomkins. The classic Jaguar was Tomkins' pride and joy. He had inherited it from his father and kept it in immaculate condition. He only drove it a few days and a few miles a year and today was one of those days. Tomkins stood up and shuffled over to greet his niece and kissed her on her cheek. He was his usual self, not smartly dressed, wearing a tatty old suit which he had bought over ten years earlier. It used to fit him, when he first bought it, but it did not fit him very well now. His fingers were stained with nicotine, his grey hair was dishevelled. He stank of whisky and had a glass in his hand when he kissed his niece. They all sat down in the room, Doctor Hughes sitting in a single seater, her parents in a three-seater and her uncle sat back in the two-seater; re-filling his glass with more whisky. Smoking was frowned upon in the house otherwise Tomkins would have lit up a cigarette, he would have to wait.

Doctor Hughes told her version of events to the two doctors in the room and her mother. Her parents already knew about the mis-diagnosis and of the investigation but they did not know what had happened during the investigation. Professor Tomkins was looking in to his emptying glass of whisky until he heard his niece mention the name of the investigator, Charlotte Mobbs. Tomkins took his eyes off his glass of whisky and looked up at his niece, suddenly taking a lot of interest in what she had to say. Kayleigh told them about the conversation she had had with Charlotte Mobbs. She told them that she was going to be struck off from the medical register but that Mobbs had told her that there was an alternative way in which she could keep her career and stay on at the surgery. There would be only a one month suspension and no detrimental comments in her file. She told them that she had transferred £20,000 to Mobbs' Swiss Bank account, immediately, and that she could not tell anyone about the arrangement or things could get very bad for her. She had told her parents, who in turn told her uncle, Professor Tomkins.

Tomkins was outraged on hearing this. "When was the investigation?" he asked her. When she told him the date, Professor Tomkins realised that he had not been aware and had not been paid by Mobbs. He did not care that it was his niece, he cared about the money more. "Don't you worry, darling" he told his niece, "I will look in to it discretely, you don't need to do anything else. I will handle it."

He would handle it alright. He was more furious by the fact that Mobbs had done this without telling him and without giving a share of the money to him, he would make her pay for this. Tomkins got up from his chair and said goodbye to his sister, brother-in-law and niece. As soon as he was outside the house, Tomkins took out a cigarette, lit it and inhaled. He discarded the cigarette butt in the driveway before opening the door to his car. He had a strict no-smoking policy in his beloved car and treated it like it was the most precious thing in his life, which it was.

Chapter Sixty

Once he sat in his car, Professor Tomkins called Detective Superintendent Tony Pallett's mobile. The call went to voicemail but he did not leave a message. He called Pallett's work number and spoke to Pallett's assistant who told him that her boss had taken a few days off due to personal reasons. It was unusual for Pallett to take time off work and Tomkins was surprised. He wanted to know whether Pallett knew about Mobbs' most recent investigation and, if so, was he too hiding it from him. Were they in it together and cutting him out?

The distance between his sister's house in Hadley Wood and Tony Pallett's house in Muswell Hill was only seven miles, so Tomkins decided to pay Pallett a visit. He parked his classic British Racing Green Jaguar XK120 outside Tony Pallett's house and walked along the path to the front door. He gently tapped the side of his car, it was a ritual which he did without realising, it was as if he was saying "Goodbye, see you soon," to his car. Tomkins rapped on the door knocker. He waited a few moments before Pallett opened the door and invited him in.

Pallett was not in a good way. He had clearly been drinking excessively and there were several plates and take-away containers piled up in the kitchen. There was no sign of his wife. Mandy Pallett had moved out and was still staying in the Hyatt Regency, London Churchill Hotel. She had run up quite an expense bill in the restaurant and bar, as well as the cost of the room. She did not care, she had her own money as she was a successful business woman in her own right, but put the hotel suite in her husband's name, using his credit card. It was the least that he should do for her, under the circumstances.

Pallett did not go into too much detail about why his wife had moved out. It was none of Tomkins' business but he was disturbed by the news which Tomkins told him about Charlotte Mobbs. Pallett had clearly not known that Mobbs had gone behind their backs with private jobs. How many other jobs had she done without telling them? Tomkins would try and find out.

They discussed the way forward and decided that Mobbs could clearly not be trusted as a member of their unofficial team. She had to be stopped, and Tomkins knew exactly how he was going to do it.

Chapter Sixty One

It had been raining over-night but it was now sunny in central London. The sky was blue and there were only a few high clouds in the sky as Andi and Chrissy walked the short walk across Westminster Bridge, from The Park Plaza Hotel to New Scotland Yard. They had reconciled their recent issues and had spent the night together in Chrissy's hotel room. The after smell of the rain was pleasant and they giggled like school girls as they avoided the puddles of rain. The Houses of Parliament looked beautiful ahead of them. There were already many tourists taking photos on Westminster Bridge using the Houses of Parliament and Big Ben as the backdrop for the photos. There were contrails in the sky from the many airplanes flying miles above their heads and planes visible, starting their final approach to Heathrow airport.

Chrissy and Andi had quickly got through their problems, it was as if nothing had changed. Chrissy had still not told Andi that she had already known of the connection between Andi and her cousin Detective Superintendent Pallet, and was not going to tell her. The previous evening had been fairly quiet, they spent most of it in a local pub, drinking wine. They had discussed the serial killer case and were hoping for a breakthrough. They did not have to wait long for the breakthrough to happen. As soon as they arrived at New Scotland Yard, the team were all there. Chrissy and Andi could tell that something had happened. It was, after all, why they were detectives. Detectives Pearce and Cross looked over to Detective Superintendent Pallett's office. The Superintendent was unexpectedly back at work. Pallett looked up as Andi and Chrissy arrived and beckoned Chrissy in to his office. He closed the blind between his office and the open office where the other detectives were based. Pallett did not tell Chrissy why he had taken time off and was certainly not going to tell her about his wife moving out or the incident with Andi, although he was pretty sure that Andi would have already told her. He did not care whether she had or had not. He had his own agenda, to bring down Charlotte Mobbs, and was going to use his department to do this for him.

Pallett told Chrissy that he had received some information about the case and that was why he had had to take some time away from the office. Chrissy knew that this was not true and also knew that she could not trust everything that her boss was saying, after the information she had received from Splinter, and Andi. She also remembered the recorded CCTV video and audio of the conversations that she had seen and heard, in The Ivy Market Grill restaurant in Covent Garden, between Pallett, Mobbs and Tomkins.

Pallett told her that one of his informers had advised him of wrong-doings and blackmail taking place in the medical profession. Chrissy knew that was true, she also knew that Pallett was involved. He told her that there was a team of two medical investigators making thousands of pounds from their victims and that one of the team had gone rogue. The team comprised of Charlotte Mobbs and Professor Clement Tomkins.

Pallett had removed all trace of calls, text messages and any connections that there may have been between himself and Tomkins, he had not had any direct contact with Mobbs apart from the lunch meeting. He was confident that no connection would be found; he did not know that Chrissy already knew of the connection.

Chrissy thanked Pallett. She left his office to go to the main detectives' office, where she advised her team what she had just been told by Pallett. Chrissy found a photo of Charlotte Mobbs on-line and printed it, before attaching it to the information board. She placed the photo alongside the photo of Professor Clement Tomkins and drew a line between the two. They were now her main suspects and they would need to be looked in to, very carefully.

Chapter Sixty Two

Detective Chief Superintendent Patricia Salter

Detective Inspector Chrissy Acton contacted Arthur Cozin to update him on how the investigation was progressing and thanked him, as well as Hannah and her team, for their assistance in the case so far. Chrissy asked Arthur to recommend a senior officer in the Met, someone that he knew and someone who Chrissy could trust. He recommended Detective Chief Superintendent Patricia Salter.

Detective Chief Superintendent Patricia Salter was in her sixties and nearing retirement from the Met, where she had served for over forty years. She was a clever and strong-minded person, who did not take fools lightly. She and Arthur Cozin had worked on many cases over the years and Arthur knew that she could be trusted. Chrissy asked Arthur Cozin for one last favour. It was to contact his daughter, Hannah, and look in to the financials and lifestyle of Detective Chief Superintendent Patricia Salter, just to be sure. Detective Chief Superintendent Patricia Salter was a higher-ranking officer than Detective Superintendent Tony Pallett and Chrissy needed to know whether she could be trusted in her move to bring down Pallett.

Splinter and his team were immediately on the case. They did a deep dive into the lifestyle and finances of Patricia Salter, checking her friends and family as well as personal and work contacts. They had to make sure that there were no connections to anyone involved in the case, and no skeletons in her closet. After many hours of searching, they came to the conclusion that Detective Chief Superintendent Patricia Salter was indeed a good cop and one that could be trusted. Hannah told her father, who in turn advised Chrissy. Chrissy contacted Detective Chief Superintendent Patricia Salter and, after a brief and discreet conversation, arranged a meeting after hours with her. They met in the Chief Superintendent's large office on the top floor of New Scotland Yard. Her office was much larger than Chrissy's and the views from the window were even better. Detective Chief Superintendent Patricia Salter was sitting behind her large desk. She had short cropped grey hair and was wearing a smart dark blue trouser suit. She offered Chrissy a drink but Chrissy declined. Chrissy explained the situation to the Chief Superintendent, saying how she knew that Detective Superintendent Tony Pallett had deliberately misled the operation and that he was involved with both Mobbs and Tomkins. She also told the Chief Superintendent that they had proof but that they did not have enough evidence which would hold up in court, yet. Detective Chief Superintendent Patricia Salter despised Detective Superintendent Tony Pallett as she thought that he had risen up through the ranks too quickly. She had always thought that he was up to no good but could not prove it; possibly now she could. Detective Chief Superintendent Patricia Salter agreed to assist Chrissy with whatever she needed to bring him down. She asked Chrissy to keep her updated and would not let Pallett know of their meeting. They had a further brief chat, including the professional connection that they both had with Arthur Cozin, he was indeed a very well-liked and well-respected person.

Chapter Sixty Three

Detective Sergeant Harry Bond was assigned the job of looking in to all aspects of Professor Tomkins' life, whist Detectives Cross and Pearce were tasked with looking in to Charlotte Mobbs. They had arranged to monitor both Mobbs' and Tomkins' phone calls and texts. In order to get authority to do this, Chrissy had by-passed Detective Superintendent Pallett and went straight above his head to Detective Chief Superintendent Patricia Salter. Chrissy and Andi would be going off the books to look in to the life and style of Detective Superintendent Tony Pallett, although Andi already knew a lot about his personal life.

Detectives Cross and Pearce had obtained the files involving Charlotte Mobbs' investigations into medical negligence. They called Mobbs to make an appointment to visit her at her home in Mill Hill as they had some questions to ask her. She was curious to know the reason why the detectives wanted to speak with her as they did not tell her over the phone. When they arrived, Pearce and Cross were surprised to see such a large house and a new Mercedes convertible in the driveway. They gave each other a look which they had acquired over the many years of working together. It was a look to suggest that something was not quite right. They rang the doorbell and Mobbs invited them in. She directed them towards the spacious reception room, overlooking the large garden. There were expensive Chesterton leather sofas, mahogany shelving display cabinets and a Steinway Classic Grand piano, in the room. It was mid-morning and not quite warm enough to sit outside, the detectives sat on one sofa whilst Mobbs sat on another.

They asked her a few general questions about what she did at her work and where she was based. They already knew the answers, but wanted to make Mobbs feel that it was a general questioning as opposed to a hard interview about Tomkins. They asked Mobbs whether she had known Doctor Harris or Professor Karen Moore and whether she had any idea as to why they had been so brutally murdered. Did she know whether they had any common enemies? At this point of the questioning, they did not want to let on to Mobbs that they knew that she was extorting money from the people she investigated.

"Have you heard of a Professor Tomkins?" Detective Pearce asked her. Mobbs' face whitened slightly when she heard the question. She initially denied any knowledge of knowing Professor Tomkins, but then said that their paths had crossed many years ago when they met at a lecture but had not seen him since. Mobbs was a shrewd person and turned the questioning around. She asked the detectives whether the professor was still practicing, was he ok and why were they asking questions about Tomkins specifically? The detectives ignored the question raised by Mobbs and Detective Pearce carried on with questions about other doctors.

"Do you know Professor Emerson Noble?" he asked. She confirmed that she had indeed investigated him a few years earlier and how unfortunate it was for such an eminent professor to be struck off like that. It was the perfect link to their next question.

"What is it like to hold the future of other people in your hands?" Detective Pearce asked Mobbs. "Did anyone of the people that you investigated try to bribe you, by paying you to change your decisions?" He continued.

Mobbs was outraged by the question and thought for a moment before carefully replying. "No-one has ever bribed me to make me change my decision," she was not lying as it was she who offered the get out clause to those who she knew could not afford to lose their career and future earnings.

Detectives Pearce and Cross got up, "Thank you for your time, we may have some more questions for you. Oh, and by the way, you have a very nice house and car, must have cost a lot of money." They said this as they left the house without giving Mobbs a chance to reply. They did not ask her directly how she could afford it, but it was insinuated. Mobbs made sure that they had left the premises when she called Detective Superintendent Tony Pallett. Mobbs shouted at Pallett over the phone, telling him that she had just been questioned by the police. "I thought that by paying you I was protected from being investigated," she

165

said. "Don't worry, they have no leads and are fishing, try and stay calm – I will sort it," he replied. Neither of them knew that the call was being monitored.

Chapter Sixty Four

Detective Sergeant Harry Bond arranged to meet with Professor Tomkins at the professor's clinic in Harley Street, on the ground floor of the same building where Professor Noble used to have his clinic. Bond collected a car from the car pool and drove the few miles to Harley Street, the traffic was heavy and he wished that he had taken the London Underground. He somehow managed to arrive on time for the ten o'clock meeting and Tomkins was waiting for him. Tomkins had told his assistants to cancel all of the morning appointments and to hold all calls. Tomkins was scruffily dressed, with a poorly fitted suit and looked physically tired. Bond made a mental note not to use Tomkins if he ever needed an open-heart surgery operation, and definitely not to use his tailor. They sat down around a conference desk in the main office. Professor Tomkins asked if Bond wanted a coffee but he declined.

Detective Sergeant Bond went straight in with the questioning. He asked Professor Tomkins a few questions about Doctor Harris. "How she was at work? Was she under any stress or pre-occupied in any way?" She had worked with both Professor Tomkins and Professor Noble, before Professor Noble had been struck off. "Had that affected her in any way?" Tomkins told the detective that it was terrible what had happened to Doctor Harris and that she had great potential; she was a good surgeon and colleague. He also said that he thought that it was unfair what had happened to Professor Noble. "Where were you when Doctor Harris was murdered?" he asked "At a Lodge meeting," Tomkins replied. It was a lie but one which could not be verified. "Do you know Charlotte Mobbs?" asked Bond. "No," replied Tomkins. The answers had been rehearsed and he gave the same answer as Mobbs had given to Detectives Pearce and Cross. Bond asked whether Tomkins had ever been investigated by Mobbs, but he had not.

Different questions were coming every minute but Tomkins was answering each one and giving away nothing. Bond was

167

writing all of the answers into his note pad. As soon as the meeting was over, Tomkins escorted Detective Sergeant Bond to the door. He waited a few moments to make sure that Bond did not return and then called Detective Superintendent Tony Pallett.

Tomkins was angry with Pallett that his name had been associated with the case and to make sure that Detective Sergeant Bond did not find out their connection. "It's what I pay you for!" Tomkins shouted to Pallett. "Don't worry," Pallett told Tomkins, "It is purely routine as Doctor Harris worked with you. They have no leads and are fishing, stay calm – I will sort it for you and Charlotte".

Neither of them knew that the call was being monitored.

Chapter Sixty Five

In the phone monitoring centre in a secure room in New Scotland Yard, the phones of Professor Tomkins and Charlotte Mobbs were being monitored. The calls which they had made to Detective Superintendent Tony Pallett had been recorded and sent to Detective Inspector Chrissy Acton and Detective Chief Superintendent Patricia Salter, who listened with interest. They now had actual proof that there was a connection between Pallett, Mobbs and Tomkins. There were conversations about payments made to Pallett from both Mobbs and Tomkins, but no proof of the murders, yet.

Detective Inspector Chrissy Acton and Detective Andi Lester were working on the fact that Mobbs and Tomkins had paid money to Detective Superintendent Pallett. They had already been told by Hannah Cozin that they had Swiss Bank accounts but the detectives could not use this and they did not have ways to access the accounts themselves. There must be a trail somewhere and they would have to try and find it. Andi suggested to Chrissy that it might be a good idea if she should speak with Mrs Pallett to see if she could assist them with the investigation. Andi had seen how angry Mrs Pallett had been when she arrived back early at their house, just as Tony Pallett had tried to sexually assault her. Andi called Mrs Pallett to make an arrangement to meet with her. She was still staying in the hotel in Portman Square close to Oxford Street. Mrs Pallett was happy to meet with them. Detective Inspector Chrissy Acton and Detective Andi Lester went to the hotel and met Mrs Pallett in the large reception area, close to the entrance. They found an empty table in a quiet area, close to the restaurant, and away from the hustle and bustle of tourists and business men and women mingling in the main reception.

Coffees were ordered and soon arrived, poured by the handsome waiter. Mrs Pallett could not take her eyes off him, both Chrissy and Andi noticed this and looked at each other with amusement. Chrissy took control of the meeting. She wanted to know the current situation between Mr and Mrs Pallett before knowing if she could tell Mrs Pallett the main reason for their meeting. Mrs Pallett was still fuming about her husband's behaviour. "I want you to destroy that bastard!" she told them, in no uncertain terms. She did not blame Andi as her husband had clearly been unfaithful to her on several occasions during their ten-year marriage. He also had a bad temper, a very bad temper, if he did not get his way. But this time it was enough, Mandy Pallett had seen first-hand how her husband had become enraged by Andi's refusal and his anger after. She was filing for divorce and had already contacted a solicitor, who had sent a letter of intention to Mr Pallett.

Mrs Pallett wanted everyone to know what sort of person her soon to be ex-husband was. This was just the news that Chrissy and Andi wanted to hear. They wanted Mrs Pallett's help, they told her what was happening and how she could assist them. Mandy Pallett was only too pleased to help them.

Chapter Sixty Six

Mandy Pallett

Mandy Pallett contacted her husband, she said that she wanted to discuss the divorce with him and arranged to meet him at their house in Muswell Hill the following day. She had already moved a lot of her clothes from the house to the hotel and dressed to impress in the most exquisite white button through dress, extending down to just above her knees. She was a tall lady, with a great figure, and wanted to let her husband know what he was missing. Her hair was styled perfectly, tied at the back, revealing the nape of her long neck.

On her way to the meeting she met with Chrissy at a pre-arranged place a few miles away from Pallett's house. Chrissy gave Mandy a tiny electronic listening device and button sized video camera which she fitted to Mandy's dress. They blended in very well and could not be seen. Chrissy checked to make sure that there was a connection and gave Mandy her final instructions. "Don't take any risks," she said. "Get out of the house as quickly and as safely as you can. We will be watching every moment." The equipment was working perfectly. Mandy Pallett took an Uber to her house in Muswell Hill. Chrissy followed the Uber in her unmarked police car and told Mrs Pallett that she would be waiting in her car, close to the Pallett's house, watching and listening. Chrissy gave final explicit instructions to Mrs Pallett, so that it was clear exactly what she had to do.

Chrissy had already cleared the under-cover operation with Detective Chief Superintendent Salter. They did not like using the public to do their work, but on this occasion, it seemed like the best option to use. Mandy Pallett placed her key in the front door lock but the lock had been changed by her husband soon after the incident with Andi and once Mandy had moved out. She rang on the door bell. A few minutes later the door opened and Tony Pallett opened the door, dressed in casual jeans and a plain shirt. He looked at her and gasped at how beautiful she looked. Mandy ignored this, they had been married for ten years and only now did he realise what he would be missing. She brushed past him as if he was not there. They went through to the same reception room where Tony Pallett had sexually assaulted Andi Lester, sitting apart from each other; she was not going to let him anywhere near her. Mandy Pallett was there for a reason, a few reasons actually.

The official reason was to talk about the divorce and to separate their belongings, who was going to get the house, the car, the money. They did not have any children. The unofficial reason was for Mrs Pallett to try to obtain some information, or even some kind of confession, about his connections with Charlotte Mobbs or Professor Clement Tomkins.

The initial conversations instigated by Tony Pallett were about where things had gone wrong in their marriage but Mandy Pallett was not interested in listening to his excuses. He had failed her on too many occasions, there was no going back. After twenty minutes of his begging her not to leave him she made her excuses to go to the bathroom on the first floor of the terraced house.

The bathroom was next to her husband's study and where she knew that he kept his private information, including his bank statements. It was his private room and she had not been in the room for several years. The door was not locked and Mandy Pallett let herself into her husband's study. She looked around for a moment, trying to remember where the bank statements were located. She made sure that the button video camera was working before she entered the room. There were some law books on the book shelf; she knew that behind the books was a wall safe, screwed in to the wall. She knew what the pass code was as she had seen her husband access the safe in the past, she made sure that she had not been spotted. Mandy hoped that her husband had not changed the code. He hadn't and soon the safe door was open. Her face was in shock when she saw the contents in the safe. Inside the safe were several bundles of cash in both fifty and twenty pound notes. She made a quick calculation and estimated that there was at least fifty thousand pounds in the safe.

She removed the cash and made sure that the button video camera was pointing in the right direction. She also took several photos with her iPhone, as evidence for her own divorce, before placing the cash back in to the safe. In the safe, there were also several photos of naked women, there were names and dates on the back of the photos. Mandy did not recognise the women, or their names. She did however, recognise the background in the photographs as being in her bedroom in her house. "You bastard." she said out loud to herself. Luckily not loud enough to have been heard by her husband. The dates on the back of the photos were familiar to her. At first, she could not remember what was special about the dates and then suddenly, like a light being switched on, she remembered the dates as the same dates when she was away on business. Her husband had clearly been cheating on her for a long time. She again took photos with her iPhone. She was furious but put the photos back into the safe, all except one as she wanted this to remind herself of what a monster she was married to.

There were also envelopes with Charlotte Mobbs' and Professor Clement Tomkins' names on the front. The envelopes were sealed and she did not have enough time to open them, as she had already been gone too long. Mandy took photos of the front of the envelopes. There were no bank statements in the safe. There was a spare set of keys in the safe, which resembled the set of keys she had seen in the entrance hallway, she took them with her, just in case. She closed the safe and went to the bathroom, treading quietly so as to avoid the creaky floorboards. She flushed the toilet and washed her hands, so that her husband would know that she had finished and that she would be coming down stairs soon.

They had a further brief but heated conversation about their divorce and Mandy left. She went out to Chrissy, who was parked in a side road away from the house so that she could not be seen by Tony Pallett. Mandy got in the car and told Chrissy what she had done; she showed her the photo of the money, which she had seen in the safe. The live feed from the camera had worked perfectly and the video evidence of the contents of the safe had been seen by Chrissy and her team back at New Scotland Yard. Chrissy asked Mandy to forward the photos to her phone, as she wanted to show them to Detective Chief Superintendent Patricia Salter when she got back to New Scotland Yard. Chrissy gave Mandy Pallett a lift back to her hotel, making sure not to drive past Pallett's house, in case he was looking out of the window as he would have recognised the car as being an unmarked police car.

When Chrissy arrived back at New Scotland Yard, she met with Detective Chief Superintendent Patricia Salter and showed her the photos which Mandy Pallett had taken in Tony Pallett's safe. Her boss had already seen the live feed from the video camera which Mandy Pallett had used.

The information was added to the recorded phone conversations but not put on the main information board, so as not to alert Detective Superintendent Pallett. There would be a separate investigation into Pallett after they had resolved the murder case.

Chapter Sixty Seven

A meeting was being held in the main detectives open office, Detective Sergeant Harry Bond was taking the lead. He was a muscly man with short cut dark blond hair, wearing a dark grey suit and white shirt with a dark blue tie. He was a few pounds overweight and his shirt buttons were trying to push through the buttonholes, he didn't mind this as he enjoyed his food. Pizza was the usual order of the day, especially if they were working overtime. Bond had a jovial character. He was always joking around but also knew when to be serious; this was the time to be serious. He had the audience which comprised of his colleagues, Detectives Pearce, Cross and Lester as well as his boss, Detective Inspector Chrissy Acton. He had been watching the CCTV cameras in The Regent's Park on the day that Doctor Harris was murdered, up until now they had a silhouette on the board who they had labelled as the mystery man.

Detective Sergeant Bond had looked over and over again at the footage and noticed that the mystery man had a slight uneven movement when he was walking. Although the mystery man's face was shielded from the cameras in each shot, he recognised the walking movement as being similar to someone they had questioned, Professor Clement Tomkins.

He went through the photos and words on the information board in front of him, deleted the words "mystery man" and replaced it with the name of Professor Tomkins with a question mark by his name. It made more sense and was also confirmed by the information which Detective Inspector Pallett had told Chrissy. Chrissy interrupted to say that, following her investigation, Professor Noble was now a victim and no longer a suspect.

Detective Sergeant Bond agreed but kept the photo of Professor Noble on the board, as he used to have a clinic in the same building as Tomkins. Detectives Pearce and Cross commented on their interview with Charlotte Mobbs; they said that she was living in a very large house with a new car outside.

After their interview they had contacted the General Medical Council to request information regarding salary pay structures, including those for people in the same role as Charlotte Mobbs. It was clear from the salary structure that there was no way that Charlotte Mobbs could have afforded to purchase her house without assistance from elsewhere. They had checked with HMRC and saw that there had been no additional earned income declared on her previous ten years' tax returns.

"So, the question is, where did the money come from in order for her to purchase the house?" asked Bond. They already knew the answer to the question. Photographs of Mobbs' house and car were placed on the information board along with pound signs and more question marks. Still too many questions but some were, at last, being answered.

Chrissy informed Detective Superintendent Pallett of the updates, neglecting to mention that she knew about the money in his safe or the monitoring of the phone calls. Once Chrissy had left his office, Detective Superintendent Pallett called Professor Tomkins to update him with the latest information.

Chapter Sixty Eight

Charlotte Mobbs was in her kitchen, eating her breakfast at around seven o'clock the following morning. She was shovelling in another fork full of pancake and maple syrup when her mobile phone rang, it was Tomkins. Tomkins had spoken with Detective Superintendent Pallett the previous evening and had been updated with the latest developments in the case, it was not looking too good for either Mobbs or himself. Pallett, on the other hand, seemed to be untouchable.

Tomkins told Mobbs that they needed to meet to discuss what they should do in order to avoid being caught. He reminded Mobbs that he had most to lose as it were he who had killed Doctor Helen Harris and Professor Karen Moore. Charlotte Mobbs had only been extorting money from her victims. They arranged to meet at Mobbs' house two days later at seven-thirty in the evening.

The phone call was being monitored at New Scotland Yard and also by Splinter and his team in their offices in the Empire State Building in New York. They had heard Tomkins confess to the murder of Professor Karen Moore, but they wanted to monitor the situation further before they arrested him.

Danno and Kaz had been busy over the past few weeks. They had been designing a computer program specifically able to piggy- back home internet systems anywhere in the world, without the main user being aware that they were being affected. They had chosen to test it on Charlotte Mobbs internet, advising Hannah, who in turn advised her father. As this was an illegal process, Arthur Cozin decided it was best not to advise Chrissy, just yet anyway.

Charlotte Mobbs had a basic internet connection along with several different virtual personal assistant technologies, in her house, some with video cameras built in. Kaz had full access to the wireless internet system, including the cameras in the virtual personal assistants. She also had full access to Mobbs' lap top and desk top web cams as well as her recently installed, state of the art, alarm system which had cameras in every room in the house.

Her mobile phone and hand-held devices could also be monitored and used as listening devices; they could access the cameras in these as well. They even had control of the ovens in the kitchen, garage door control and heating systems of the house and swimming pool. If it was connected, they had access. They were watching Mobbs' every move, in and out of the house. They had even managed to access and over-ride, if necessary, the controls of her car and cameras. They were very pleased with themselves and high-fived their achievement.

Charlotte Mobbs finished her breakfast with a gulp of her third cup of coffee, each with two heaped teaspoons of sugar and full fat milk. She went back to her bedroom and undressed to take a shower, admiring her naked body in the full-length mirror. The shower did not take long as Charlotte Mobbs had work to do before she met with Tomkins later that week. She knew that he was a murderer and had to be careful, she had plans for him. She was going to buy a gun from one of her contacts.

Chapter Sixty Nine

"G"

Charlotte Mobbs finished her shower and got dressed into the most unflattering pair of dark blue denim jeans and a floral blue and pink blouse. She sent a text message to an un-named contact in her phone, the contact was known by the capital letter "G". The cryptic text read "I need one, I will be there at ten." There was no reply to the text, but she did not expect one. She went to the wall safe in her bedroom, opened it and took out £500 in cash, all shiny new twenty pound notes. She folded the notes and put them in to an envelope before putting the envelope in to her jeans pocket, along with a pair of light blue latex medical gloves and a pocket size packet of wet wipes.

Mobbs opened the front door to her house and walked past the gleaming white Mercedes convertible, sitting proudly in the driveway in front of her house. She walked a few hundred yards along the road to a beaten up old dark green un-washed, Mini. The small car was parked under a tree. There must have been a bird's nest in the tree because the car was covered with bird droppings. She ignored the condition of the car, it was a perfect car and cover for her not to be noticed, unlike the new Mercedes in her driveway. She took the packet of wet wipes and a key from her pocket and wiped the door handle before opening the door to the Mini. She reached into the glove box and found a spare sanitiser gel, which she used to wipe the steering wheel, she inserted the key in to the ignition and turned it.

She kept the car with a full tank of petrol, just in case she needed it. The car started straight away, despite the fact that it had not been driven for several weeks. This was her car to drive when she did not want to be recognised. She had owned it for several years and bought it for cash, from a local second-hand car dealer.

At the time she bought the car she could fit in it with no problem, now it was a bit of a squeeze to get in. The Mini was a manual car with a central gear stick, the stick would rub against her left leg every time she changed gear, this annoyed her. She told herself to get a larger car for next time, or an automatic; she could certainly afford one. She tried not to use too many main roads and she made lots of unnecessary turns, to make sure that she was not being followed. Unfortunately for her, she was being followed by the local street cameras which were being constantly monitored by Splinter.

The journey to "G"'s flat took just under twenty minutes. He lived in a housing estate in Barnet, built by the local authority in the 1960's. The estate comprised of high and low-rise concrete buildings, each with multiple flats, some of which were privately owned but most were still owned by the local authority. Mobbs parked her Mini on the estate. It was probably un-safe to park there but she didn't care if anything happened, it was a cheap run around car and not her prized Mercedes. She didn't even lock the door because, if someone wanted to break in, they would. There was nothing of value in the car.

It was exactly ten o'clock when Mobbs went to the communal front door of the high rise building nearest to where she had parked her car. She re-applied the sanitiser gel to her hands before pressing the buzzer to Flat 33. The communal front door unlocked, she pushed it open and entered the building. Flat 33 was a duplex flat with the entrance, kitchen and lounge on the fourth floor and the bedrooms on the fifth floor. The lift was not working and there was a sign saying "out of order". The sign looked like it had been there for several months. The corridor and communal areas were filthy and smelled of urine, it was disgusting. Mobbs held her nose as she slowly climbed the eight half flights of stairs to the fourth floor, trying not to touch the stair rails as they were so dirty and full of germs. Once she reached the fourth floor level, she stopped at the top of the stairs, to regain her breath. After a few deep breaths, she walked the few yards along the corridor to Flat 33. The door to the flat was open and Mobbs walked inside.

"G" was a muscular, tall six foot four inch man, and someone who you would not want to get on the wrong side of. His head was shaved and had a large tattoo of a hammer and sickle on his forehead. He was proud of his Russian heritage. His heavily muscled arms were covered with so many tattoos that you could not see the flesh of his arms. He had lived in England for most of his life after being abandoned by his parents, as a young boy in Russia. His life in England was not good and he spent more time in prison than out, for Grievous Bodily Harm and Actual Bodily Harm as well as for armed bank robbery. If you wanted anything from the black market, whether drugs or weapons, "G" was your man.

Mobbs had come across "G" when one of his associates needed a bullet removed for a gunshot wound. The doctor performing the operation was supposed to have reported the incident to the police, but he did not. Mobbs found out about this through an informer who was present at the time of the surgery. It was the first time that Mobbs had accepted money for her silence – the first of many. Inside the kitchen, "G" was pouring himself an early morning cheap scotch whisky, straight. The kitchen was extremely basic with a solitary very old double cupboard, a filthy fridge which had seen better days and a sink and drainer unit with a cupboard below. There were several old take-away cartons on the small table in the kitchen, most with left-over food in them. "G" offered Mobbs some whisky, but she declined as she would be driving back home straight away and did not want to be pulled over by the police, for any reason.

They went from the kitchen to the lounge at the back of the flat. On the way to the lounge, Mobbs passed a staircase which led to the bedrooms on the floor above, she looked up but carried on walking to the lounge. "G" saw her look at the stairs. "You want a bit of action in the bedroom?" He asked her, with a strong Russian accent to his broken English; and winked at her. She looked at his tattooed head and arms and politely declined.

The lounge had one chair and one double seater sofa as well as a small dining table. The room was filthy and Mobbs reminded herself to take another shower when she got back home. "G" asked Mobbs to sit down whilst he went upstairs to get the goods, she looked at the condition of the chairs and decided that it was best for her to stand. She rubbed more sanitiser gel in to her hands.

"G" returned after a few minutes and put a large black box onto the table. He took out several pistols and boxes of bullets for each pistol. He placed them on the table for Mobbs to have a closer look. There were various Glocks, Smith and Wesson's and even an old Colt. It was evident that all of the pistols had been fired, but Mobbs was not put off by this. Mobbs pulled out the blue latex gloves from her jeans pocket and pulled them on to her hands, they were a tight fit but after a few pulls they were on. She then picked up each pistol, feeling the weight of the pistol and the ease of trigger to suit her needs. She noticed that the serial numbers had been filed off from each of the pistols, but did not care. She only needed the pistol for one job and would discard it straight away. The final pistol which Mobbs picked up was a Smith and Wesson SD40 grey frame finish 9mm pistol, it felt comfortable in her hand. She released the magazine and saw that there were no bullets inside. "G" handed her a box of bullets and Mobbs filled the magazine to capacity with fourteen bullets to check the weight; it was not too heavy and she decided that this was the pistol for her.

"G" took the pistol back and emptied the magazine. He placed the bullets back into a box which contained even more bullets. Mobbs took the envelope from her pocket, opened it and handed the folded cash to "G". He counted the cash to make sure that it was all there, it was. He put the pistol and bullets in a plain brown bag and again suggested that they go upstairs for a little fun. Mobbs again declined. She took the brown bag and its contents from him, thanked him and left the flat. She walked down the eight half flights of stairs to the ground floor, opened the door to her Mini and returned home, checking all the while that she was not being followed.

She was now ready for her meeting with Tomkins.

Chapter Seventy

Professor Clement Tomkins

Professor Clement Tomkins lived alone in a large old detached house in Totteridge, a wealthy neighbourhood to the north of London, and only a few miles away from Mobbs' house in Mill Hill. Tomkins had inherited the house and the Jaguar car, when his father died several years earlier.

Despite the fact that Tomkins had earned good money as a surgeon, he had not spent it on the house. He enjoyed spending his money on drugs, alcohol and cigarettes. The house was too large for him as it had seven bedrooms and five reception rooms. He lived there by himself and spent most of the time in one room, his armoury. The armoury was in a former cellar, situated beneath the house and accessed from a concealed door in the dark oak panelled wall in the reception hallway, close to the front door. The access staircase was narrow and dark. The stairs leading down to the armoury creaked. Tomkins liked this, as it meant that he would know if someone was coming down to the armoury without his advanced knowledge.

Professor Tomkins had a fascination for knives and in the armoury was his proud collection of knives. The armoury was a long but narrow room with only a small window, just below ceiling level at the top of the side wall. From the outside, the window was just above ground level. The glass was obscured so that no-one could see in, it was also protected by rusty metal railings. The armoury room was the only room in the house in which Tomkins had spent any money. There were motion-controlled spotlights in the ceiling, alarm pads buried in the floor and motion detectors. The plastered walls had modern bullet proof glass display cabinets, some of which were locked with finger print and iris recognition controls, whilst others had more traditional key and combination locks. Inside the most heavily

183

protected cabinets were Tomkins' most precious knives, including the six-inch serrated hunting knife which he had used to kill Doctor Harris and Professor Moore. In one of the other cabinets were equally as dangerous knives ranging from clip point to straight backs. In another, highly protected cabinet, were a range of machetes with blades ranging from ten inches to twenty nine inches long. Some of the knives had blood stains on their blades, including an eight-inch chef's knife.

Professor Tomkins' interest in knives started when he was a young boy, in the same family home where he lives now. He used to watch his mother slice open fish and gut them in the kitchen, prior to cooking them for dinner. He used to study his father when he sliced the roast beef when they had their Sunday roast. He was fascinated by the way the knife cut through the flesh and meat so easily. He paid particular attention to the way both of his parents sharpened the knives, prior to using them. The range of kitchen knives was vast and each had a different use, bread knives, pairing, carving, utility, cleaving, boning. All of the knives were placed neatly in a wooden knife block.

Tomkins first use of a knife was when he was a child, using a small vegetable paring knife which he used to carve his initials into the willow tree close to the end of their long garden. He also carved his initials in the panels of the wooden shed at the end of the garden. He was an only child and did not make friends easily. He went to the local school but the other children thought that he was strange, they were correct. His use of small knives progressed to larger knives. He dissected dead mice, some of which were killed by the family cat and some of which he had killed. He did this in the wooden shed at the end of the garden. He had made the shed into his own area; his parents were not allowed in and he made sure of this by purchasing and fixing a padlock to the door. His curiosity with knives continued over time and his prey got larger. One day, the family cat made the mistake of entering the garden shed when Tomkins was inside. Tomkins was caught by surprise. He was dissecting a squirrel at the time but he then looked at the cat and knew his next victim. The cat was never seen again.

Tomkins had discovered a disused second World War Two air raid shelter beneath the end of the garden, close to the wooden shed. He used this to bury his dissected subjects. His parents did not know of the existence of the air raid shelter, as the entrance was well concealed by the overgrowth. It was his interest in knives which made Tomkins consider a career as a surgeon, so that he could cut people open. He went to Oxford university and medical school and qualified as a surgeon. He finally specialised in open heart surgery repair, his ease of use of the scalpel was immediate.

Chapter Seventy One

Twenty Five Years Earlier

Clement Tomkins had returned home earlier than expected from medical school one summer day. His father was away on a two-day business workshop and was not due back until the following day. Tomkins entered the house and expected to see his mother in the kitchen, preparing his tea. His mother was not in the kitchen, this was not normal and Tomkins was curious to find out why. He looked around the ground floor rooms of the house but there was no-one there. He heard a creaking noise in the floorboards of one of the first floor bedrooms. He was scared and picked up the eight-inch chef's knife from the kitchen and went upstairs. He opened the door to his parent's bedroom and saw a sight that would remain with him forever. His mother was naked and lying on top of the bed with her legs wide open. A young man, about the same age as Tomkins, had his face buried in between her legs – he too was naked. His mother was squirming and moaning with the pleasure that she was receiving from the tongue of the younger man. They were both unaware of his presence in the room.

Tomkins was outraged at the sight and of his mother being unfaithful to his father. He ran towards the bed and plunged the blade of the eight-inch chef's knife several times into the base of the neck of the man. He then used the same knife to kill his mother by stabbing her directly in her heart. They were both dead, immediately.

There was blood all over the bed, luckily for him it had not yet spread to the carpet. This was the first time that Tomkins had murdered a human, previously it had been mice, squirrels and cats.

At first, he felt sick and vomited in to the sink in the en-suite bathroom. After a while his thoughts changed and he actually felt proud of himself. His mother had been cheating on his father and he had, in his mind, done the right thing. He had to think straight and dispose of the bodies. The bodies were heavier than he expected, he could not move them in their current size. He decided that in order to move them, he would have to cut them in to smaller pieces. He knew that he had time on his side as his father was not due back until the following day. He carried the bodies into the bathroom and placed his mother's body into the bath first. He took the meat cleaver from the kitchen knife block and cut the limbs off the dead bodies of his mother and her lover, watching as the blood poured out of her body and down the plughole. He found several large bed-sheets in the airing cupboard and placed them on the floor of the bathroom, placed the body parts and wrapped them in the sheets. He did the same to his mother's lover. One piece at a time he took the body parts in to the garden and in to the secret air raid shelter, no-one would find them there.

The whole moving procedure took several hours, it was now evening and nearing twilight. He sat in the kitchen and poured himself a well-deserved whisky, neat. Once he had finished the whisky, he returned to the crime scene in the bedroom, the bed sheets were soaked with blood. He stripped the bed completely and put the blood-stained sheets in to the washing machine on a hot wash. He remembered seeing his mother do this when she had blood on the sheets from one of her periods. It worked for her then and it should work for him now, he thought. He washed the sheets several times, but there were still traces of blood. He took the sheets into the garden and placed them into the bonfire. He checked the bed and bedroom floor to make sure that he had not missed any blood, he could not see any.

The clothes of the man who had been pleasuring his mother, were laid out neatly on a chair in the bedroom. He searched the pockets and found a leather wallet with the initials AV engraved on the outside. Inside the wallet was sixty pounds in cash along with a driver's licence, with the name Alex Viking, aged 26 with a local address. Tomkins took the cash out of the wallet and put it in his own pocket. He took the clothes and wallet to the end of the garden and burned them in the bonfire with the sheets. He took his mother's passport out of the safe, along with some cash. He took all of her clothes from the bedroom wardrobes and drawers, along with a suitcase from the loft. He put the cash from the safe in his pocket.

Tomkins wrote a note to his father pretending to be from his mother; explaining that she was not happy and did not love him anymore. Tomkins was good at forging his mother's handwriting and signature from when he was at school, wanting to take a day off, pretending to be ill. The note went on to say that she had left him and gone abroad to spend time with her elderly mother, who lived in Canada, and that he should not to come looking for her. There was no forwarding address or contact number. He burned all of his mother's clothes, along with the suitcase, in the bonfire along with her lover's clothes and bed sheets.

When his father arrived home the following day, Tomkins explained to him that he had been there when his mother had left and witnessed her take her passport and cash from the safe along with clothes and suitcases. Clement Tomkins told his father that his mother had asked him to give the note to his father. His father sat down and read the note. He was distraught; he loved his wife and respected her decision to leave, if that was what would make her happy.

A few days after Tomkins had killed his mother and her lover, two policemen knocked on their door. Clement Tomkins was not there and his father answered the door. The policeman showed him a photograph of Alex Viking and asked if he recognised the man as he was missing and had been recently seen in the neighbourhood. Tomkins' father took a long look at the photograph and told the policeman that he did not recognise the man. The policemen thanked him for his co-operation and never returned.

His father never moved on from his wife leaving him. He became a recluse, never to leave the house again, until he died several years later. The house and all of his possessions were left to his only child, Clement Tomkins.

Tomkins could not believe how easy it was to fool his father and could not believe how easy it had been to kill not one, but two people and to get away with it.

Chapter Seventy Two

Splinter advised Hannah of the phone conversation between Professor Tomkins and Charlotte Mobbs as well as the text messages between her and an unknown number. Hannah immediately contacted her father in London. She told her father about the meeting which was arranged in two days' time at seven o'clock at Mobbs' house. She also told him that they had monitored Mobbs driving to a nearby local authority estate and that she was carrying a package when she left the building, which she did not have when she entered. Splinter had made a note of the number of the flat where Mobbs had gone to and Hannah passed this information to her father.

Arthur Cozin called Detective Inspector Chrissy Acton with the information which he had just received from his daughter. Chrissy had already been advised about the meeting as they were also monitoring Mobbs' phone. She did not know that Mobbs had been to collect something from a flat in a nearby local authority estate and was grateful when Arthur Cozin told her of the estate and flat number where Mobbs had visited, the address sounded familiar to her. Once she finished talking to Arthur Cozin, Chrissy typed in the address of the flat in to the police computer. The name of the flat owner came up, it was Olek Gregorski, alias "G". The computer also showed that "G" had an arrest sheet dating back over several years, and a prison record just as long. He was a known gun dealer; this was alarming news for Chrissy as she knew about the meeting between Mobbs and Tomkins in a few days' time. She immediately arranged for a team of armed police to meet her, as well as Detectives Pearce, Cross and Andi Lester at Olek Gregorski's flat. They were there within fifteen minutes, there was an officer with a battering ram, just in case.

Chrissy knocked on the door of the fourth floor flat. "Police, open up!" she announced. The armed officers were waiting in the external corridor, telling other residents to stay inside their flats. There was no reply but Chrissy could see the twitch of a curtain from within the flat, she knew that someone was in. As Gregorski had refused to acknowledge Chrissy; she instructed the officer with the battering ram to use it. Within seconds, the door was forced open. "Armed police, we will shoot!" they shouted as they entered the flat. Gregorski came out from the bathroom, drying his shaved head and with a towel around his waist. He pretended that he was having a shower and looked surprised to see the police in his house. He had actually been disposing of his stash of cocaine down the toilet. He was told to get dressed and sit in the lounge, which he did. He did not have too much choice as there were armed police all around. Chrissy and Andi entered the room. He looked at them and made a sexual gesture towards them with his pierced tongue. The gesture was ignored by the police detectives. "You want action in the bedroom, I will take you both at the same time," he said with a strong Russian accent to his broken English. He dropped the towel around his waist to the floor, revealing a very large penis. "Put the towel back on, now, or I will arrest you," Chrissy replied in a very stern voice. "G" pulled the towel from the floor and tied it around his waist.

Chrissy showed "G" a photo of Charlotte Mobbs and asked him if he recognised her. At first, he denied knowing her but when Andi reminded him that Mobbs had been seen entering his flat earlier, he suddenly remembered. Chrissy showed "G" a warrant, which she had obtained en-route to the flat. She asked detectives Pearce and Cross to search the flat. They put on their latex gloves and went upstairs to the bedroom area. Pearce searched the front bedroom whilst Cross searched the rear. They were meticulous in their technique; they had clearly done this many times. The cupboards in the bedrooms were filthy, stained with nicotine from the cigarettes and other stains which they did not even try to guess what they were from. They found nothing of interest. Chrissy shouted upstairs asking Detective Cross to get some clothes for "G". Detective Cross brought down a pair of jeans and a T-shirt. "Put these on," he said.

There was a bathroom and cupboard in the upper landing area still to be searched. Tucked away at the top of the cupboard, next to an old water tank and hidden behind dirty sheets and blankets, was a large black box. Detective Pearce opened the box and saw four pistols and boxes of bullets for each pistol. They took the box downstairs to the room where Chrissy and Andi were questioning "G". When "G" saw what they had found he denied all knowledge of the contents of the box, he told them that he was looking after the box for a friend. Chrissy did not fall for his excuse and told him that, due to his criminal record, and prison history, he would be sent to prison for just having the weapons in his possession. Unless he co-operated with her.

With this in mind, "G" told Chrissy that he had sold a Smith and Wesson SD40 grey frame finish 9mm pistol, and a box of bullets, to Charlotte Mobbs. Chrissy asked Gregorski to stand up. His six foot four inch height dwarfed her five foot nine but she read him his rights. She handcuffed him and arrested him, for possession of a deadly weapon and for not having a firearm's certificate. Gregorski struggled but was taken away in a police car to be further interviewed at the local police station. Crowds were gathering outside the flat and the scene was starting to get nasty. "Police brutality!" was being shouted at the police; bottles and stones were hurled towards them. Police with riot gear were holding the crowds back, just long enough for the detectives to leave.

Chapter Seventy Three

Detective Superintendent Tony Pallett had been listening to the police radio transmissions when he overheard the name of Charlotte Mobbs mentioned in an ongoing firearms investigation. He followed up on the information with the local control officer, who he knew personally. He wondered why he had not been advised by Chrissy about the operation and made a mental note to ask her when she returned. Instead of phoning Charlotte Mobbs to advise her that the police knew she had acquired a pistol, he called Clement Tomkins. They both belonged to the same Freemasons Lodge and it was Tomkins who got him involved in their scam and had made him lots of money in the process. His loyalty was more with Tomkins than Mobbs, but only just.

Tomkins was in his armoury room in the basement of his house in Totteridge, when re received the call from Pallet. He was cleaning the blood off, and sharpening, his favoured six-inch serrated hunting knife. Tomkins took the news about the gun well and told Pallett that he was meeting with Mobbs in a few days' time to discuss the best way forward.

He had his own plan for Charlotte Mobbs, but with this additional information he knew that he would need to take a bullet proof vest with him to the meeting with her. He had acquired a lot of items over the years and had a selection of knife and bullet proof vests in his armoury room, such was his interest in the subject. He had recently purchased a brand new, military grade bullet and stab proof waistcoat style body armour with front, rear and side protection against heavy handguns and knives as well as high velocity larger bore guns and shotguns. It could be worn under his shirt and she would not know that he was wearing it. He would be well prepared for Charlotte Mobbs and her weapons.

Tomkins carried on cleaning his knives. He was very careful when he cleaned the eight-inch chef's knife with which he killed his mother and her lover. He spent a few moments remembering the day when he killed them, he had not used this knife since then.

The police officer in Police HQ, monitoring the call made by Pallett to Tomkins, wrote down the conversation and time of the call. He passed this to his superior officer, who in turn advised Detective Chief Superintendent Patricia Salter. Detective Chief Superintendent Salter had been advised of all of the phone conversations relevant to the case involving Pallett, Mobbs and Tomkins. Salter knew of the meeting which was to take place between Mobbs and Tomkins at Mobbs' house, a few days later. When Chrissy and her team arrived back at New Scotland Yard, Detective Chief Superintendent Patricia Salter requested Chrissy to come to her office immediately, without notifying anyone else. She had a plan and wanted to discuss it with Chrissy.

Chapter Seventy Four

Later that afternoon, Detective Superintendent Tony Pallett was giving a lecture at Peel Centre, the Metropolitan Police Training Centre in Hendon. It had only been arranged a few days earlier as the police officer who was supposed to be the speaker had been injured, whilst on duty at a local demonstration. The person who insisted that he took over was Detective Chief Superintendent Patricia Salter and it was something which he had to attend. Ironically, he was giving a talk on ethics to the new police cadets. Detective Chief Superintendent Salter had also arranged for a police officer to drive Pallett to the Training Centre and to report back to her as soon as the lecture was over. She had arranged this specifically in order for her and a team of forensic officers to go to Pallett's house in Muswell Hill, to see what they could find.

DCS Salter had obtained a search warrant for Tony Pallett's house and, a few minutes after Tony Pallett left Police HQ, with his driver, DCS Salter, Chrissy and Andi left to go to Muswell Hill. On the way, they stopped at the Churchill Hotel in Portman Square, to obtain the front door key from Mandy Pallett, which she had taken from the safe when she had been to the house. Mandy Pallett also gave them the alarm code and code to the safe. She wanted to go to her house with the police but Detective Chief Superintendent Salter refused her request.

When they got to Tony Pallett's house the forensics team and a tactical support team were already waiting. Chrissy put the key in to the front door lock, it turned and the door opened straight away. The alarm started to beep but the beeping stopped as soon as Chrissy had typed in the code which Mandy had given her. Chrissy led the way up to the room where the safe was located. The safe was exactly where Mandy Pallett had told them, behind the law books on the book shelf, screwed in to the wall. Chrissy put in the pass code and opened the safe. Inside the safe were the same bundles of cash in both fifty pound and twenty pound notes, which Mandy had photographed. Chrissy removed all of the cash and put it in to a large, clear plastic, evidence bag which she then sealed. The letters addressed to Charlotte Mobbs and Clement Tomkins were sealed but Chrissy opened them and read the words aloud. Both letters read the same, with the exception of who they were addressed to. Each letter was a copy of the letters which Pallett had already sent to Mobbs and Tomkins. They were blackmail letters saying that he knew what Mobbs and Tomkins were doing and that, unless they paid him a percentage of their take, he would have no choice but to arrest them. Chrissy took the photos from the safe, they were of naked women. The names of the women were on the back of the photos, along with dates; she would follow this up later. The letters and photos were put into small, clear plastic, evidence bags which Chrissy then sealed. Andi was searching the desk in the study and had opened the drawers, there was nothing of interest in the drawers but she felt underneath the drawer and found an envelope attached to the underside. She opened the envelope and found a key which looked like it was from a safe deposit box. There were numbers and letters inscribed on the key but no clue as to where the safe deposit might be located; the key was put into a small evidence bag.

There was another small key in the desk drawer. Andi took the key and walked over to the three-drawer dark grey filing cabinet, which was in the corner of the room by the window. The filing cabinet was locked but the key in her hand fitted the lock and it opened easily. Inside the top drawer were several paper files, each with neatly handwritten tabs. One of the tabs was marked "bank accounts." Andi opened the file and inside she found several bank statements each with different account numbers. Each bank account had several thousand pounds entering and exiting, there were handwritten comments by each entry. Chrissy looked at what Andi had found and recognised the handwriting as being that of her boss, Tony Pallett. The bank statements were put in to another evidence bag. Andi then searched the rest of the room, removing books from shelves, there was nothing of interest.

The computer on the desk proved to be a bit more of a problem as it was password protected. Andi called Mandy Pallett and asked her if she knew what the password might be. Mandy told her to try the word "Maldives", as it was where she and her husband had honeymooned when they were still in love. It worked and soon the computer lit up showing hundreds of yellow folder icons on the desktop screen. Each folder had a separate name. Andi recognised some of the names, her name was on one of the folders. Detective Chief Superintendent Patricia Salter's name was on another and she also recognised the names of other female police officers, on other folders. She opened the folder with her name on and stood back in shock as she saw the contents. There was a video of her and Pallett having sex in the hotel room after his promotion party. She had no idea that it was being filmed, she had not even seen the hidden camera in the bedroom. She did not open the folder with Detective Chief Superintendent Patricia Salter's name on it, out of respect for her senior officer, and could only assume what was in it. Andi signalled for Chrissy to come over to the computer and showed Chrissy the video in her folder and the names on the other folders. Andi wanted to delete the folder and its contents but Chrissy talked her out of the idea. Chrissy knew that this was painful for her girlfriend to see, but they could not delete it as it would be used as evidence against Pallett. She called Detective Chief Superintendent Patricia Salter in to the room and showed her the folders, stepping back so as not to see the content of her boss's folder. Salter opened the file with her name on it and watched the video content. She asked Chrissy to turn off the computer as she had seen enough to make an immediate arrest of Detective Superintendent Tony Pallett. The computer was turned off and removed from the premises. The forensics team continued to search the house whilst Chrissy, Andi and Detective Chief Superintendent Salter left the building. They still had the key which Chrissy had found hidden beneath the desk drawer in Pallett's office. They did not know where the safe deposit box was located, or what they would find in it, once it was opened.

Chapter Seventy Five

It was six miles from Tony Pallett's house in Muswell Hill to The Peel Training Centre in Hendon; but with sirens blaring and blue lights flashing, it took only fifteen minutes for the two unmarked police cars to make the journey. Red traffic lights were carefully ignored and traffic moved out of their way, pulling over to the side of the road to let them pass. Inside the lead car was Detective Chief Superintendent Patricia Salter, driven by her professional driver. The second car was driven by Chrissy with Andi in the passenger seat. Chrissy was an experienced driver but even she had a few problems keeping up with the lead car, such was the speed and urgency of the situation.

The cars arrived at the Training Centre and stopped by the entrance to the dark brick and glass Police Academy building. Detective Chief Superintendent Patricia Salter led the way into the building where all of the officers in the reception area stood up and saluted her as she entered the room. She saluted back but did not stop to talk. DCS Salter, Chrissy, Andi, along with four armed officers entered the room where Detective Superintendent Tony Pallett was giving his lecture to over one hundred fresh faced police cadets.

The lights had been dimmed as he was talking through a slide show with a projection on to the plain wall at the end of the room. Andi turned up the lights and Detective Chief Superintendent Patricia Salter started to walk over to Tony Pallett. The police cadets in the room all stood up to acknowledge the senior officer in the room. Pallett looked up to see why the lights had been turned on and was surprised to see the three female officers along with armed officers approach him. He froze for a second as he did not know what they knew.

DCS Salter walked up to Pallett. "You're under arrest for blackmail, concealing evidence as well as conspiracy to murder and perverting the course of justice!" she announced. There were several gasps of shock from the cadets in the room as she read him his rights and handcuffed him.

"Don't do this," Pallett whispered to her. "I have a video of you which will humiliate you were it made public," he continued. "Don't worry, I've already seen it and I'm not ashamed," she replied as she handed Detective Superintendent Tony Pallett to the armed officers to take him into custody. His phone was taken from him so that he could not warn Mobbs or Tomkins.

Chapter Seventy Six

The questions kept coming at Tony Pallett in the interview room at the local police station. He was handcuffed to a metal bar at the table; on the opposite side of the table was Detective Chief Superintendent Patricia Salter. Pallett was used to interrogating suspects; he did this very well but he was not good at being interrogated himself and insisted that a union representative was present during the interviewing sessions. DCS Salter told Pallett that they knew about his part in the blackmail scam carried out by Mobbs and Tomkins. She produced the photographic evidence which they had found in his safe; the money, the photographs, the blackmail notes to Tomkins and Mobbs as well as the bank statements. Pallett did however have one final bargaining tool on his side. He assumed that Detective Chief Superintendent Patricia Salter did not know what the key, which they found under his desk drawer in his office, was for. He asked them for a reduced prison sentence if he told them what the key was for. Unfortunately for Pallett, the team back at New Scotland Yard had already worked it out. The key had several numbers and some letters on it and Detective Sergeant Bond had cracked the code. It was clearly from a safe deposit box and Bond had input the numbers and letters in to several web sites until he found out where the box was located. It was the local High Street bank, close to where Pallett lived. A warrant was granted and Detective Sergeant Bond went, with Detective Cross, to the bank where the safe deposit box was held.

They had already called ahead and showed their ids and warrant to the bank manager when they arrived. The bank manager escorted them to a small room and brought the large box to them. He placed it on the table in front of the detectives and left the room. As soon as the bank manager had left the room the detectives opened the safe deposit box. It was brimming full with fifty and twenty pound notes, even more money than they had found in his safe at home, along with gold bars. The detectives photographed the contents of the safe deposit box and sent the photo to DCS Salter, before putting it in an evidence bag and returned to New Scotland Yard. DCS Salter showed the photo to Pallett. There was nowhere left for Pallett to go, except to prison. It was not looking good for Pallett; his career was over and he was going to jail for a very long time. His wife was divorcing him. He was ruined.

Chapter Seventy Seven

Professor Noble had decided that, instead of going for a run in Hampstead Heath, he would try out the new exercise bike which had been recently delivered and set up in his home gymnasium, only a few days earlier. He changed in to his black track suit and trainers. It wasn't a normal home gymnasium; it was the size of a professional gym where people would expect to pay hundreds of pounds membership. As well as the newly installed exercise bike, there was a treadmill, weights, a punch bag, rowing machine as well as abdominal trainers. Everything that you could want in a gym. There was a large flat TV screen attached to the wall in front of the machine. The TV was connected by Bluetooth to the exercise bike and was set up to show bike rides from all around the world. It was as if you were on a real road, it was so life-like. The screen showed the incline and distance travelled, you even could adjust the wind speed, weather and temperature. There were similar TV screens set up in front of the treadmill and rowing machine. There were stadium tracks and even swimming the English Channel, if that was what you wanted. Today, the professor was riding his exercise bike on Route 23, Westlake Boulevard and Mulholland Highway from Westlake Village, Ventura County to the Pacific Coast Highway, just north of Malibu in California.

He had set the weather to a cool 18 degrees Celsius and set the time to six o'clock in the morning, as this was the time in England. He let the computer in the exercise bike sort out the logistics and was soon on his way. The journey started from the Westlake Village Inn hotel, in Agoura Road and left on to Route 23. There were normal houses on both sides of a normal residential street, before the road suddenly narrowed considerably. It was a very winding route of around twelve miles with sheer drops, first on the left and then on the right, as the road meandered through the canyons and mountains. The incline was extremely steep, far steeper than he had ridden before and he was struggling in places. He was however, very pleased with his new machine. The views were amazing, especially when the deep blue Pacific Ocean came into view around a bend as he started the decline. He had noticed road signs on the route to a Wine Safari as well as various trails, he also realised that there were very few houses around. It was about ninety minutes before he reached the PCH and turned off the screen. He was sweating profusely, despite the cooling fan which he had attached to the exercise bike. He decided that he would like to visit this place for real, and soon. Whilst the professor had been exercising, Elizabeth had been working in the kitchen, baking a Victoria sponge cake for their visitors. Hilda and Arthur Cozin had become good friends with Elizabeth and Emerson Noble since the investigation had started, especially with their daughter, Hannah, being of so much assistance. They were coming round for tea at three o'clock. The professor put a towel around his neck and followed the smell of the freshly baked cake to the kitchen. He walked up to Elizabeth and put his arms around her. He kissed her. "I love you," he said affectionately. Elizabeth smiled, returning the affectionate comment and pushing him away, as he was still very sweaty following his bike ride. "Go and take a shower, our guests aren't due for a few hours. I will join you in the shower, in a few minutes," she told him. He ran to the shower and waited eagerly for his wife.

Chapter Seventy Eight

At precisely three o'clock a black taxi cab arrived at the gates of the Noble's large house in The Bishops Avenue. Arthur Cozin got out of the taxi and pressed the buzzer on the entry phone, the gates opened slowly and Arthur Cozin got back in to the black taxi. The driver continued up to the front door, which was open slightly. They paid the taxi driver, giving him a nice tip. The Noble's embraced The Cozin's like old friends, despite the fact that they had only recently met, and went in to the drawing room. At their request, the professor poured a double shot of whisky, on the rocks, in to a tumbler glass for Arthur Cozin and a single shot of vodka in to a tumbler glass with tonic for Hilda. He poured the same for himself and Elizabeth.

The conversation was easy, despite this being the first time that the four had met - prior to this it was to discuss the investigation only - Hilda and Elizabeth had not met before. The initial conversations were about their respective children and how proud of them they all were. Time flew by and Elizabeth excused herself to get the tea, Hilda followed her in to the kitchen. The tea set was a blue floral design, 1920's art deco Royal Doulton set which had been handed down from Elizabeth's parents to Elizabeth, when they passed away. The tea set was beautiful and hardly used, it was only brought out for special occasions. Hilda took the freshly baked Victoria sponge cake and plates in to the drawing room whilst Elizabeth took the teapot, cups and saucers in on a tray. Tea was poured and the conversation flowed, until Arthur's phone rang – it was Hannah calling on Facetime from New York.

Arthur told Hannah that he was at Professor Noble's house, to which Hannah said that she already knew and that was why she was calling. She had news for Professor Noble as well. They went to the TV room where Arthur followed the instructions from his daughter how to Air Play the phone to connect to the TV screen. They sat down and waited whilst the connection between the iPhone and TV started. Within seconds, Hannah's face showed on the large TV screen on the wall. Hannah could see her parents and the Nobles sitting on the sofas watching her, she was the centre of attention. Hannah had been following the case very carefully and told her audience of the latest situation. She told them that Detective Superintendent Tony Pallett had just been arrested, in front of an entire class of police cadets. All of the crimes for which he had been arrested, were listed. She also told them that Charlotte Mobbs had purchased a gun and that there was a meeting arranged for the following evening between Mobbs and Tomkins at Mobbs' house. "The final showdown" as she liked to call it. Her audience was listening intently and watching with amazement, they could not believe what they were hearing. Arthur Cozin had worked with Tony Pallett. He knew that Pallett was not a nice person, but did not realise just how bad and crooked he had become. He was so proud of his daughter and told her so. Hilda and Arthur told Hannah that they wanted to fly out to New York and meet up again as soon as possible, but agreed to wait for the conclusion of the case first.

Chapter Seventy Nine

It started off as a normal working day for Professor Clement Tomkins. He had a full morning of appointments in his Harley Street surgery, including two open heart surgery repair operations, and three consultations. Tomkins left his house in Totteridge at around six thirty in the morning. It was a cool but dry morning as he shuffled the short distance to the nearby Totteridge and Whetstone station on the London Underground system. He grabbed a copy of the free Metro newspaper at the entrance to the station and, with a weathered black leather briefcase in his hand, he walked down the steps to the platform where the 06:52 southbound Northern Line train was waiting. Tomkins had the timing down perfectly. He had used the same route for so many years, he could have done it blindfolded. The destination station shown on the front of the train was Battersea Power Station, part of the recent extension at the southern end of the extended section of the Northern Line in order to access the new American Embassy at Nine Elms and the nearby Battersea Power Station redevelopment.

The train had started its journey at High Barnet, which was only one stop north of Totteridge and Whetstone. As a result of this, and also because of the time of day, there were only a few passengers on the train with him. He chose a window seat in a carriage towards the rear of the train and sat facing the direction in which the train was to travel. He decided that he did not want to read the newspaper just yet, he had a lot of thinking to do about his upcoming meeting with Charlotte Mobbs. Tomkins opened his briefcase and put the newspaper inside next to his trusty six-inch serrated hunting knife, which was shining after its recent cleaning. He stared out of the window, watching the trees and backs of houses pass by. There were twelve stops to Warren Street station; the first four of the stations were overground, before entering the tunnel just before Highgate Station. More passengers got on the train at each station until the train was full, including the standing areas.

There was a slight delay at Camden station caused by a passenger trying to get on to the train when the doors were virtually closed. The doors opened and closed several times until the passenger managed to squeeze in to the tightly filled carriage, like sardines. It took just under 30 minutes for the train to travel to Warren Street station. The train was still full as many of the passengers were going beyond Warren Street to the shopping areas of Tottenham Court Road and Leicester Square, in central London. Outside Warren Street station Tomkins hailed down a black taxi cab and took the short five minute journey along Euston Road and Marylebone Road, turning left into the one way street of Harley Street, to his clinic.

It was just after seven thirty when he arrived at his surgery in Harley Street. He was the first person to arrive as the concierge to the building usually arrived at around eight o'clock. He unlocked the main front door of the building. Everything seemed normal until he got to the front door of his ground floor surgery, he noticed that the door was slightly ajar. Something was wrong. He pushed the door open quietly, as he was not sure whether anyone was inside. Professor Tomkins' offices had been turned upside down; drawers were open and papers had been thrown all over the floor. Someone had clearly been looking for something; he did not know who it could have been, or why.

He went in to his private office and saw that his safe had been opened. It was a state of the art safe and could not be opened without a sequence of several codes. Only he knew the codes, or at least that was what he thought. The safe was empty. Inside the safe there had been several thousands of pounds in cash along with an envelope with incriminating evidence against Charlotte Mobbs which he had kept to use against her, just in case. Tomkins heard a noise coming from the rear office and entered the room slowly, just as a man was exiting through the rear window carrying a bag. The bag was brimming at the top with the items which he had just stolen from the surgery and safe. The man was tall and muscular. As the man turned to see who was there, Tomkins could just see part of a large tattoo of a hammer and sickle on his forehead. He could also see the heavily muscled arms, which were covered with tattoos. The man ran to the alleyway behind the building and off in to the distance. Tomkins could not run and could not get near him. He sat down and pondered what to do. He called his friend, Detective Superintendent Tony Pallett but the call went straight to voicemail. He didn't know that Pallett had been arrested. Should he call the police? They would only ask questions about what was stolen and what he had in his safe. He looked at the CCTV footage on a small old-fashioned black and white monitor in his office. He saw the man on the CCTV enter his surgery, using a key. He then saw him rifle through the drawers in his office and put some papers into his bag. He then saw the heavily tattooed man pull out a piece of paper from his jeans pocket and walk to the safe. The man looked at the paper and typed in a sequence of numbers so that the safe opened, first time.

Tomkins did not recognise the man and wondered how he had obtained the codes. He saw the man put the cash in his jean's pockets and the envelope in his bag, along with the papers. Not sure of what to do for the best he called 999 and asked the operator to put him through to the police. His call was initially put through to the nearest police station in Savile Row. The policeman who answered the call in the Savile Row police station asked for his name. When he typed the name "Tomkins" in to the system it came up with a red flag notice. A link came on to the screen telling the policeman to put all calls through to Detective Inspector Chrissy Acton at New Scotland Yard.

Chapter Eighty

Detective Inspector Chrissy Acton had just arrived at her office when the inter-office phone rang. It was Savile Row police station advising her that they had Professor Tomkins on hold. She took the call immediately and listened to Tomkins telling her about the break-in. She immediately recognised the man based on the description that Tomkins had given as Olek Gregorski, the man who had sold the gun to Charlotte Mobbs. Gregorski had been arrested at his flat and taken in for questioning for possession of deadly weapons and without having a firearm's certificate. He had made his allotted phone call to Charlotte Mobbs who arranged for a very expensive solicitor to attend the interview. Gregorski had been released with a caution, after his solicitor had questioned the circumstances of his arrest. "Don't disturb anything," DI Acton told Tomkins, "I will send a team to meet you in your surgery," she continued. Detectives Pearce and Cross were dispatched to Harley Street, along with local officers from Savile Row. D! Acton was working on far more important things. She was preparing her strategy for the seven o'clock meeting later that day, between Charlotte Mobbs and Professor Tomkins.

There was a police cordon in front of the building and a crowd gathering outside Tomkins' surgery in Harley Street when Detectives Pearce and Cross arrived in their unmarked police car. Curtains and blinds were twitching from the buildings on the opposite side of the road, with the neighbours wondering what all of the excitement was about. Detectives Pearce and Cross showed their id's and entered the communal entrance area of the listed building where they were greeted by the concierge. They asked the concierge whether he had seen anything that morning but as he had not been there when the burglary took place, he could not assist them. It was not a 24 hour concierge service and he had arrived slightly later than his usual time, at around eight thirty. He showed the detectives the way to Professor Tomkins' surgery.

Tomkins had sent his staff home but made sure that any appointments for the day had been cancelled before they left. He had not touched anything since his call to the police. A team of forensic experts were already in the building, checking for fingerprints, when Detectives Pearce and Cross entered the surgery. They took notes from Tomkins and asked him if he knew what had been stolen. Tomkins told them that the items stolen were work related and contained personal information about his patients and staff. He did not mention the money taken from the safe, or the incriminating evidence he had against Charlotte Mobbs. The detectives looked at the CCTV footage from the communal area, showing the tattooed man enter the building, using a key. The internal CCTV footage showed the same man opening the safe, using a key code from a piece of paper. They saw him take what looked like rolls of bank notes from the safe and an envelope, but the pictures were unclear. They asked Professor Tomkins what the cash was for but Tomkins shrugged his shoulders and said that it was petty cash for the office tea fund. The detectives knew that this was not true. They wrote down a few notes and took the CCTV footage with them, back to New Scotland Yard. They asked Tomkins to arrange for a full list of items stolen and to call them when he had done so. Detective Cross gave Tomkins his card with his direct phone number. The detectives knew the identity of the thief and knew of his connection to Charlotte Mobbs, but did not pass this information to Tomkins. They noticed the traffic cameras in the road and surrounding roads and made a note to get the footage sent to them. Once the detectives and forensic team had left, Tomkins started to tidy up. He was fuming; not because of the money being stolen but the contents of the envelope, this was worth more than the money to him. He opened his brief case and looked at his six-inch serrated hunting knife, this relaxed him slightly as he ran the tip of his index finger over the sharp blade. It made him concentrate on his meeting with Charlotte Mobbs later that evening.

When the surgery was tidy, he made sure that the doors and windows were locked. He changed the code to the safe and left the building, saying goodbye to the concierge on the way out. He dialled Detective Superintendent Tony Pallett's number on his phone but it again went straight to voicemail. "Where are you, when I need you most?" he asked himself. Unsure what to do, he walked the short distance to Marylebone High Street where he found a local café and ordered a strong black coffee. He sat at a small round table in front of the café, people watching whilst all the time nursing his weathered black brief case. After half an hour he took another taxi to Warren Street station and returned home to his house, in time for a late lunch, and to prepare himself for his meeting with Charlotte Mobbs.

Chapter Eighty One

A few days earlier

After he was released from custody, Olek Gregorski had called Charlotte Mobbs to thank her for arranging the solicitor and asked if she wanted anything in return. Mobbs thought for a second and said that there was something that he could do for her. They arranged to meet at a nearby supermarket car park, a neutral place where no-one would see them. Mobbs turned up in her Mini and parked at the far end of the car park. "G" arrived a few minutes later in an inconspicuous, ten year old, grey Ford Focus. Although it was daytime, Mobbs flashed the headlights on the Mini to let "G" know that she was there. "G" parked in the empty parking bay next to Mobbs' mini. He opened the door and walked to the Mini. The door was not locked and "G" opened the door. He sat in the car, despite the lack of room inside for such a tall man. Mobbs gave him an envelope, which he opened immediately. Inside the envelope was a piece of paper with an address, it was the address of Professor Clement Tomkins' surgery in Harley Street, along with two keys. One key was for the communal street door and one for the surgery door. There was also another piece of paper with several codes written down; these were the codes of the safe in Tomkins' surgery.

Mobbs had obtained the keys and the safe code information when she had recently interviewed Professor Clifton, who's practice was in the same building as Tomkins. There had been a ten-minute break when she had left Noble's surgery during the investigation and she met with Tomkins. Whilst she had been talking with Tomkins, he had opened his safe on the wall in front of her. She noticed that he had opened a drawer in his desk before typing in the codes to open the safe. When Tomkins was looking in his safe, he had his back to her. Mobbs took that moment to open the drawer carefully and quietly. She took a photograph of the numbers on the paper with her iPhone camera, just in case she ever needed to look in his safe. There was also a set of keys in the drawer, labelled spare office keys, Mobbs took these and put them in to her handbag.

Mobbs had overheard a conversation between Tomkins and Pallett during their lunch at The Ivy Garden in Covent Garden. Mobbs had left the table to use the toilet facilities and, as she returned to the table, she heard Tomkins tell Pallett that he kept some incriminating information on Mobbs in an envelope in his work safe. Tomkins and Pallett were unaware that Mobbs had heard this. Mobbs wanted to see what it was that Tomkins had and she wanted to know before she had her meeting with him. She knew that Tomkins was a man of routine and liked to start work early. She told "G" to use the keys to enter the surgery and the codes to open the safe. Mobbs told him to make it look like a routine burglary and to "rough up" the place a bit. "You can keep whatever cash you find in the safe, that will be your reward for the job, but bring the envelope in the safe to me," she said to him. "Call me when you're finished." The heavily tattooed man exited the Mini, got back into his Ford Focus and drove out of the car park. Mobbs took out her hand sanitiser gel and wiped the seat where "G" had been sitting, and drove off.

Chapter Eighty Two

On the day of the robbery at Tomkins' surgery, "G" parked his grey Ford Focus in The Regent's Park at 06:45. He dodged the fast- moving traffic as he crossed over the already busy Marylebone Road and walked the short distance to Harley Street. It was a cool but dry morning. He was wearing blue denim jeans and a white T-shirt, with a blue denim jacket which only partially covered his muscular and tattooed arms. He checked his pockets to make sure that he had the correct address and codes to the safe, he did. "G" let himself in to the Harley Street building and surgery at around 7am, using the keys provided by Mobbs. There was no-one around but he kept his head down, so as not to be recognised by the CCTV cameras. Once inside the surgery he went to the office and opened a few drawers. He threw papers on the floor as well as putting some in his bag, this was just for effect as he was not interested in the content of the papers. He was interested in the contents of the safe.

One of the papers from the drawer was headed paper and had the home address of Professor Tomkins written at the bottom, he took this just in case he may need the address later. He found the safe and pulled out the paper from his jeans with the safe codes. He typed the numbers in and the safe door opened immediately. He looked in the safe and saw a lot of cash. He flicked through the twenty and fifty pound notes and estimated that there was around twenty thousand pounds. "A good day's work," he thought. He put the cash in his jeans pockets and found a large envelope with Charlotte Mobbs' name on it. The envelope was not sealed, he opened it to see what it was that Charlotte Mobbs wanted so badly. Inside the envelope was a letter from a private investigator to Tomkins and attachments including copies of Mobbs' Swiss bank account statements. There was a copy of her work itinerary with dates relating to the payments in to her account. There was also confirmation of her home address along with some long-range photos of Mobbs, in a bikini, pleasuring herself around her swimming pool in her garden. "G" studied the photo for a bit longer than was necessary and felt a sudden twinge in his groin. He took photographs of the contents of the envelope with his iPhone camera and put the photo and contents back in to the envelope. There was plenty of time for fun later, he thought. He had just finished and was ready to leave, when he heard a noise in the building. He looked at his watch and knew that it must be Professor Tomkins. "G" had taken longer than expected as he had stopped to read the contents of the envelope and take photos. He sealed the envelope and put it in to his bag. Just as Tomkins entered the office, "G" opened the window at the rear and ran out. He looked back and saw the professor and realised that the professor must also have seen him; that was not good. He got as far away from the building as he could and made sure that he was not being followed by Tomkins, before he texted Mobbs. "Job done," the message read. He did not tell her that he had looked at the contents inside the envelope and had certainly not told her that he had taken a photograph of the contents. "Meet me in the same car park as before, in one hour," she replied.

The same parking bays were free but this time "G" got there first and waited a few minutes for Mobbs to arrive. "G" had reverse parked so that the two driver's windows were next to each other. He pressed a button and the window lowered. Mobbs did not have such a luxury and struggled to roll down her window with the handle. "G" nodded in acknowledgement and passed the envelope through the open car windows to Mobbs. "Well done, thanks," she said; flicking through the contents of the envelope before "G" drove off. He had acquired a lot of money and wanted to spend it. The police had confiscated his remaining weapons and he had flushed his drugs down the toilet. He wanted to replace them and knew exactly where to go.

Chapter Eighty Three

The formal briefing room was on the top floor of New Scotland Yard. It had large windows with expansive views of the River Thames and the London Eye on the opposite bank of the river. The streets below were bustling with commuters scurrying to get to their workplaces and tourists taking photos of the Houses of Parliament. Red London buses were queueing at the bus stops full with people going about their daily business; all completely unaware of the discussions taking place in New Scotland Yard. The room was large and had been set out with a rectangle of tables spanning the entire length of the room. There was a large TV monitor on the wall, with a notice board beside the monitor. Inside the formal briefing room DI Chrissy Acton was talking with DCS Patricia Salter when Detective Chief Superintendent Adam Robson entered the room. DCS Robson was in charge of SCO19, a highly trained police tactical support team. There were also other respected members of his team in the briefing room. They were in the room to finalise their tactics for the meeting between Charlotte Mobbs and Clement Tomkins at Mobbs' house, later that day.

DCS Robson was slightly older than Chrissy Acton. He had been recently promoted to Detective Chief Superintendent due to the success he had during several recent high profile armed incidents in London. He was well known at New Scotland Yard and throughout the Met, and was well trusted. The TV monitor was split in to several screens. There was a live feed from the CCTV cameras in the roads where both Mobbs' and Tomkins' houses were located, as well as the roads in the surrounding areas. There was a screen shot from Google Maps, showing the likely routes between the two houses - they were only a few miles apart. On the notice board were photos of Mobbs and Tomkins, along with photos of Tomkins' car and a time line including the scheduled meeting at 7pm. They had agreed that a full team of officers would be required and a full range of weapons from the

Glock 17 self-loading pistol, the standard sidearm for SCO19, to the Heckler & Koch MP5 sub machine gun.

Despite the time of the meeting, it was decided that the officers would set up early and be waiting out of sight, they would be taking no chances. The briefing lasted for over an hour and all potential possibilities were discussed. After the meeting was over, the three senior detectives left the briefing room and went to Chrissy Acton's office where DCS Robson was introduced to the rest of her team. Detectives Pearce and Cross had returned from Harley Street and were sharing their findings with their colleagues from the early morning robbery, when they were interrupted by their senior officers. Detective Inspector Chrissy Acton took charge and updated her team with the tactics which had been discussed during the meeting in the briefing room. She was curious as to why Olek Gregorski had been spotted at the surgery but had more important matters to discuss.

Chapter Eighty Four

Professor Tomkins had returned home from his unexpectedly shortened day at his surgery; the annoyance of the break-in still playing on his mind. He put his brief case on the kitchen table in front of him. Who was the person who had broken in to his office? How did he know the codes to the safe and why did he take the envelope? He could understand why someone would want to take the cash. He knew what was in the envelope and also knew that the contents would affect only one person, Charlotte Mobbs. The timing was not a coincidence, the same day as his meeting with Mobbs. He knew that he no longer had a hold on her; he knew what he had to do. He opened his briefcase and took out the shiny six-inch serrated hunting knife. He smiled as he remembered what he had used the knife for in the past, and who he had killed. He touched the sharp point with the tip of his finger and made himself bleed. He was not put off by this as he wiped the blood away with a clean dampened cloth from the sink.

Tomkins walked slowly to the entrance hall and pushed a concealed button close to the edge of one of the panels on the dark oak panelled walls. The panelling opened slowly on its hinges and exposed the staircase leading down to his armoury. Inside the armoury Tomkins picked out his recently acquired military grade bullet and stab waistcoat style body armour, along with the eight-inch chef's knife. The very same knife which he had used to kill his mother and her lover twenty years earlier. He cleaned both of the knives in his armoury until they shined so brightly that he could see his face in them. He tried on the body armour and was pleased that it still fit him, despite him having put on a few pounds in weight since he had bought it. Still wearing the body armour and carrying both knives, Tomkins shuffled up the staircase from the armoury to the entrance hall and closed the panel in the wall panelling behind him, until he heard it click shut. He took off the body armour and placed it, along with the knives, onto the kitchen table. He then went upstairs to shower and shave, whilst working out his strategy for his meeting with Mobbs. He dried his body and got dressed in to a pair of blue casual trousers and a white shirt, no socks and a pair of brown boat deck shoes. He assumed that Mobbs would have her own plan for him, following the break-in at his surgery and the stolen envelope. He knew that she had recently bought a gun. He also knew that Mobbs was shrewd and that he would have to be very clever and careful to get the better of her.

He made his way back to the kitchen and was preparing a sandwich, when an intruder alarm lit up. Tomkins had employed a contractor to install a motion detector intruder alarm system for the garden and house several years earlier and this was the first time that that it had picked up anything unusual. The alarm had picked up movement at the end of his garden. He looked out of the window but could see nothing. Suddenly he heard a noise. It was a metal hitting metal noise; faint, but loud enough to have startled a few of the birds. Tomkins looked again and this time he saw something, or someone, moving in his garden. He grabbed a pair of binoculars, which he kept in a cupboard in the kitchen and ducked down behind the kitchen table so that he could not be seen. He looked through the binoculars and could just make out that there was a man hiding in the trees towards the end of the garden, close to the area where the bones were buried. The person was holding something in his hand but could not quite make out what it was, was it a gun? He could see the large tattoos on the man's large muscular arms and immediately recognised the tattoos as those belonging to the same man who had broken in to his surgery and taken the money and envelope from his safe, only a few hours earlier. The man was now standing still, watching the house. Tomkins ducked down as he did not want the man to know that he was also being watched. After a few minutes, the tattooed man moved towards the wooden shed and air raid shelter, still being covered by the growth of trees in the garden. Tomkins was watching his every move.

Chapter Eighty Five

A few hours earlier

After "G" had finished his brief rendezvous with Mobbs in the supermarket car park he drove his grey Ford Focus to a railway arch close to the canals in Hackney Wick, a part of east London. The railway arch had been converted in to a car workshop and office and was where he had his contacts for acquiring drugs and weapons. The traffic was light and it took just over thirty minutes to drive to meet his contact. He parked directly in front of the railway arch and made his way in to the workshop. "G" had called in advance and made his order for Cocaine and a pistol. Not just any old pistol, he wanted a Glock 17 police pistol and bullets. He also wanted a silencer for the Glock.

The area used to house factories and workshops but since the arrival of the Olympic Stadium in 2012 the area had been regenerated. Despite there now being and abundance of upmarket flats and recently opened restaurants, along with the opening of the large shopping centre of Westfield, Stratford, there were still a few remaining places where, if you had contacts, you could buy anything. He met with an equally tattooed man, Janus, alias "J", whom he had known for several years. "J" was also originally from Russia and, despite them both being over six foot tall and heavily tattooed, they greeted each other with a kiss on both cheeks, in the traditional Russian way. Before they did business, they sat down in the office at the rear of the workshop and "J" opened a bottle of Stolichnaya Vodka. He poured the vodka into two shot glasses and they toasted each other. "Nazdrovia!" they both shouted. A few glasses of vodka later, "J" unlocked a metal cupboard in the office and took out a packet containing a Glock 17 pistol, a silencer and a box of bullets. He handed the pistol to "G". The serial numbers on the

Glock had been filed away so that there was no trail of where the gun had come from. It was obvious from the condition of the pistol that it was not new and had been fired several times before. "G" picked up the Glock and looked at it carefully. He checked to see whether it was loaded, it was not. He attached the silencer and aimed the pistol at "J". He pulled the trigger, Click. "J" laughed; he knew that "G" would do this as he had done the same thing every time that he had bought a gun from him. Janus pulled open a drawer from the tatty desk in his office and produced two packets; one of clean uncut pure white powder and one which was greyer in colour and clearly cut. He made a narrow line on the table from both packets. "G" took out one of the recently acquired fifty-pound notes from his pocket and rolled it up in to a small tube. He snorted first the pure white Cocaine, waited a minute and then the snorted the cut greyer version through the bank note and in to his nose. He rubbed his nose and sniffed to make sure that the contents had gone fully in to his body.

"This is good shit!" "G" said. He was pleased with what he had tested and pulled an envelope, with fifty-pound notes out of his jean's pocket. He gave the money to "J" who counted it to make sure that it was the agreed amount, it was. They had another shot of vodka before "G" got up, took the pistol, bullets and Cocaine, and walked to his grey Ford Focus. "Do svidaniya, comrade," he said to "J" as he got in to his car.

Chapter Eighty-Six

His car did not have a Sat Nav, so "G" typed Professor Tomkins' address in to the sat nav in his mobile phone. He had obtained the address when he took some of the headed paper from the professor's surgery. He arrived at Professor Tomkins house in Totteridge and parked in a side road around the corner from the house. He had taken off his denim jacket, making his large muscles and tattoos visible for all to see. There was an opening in the prickly hedge in the garden boundary of the property adjacent to Tomkins' rear garden. He forced his way through the hedge but caught the top of his heavily tattooed arm on one of the sharp edges of the hedge. There was a trickle of blood running from his shoulder down to his elbow, the red blood made a nice contrasting pattern with his tattoo. "G" was not bothered by this as he entered the large garden. There were many trees at the end of the garden; he carefully manoeuvred his way to them so that he could hide and wait to assess the situation. "G" was standing on a raised area at the end of the garden, it looked like it was hiding something below. He had no way of knowing what was buried beneath his feet. He moved to one side and saw a concrete door below the raised lawn area. He tried the door handle but it was locked and would not turn. There was a padlock on the rusty door hooks. The padlock was a very heavy-duty padlock and looked new as it was so clean, he thought that this was unusual and his curiosity got the better of him. He looked around for some way of breaking in to the concrete structure to see why it needed such a heavy-duty padlock.

"G" searched for a few minutes but there was nothing strong enough to break the padlock. He took out the Glock from his pocket and attached the silencer which was in his other pocket. He checked the bullet clip and saw that it was full. He stood back six feet and aimed the Glock at the padlock. It was a perfect first shot as the padlock clip shattered under the pressure of the bullet. The shot had made a noise, a metal-on-metal noise. He stopped and looked around to see whether anyone had seen or heard him, nothing – or at least that was what he had thought. He did not know that he had already triggered the motion sensor intruder alarm system and that he was being watched. "G" tried to open the door; it was very heavy and clearly had not been opened for some time. He eventually managed to prise the door open and he was greeted by the stench of death and human bones. He stepped back away from the open door, holding his hands against his nose and mouth. The smell was so putrid that he was gagging. "What the fuck!" he exclaimed. What had he come across? Who did the bones belong to? Who was this man, Professor Tomkins? He had so many questions. He closed the heavy concrete door and brushed away the many cobwebs which had clung to his clothing and hair. Before he had a chance to turn around, he felt a metal object on his throat. Professor Tomkins was standing behind him holding a knife, with the pointed blade pressing in to "G"'s throat. Not his usual trusted six-inch serrated hunting knife but a carving knife which he had picked up from the kitchen wooden knife block. Tomkins had seen "G" in the garden and saw him open the air raid shelter. He knew what "G" must have found inside. "Drop the gun!" shouted Tomkins. "G" did as he was told. "G" was taller and stronger than Tomkins but Tomkins had a knife to his throat and he was weighing up the situation, before he made his move.

Tomkins tried to pick up the gun from the floor and "G" saw his chance. He fought with Tomkins to try and reach the gun first. There was a struggle with both men on the floor, each desperately trying to reach the gun. The struggle continued for a few minutes until they both had their hands on a section of the Glock; but only one of them had their fingers on the trigger. The silencer was still attached and there was no noise as "G" fell back on to the floor with blood pouring from the top of his left arm. The bullet had scratched the surface of his arm and blood was running down his arm; it matched the blood pattern on his other arm where it had been caught on the hedge. Tomkins picked up his knife from the grass and pointed the Glock at "G"'s face. He gestured with it for "G" to follow, in front of him, in to the house. Reluctantly "G" followed his instructions and, holding his bullet-damaged and bloodied arm, they went in to the house.

Chapter Eighty-Seven

After her brief meeting with "G" in the supermarket car park, Charlotte Mobbs opened the envelope which he had given her and pulled out the contents. She read the letter from the private investigator to Tomkins and looked at the attachments, including copies of her Swiss bank account statements and her work itinerary with dates relating to the payments in to her account. She saw the confirmation of her home address along with the long-range photos in which she was pleasuring herself in her garden, around her swimming pool. She smiled. "You dirty bastard Tomkins", she thought to herself. She kept the photos out, admiring herself, and put the other contents back in to the envelope. Mobbs drove the few miles back to her house in Mill Hill, content with the knowledge that, with this information away from Tomkins, he no longer had any control over her. She did not know that "G" had taken a photograph of the contents.

She had put the photos on the front passenger seat beside her and was looking at them as she drove. As she was driving, Mobbs lifted up the hem line of her long black dress with her left hand, whilst she held the steering wheel with her right hand. She put her left hand up her between her thighs and felt that she was getting wet. Her mind was on her pleasure and not concentrating on the road. She didn't follow the bend in the road and didn't see the car coming towards her. She was on the wrong side of the road and nearly hit the oncoming car. If it was not for the quick mindedness of the other car swerving away from her, there would have been a very nasty head-on collision. Mobbs slammed on the brakes and made a few unpleasant gestures to the other driver, as if it were his fault. She continued her journey home, this time concentrating on the road. She would continue with the pleasure later. She parked her Mini a few hundred yards away from her house, got out of the car, and wiped the handles and steering wheel with the wet wipes. She did not spot the unmarked van with blacked out windows, which was parked in the side road. Inside the van was a police surveillance team, setting up controls for later. They watched Mobbs park her car and get out. They saw her re-arrange her dress and watched it settle to just above the ground surface. In her hand they saw the envelope and photos. The surveillance team were taking photos of her every move, with the long telephoto lens on their camera. As well as being stored on the SD card in the camera, the photos were also automatically uploaded on to the computer in the van. Within seconds, the photos could be seen by Detective Inspector Chrissy Acton and her team at New Scotland Yard.

Mobbs walked the short distance to her house and looked around as she walked. She was paranoid, but did not see anything unusual. She opened her front door and walked through the spacious hallway in to the kitchen. She was craving a strong coffee but first she put the envelope and photos on to the kitchen table. She took the contents out of the envelope and re-read them. She made a note of the private detective's details, he was good. He had found out lots of information about her and taken photos of her, without her having any idea that she was being watched. She may need his services in the future. Mobbs looked at her bank statements and diary dates and shredded them in the diamond cut shredder which she kept in her home office. She kept the photos of herself and looked at them again. The warm feelings in her stomach and between her legs started again; she took the photos upstairs to her bedroom.

She opened the drawer by the side of her bed and took out her vibrator. She lay back on her large king size bed and pulled up her long dress so that it exposed her stomach. She played with herself as she looked at the photos taken by the private detective. She came, within seconds of touching herself. Her body was still shaking from her orgasm, when she heard the doorbell ring. She got up from her bed, looked out of the bedroom window and saw a van in her driveway. On the side of the van there was a logo of a drainage company and there were two men, with company overalls, standing by her front door. One of the workmen had a clipboard, whilst the other was carrying a toolbox in his hand. Mobbs opened her bedroom window. "I'll be down in a minute, I'm just coming," she told the men. She smiled to herself at that comment. She pulled her dress down and, with her legs still trembling, she walked slowly downstairs and opened the door to the two men.

The drains workmen showed their id's. "There's been complaints from the neighbours about blocked drains in the road," one of the men announced. "Our investigations suggest that the blockage was coming from your drains," he continued.. They wanted to lift the drain covers and check the system. Mobbs let them lift the drain covers in the front driveway and then in the rear garden. Once they had finished, they asked to check the bathrooms in the house. Mobbs let them in. One of the men asked Mobbs to check the paperwork. They went to the kitchen and sat at the table, whilst the other man went, with his toolbox, in to the bathrooms. There were three bathrooms on the first floor of the house, including the en-suite bathroom to the main bedroom, where Mobbs had been when they arrived. The workman walked past the bed and saw the vibrator on the bed with the tip glistening, he smiled. He went in to the bathroom and opened his toolbox. Inside the toolbox were screwdrivers and specialist plumbing tools which concealed a separate secret compartment, which he opened. The secret compartment in the toolbox contained the latest, state of the art, tiny button cameras and listening devices. He did not have time to fix them into walls, which would have been the best option, so he looked around for places to put the devices. He attached them to the edge of mirrors and cabinets in each of the bathrooms, one at the top of the wardrobe in each bedroom, and one above a picture in the first-floor landing. He tapped each of the listening devices as he fixed them and got a signal back from the unmarked police surveillance van parked along the street. The equipment was working and he put his face right up to the camera lens to scare the team.

Once he had finished, he flushed all of the toilets, so that Mobbs would believe that he was doing his drainage tests. He then went to the ground floor toilet area and placed a further camera and listening device there and also in the reception rooms beside the photo album of Mobbs and her three black cats. Once he had finished doing this, he went back to the kitchen and met up with his colleague. "Problem solved," he announced. "There's no charge it's covered by the council," he continued.

They thanked Mobbs for her co-operation and she signed the paperwork. The two men got back in their van and drove off, stopping next to the unmarked van with blacked out windows which was parked further down the street. The man with the clipboard got out and entered the back of the unmarked van. The other man drove off; his job was done.

Chapter Eighty-Eight

The unmarked van with blacked out windows resembled a fully working office. There were three police officers looking at several TV monitors; each of the monitors had split screens showing the images from each of the cameras, recently placed in Mobbs' house. The officers had headphones covering their ears and were listening to hear any sound which might be made inside the house. They had witnessed their colleague placing the surveillance equipment in specific locations inside the house and were secretly impressed with the system as it started to work immediately. The picture quality was the not the latest technology but the clarity of the pictures was good enough. The sound quality was not top of the range Dolby, but it was also good enough for their purposes. The drains workman entered the van; he was a colleague of the three officers already inside the van and acknowledged his co-workers by name. He sat down beside his colleagues and looked at one of the screens. He could see the live feed from the cameras which he had just placed throughout Mobbs' house. The live feed could also be seen by Detective Inspector Chrissy Acton and her team at New Scotland Yard, watching on the large screen in the main office. They watched Mobbs in her kitchen as she made herself a cup of coffee. The camera which had been placed in the reception room only just covered that area, but it was enough and the quality of picture was good. The sound quality was good enough, they could even hear the kettle boil. They watched Mobbs as she put copious amounts of sugar in her coffee. They then watched as she went to the biscuit jar and took out several chocolate digestive biscuits, which she then dunked in to the hot coffee.

Mobbs sat at the large kitchen table and looked through the paperwork which she had been given by the drain's contractor. She studied it carefully, reading it once and then again. Something did not seem quite right but she could not put her finger on it. She saw a phone number at the bottom of the front page and dialled the number from her iPhone. The number rang three times and was then answered by a female voice on the other end of the call. The voice was one of the officers in the surveillance van. The officer answering the call pretended to work for the drainage company and put Mobbs at her ease. She told Mobbs that the drains problem had indeed been resolved and thanked her for her co-operation. Mobbs finished the call but was not satisfied, she was experienced in blackmailing and conning people out of money; she still felt that something was not right. She picked up her coffee cup and went upstairs to her bedroom, also noticing her vibrator on the bed. She went in to the en-suite bathroom where the drains man had been and noticed that some personal items in the bathroom had been moved. Only slightly but enough to make her look closer. She saw a small item by the mirror, which had not been there earlier. She did not touch it or go too close to it but went to the other rooms where the workman had been. She looked around and noticed the same items in those rooms as well. She knew that she was being watched and would have to think carefully what to do next. She went back to the kitchen and finished her coffee, weighing up the possible outcomes of her next actions. Mobbs went back in to the rooms where each of the cameras had been placed and looked in to the cameras, with a wry smile on her face.

She threw each camera and listening device in to the toilet in the bathrooms where they had been placed and flushed, making sure that the devices had been fully flushed away. "Nice try," she said out loud to herself. "Thanks Pallett," she continued. As each camera was flushed down the toilet, the pictures on the TV monitors in the surveillance van, and at New Scotland Yard, fizzled out and went blank, one by one, until there was nothing on the screens.

Chapter Eighty-Nine

Detective Inspector Chrissy Acton and her team at New Scotland Yard watched the pictures on the large monitor go blank, one at a time. She knew that Mobbs had found the cameras and listening devices and was angry. She was so angry that she started thumping the desk in front of her and shouting through the comms to the officers in the surveillance van. The detectives in her team around her had not seen that side of her for a very long time and they did not like it, she scared them when she was like this. They said that she had a certain voice which she used when she was angry, this was that voice. They knew that the best thing was for them to leave their boss alone to reflect and come up with a solution to the problem; she usually did as she was a very experienced police detective. DI Acton got up and walked to her office and shut the door behind her, she needed time to think. She only needed a few minutes. She checked the contact list on her iPhone and scrolled down until she found the name of Hannah Cozin. She looked at her watch and knew that it would be OK to call, even with the five-hour time difference between London and New York. She pressed the call button and within seconds Hannah Cozin's phone was ringing. Hannah looked at the screen on her iPhone, saw Chrissy's name and answered immediately. She answered the call with a whispering voice.

Hannah was on a stake-out in her car, watching a high-profile multi-millionaire businessman cheating on his wife. Her client was the man's wife who was also wealthy in her own right. Hannah's car was parked outside a motel on the outskirts of New Jersey, when the couple arrived in separate cars. She had been listening in to the conversations and reading text messages between the man and his lover for over two weeks and knew exactly what time and place they were meeting. It was a regular meeting every two days, always at the same time and place. At an earlier rendezvous Hannah had taken photos of the lovers arriving separately at the motel, pretending that they did not know each other. Each time it was the man who went to the reception area to book the key and pay for the room, in cash. Hannah had photos of them both entering the same room, room 10, but up until now she did not have a photo of them actually having sex with each other. The photos she had taken so far would not be able to be used in evidence by a divorce lawyer as the couple could say that they were simply playing backgammon, or that it was a work meeting. She needed the "money shot" and she had done this before. She cast her mind back to the hotel in New York where she photographed James Hopkiss having sex with the two beautiful escorts. She needed the same photographic evidence to close this case.

Chrissy updated Hannah on the situation in London and told her what had happened, with the cameras. Hannah put Chrissy on hold whilst she contacted Splinter; after a few moments Hannah spoke again with Chrissy. "Splinter already has control of the electrical equipment in Mobbs' house," she told Chrissy. "He was aware that Mobbs had found the equipment placed in the house by the police officers posing as drains men. "Amateurs", was the word he used to describe the workmen," she continued. The good news for Chrissy was that Splinter was prepared to share his surveillance access to Mobbs house with the Metropolitan Police, for a fee. Chrissy was not in a position to argue and agreed; she would have to explain this to her boss later.

Hannah cut off the call to Chrissy and walked up to the window of the motel. There was a slight break in the curtain and she could see that the man and woman, who she was following, were getting naked. She went to the reception area and gave the clerk behind the desk a one-hundred-dollar bill with the semi-smiling face of Benjamin Franklin staring at him. "I've lost the key to my room, room 10," she told the clerk. "I want to surprise my boyfriend," she continued. The man did not look up; he accepted the money and handed a spare key to room 10 to Hannah.

Hannah went back to her car to retrieve her camera and walked across the car park from her car to room 10. She looked through the window again and, sure enough, the couple were getting busy. She could see the man lying on the bed with the woman straddled with one leg on either side of his naked body. She was riding him like a cowgirl would ride a horse, her long blonde hair thrashing from side to side, her body rising and falling in a steady rhythm. They were so busy enjoying each other's bodies that they did not notice the door opening and Hannah tip-toeing quietly into the room. Hannah took the "money shot" photo many times and left the room with the couple still unaware that they had been caught in the act.

Chapter Ninety

"G" walked ahead of Professor Tomkins, aware of the gun to his back but also fully aware that he was much stronger than the man holding the gun. He knew that he could overwhelm Tomkins at any time he chose. But he chose not to. He was fascinated by the man with the gun and the secrets that were hidden in the garden, so he walked ahead of the professor and in to the kitchen. He wanted to know more about this strange man and how his mind worked. Professor Tomkins told "G" to sit down at the kitchen table whilst he went to one of the cupboards and brought out a larger than average first aid kit. At the far end of the table were the body armour and knives, which the professor had taken out from his armoury, for his meeting with Charlotte Mobbs. "G" saw these and was surprised and intrigued by what he saw. He was fascinated by Tomkins.

Tomkins looked at the gunshot wound and decided that it was a surface wound only. The damage was superficial but needed stitches as the tear was a few inches long and was still bleeding. He gave "G" a clean towel and told him to press hard on the wound to stop the bleeding. The bullet was lucky not to have caused more damage and had missed the main artery by a few inches. Tomkins took out an anti-septic spray and a local anaesthetic syringe from the first aid kit, along with a needle and thread. He put some fresh water in the kettle and boiled it. Once the kettle had boiled Tomkins sterilised the needle and put on a pair of medical grade latex gloves. He walked up to "G" and removed the blood-stained towel; he was pleased to see that the bleeding had virtually stopped. He cleaned the wound in "G"'s arm, making sure that any debris had been removed. Tomkins injected the local anaesthetic and sprayed it with the anti-septic spray. Once satisfied that the wound was clean and that the needle was sterilised, he started to stitch the wound. Tomkins knew exactly what to do as he stitched his patients every day after their surgery, he could do it with his eyes closed if necessary. He pinched the skin on either side of the wound and punctured the skin about four millimetres away from the wound. He pulled the needle through to the other side of the wound pulling tight, like a purse string, and leaving enough length to tie off the individual stitch.

"G" was a strong man but the sight of the stitches going in to his upper arm made him light headed and feeling faint. Tomkins repeated the stitching several times, until he was satisfied that the entire length of the wound had been covered. Once he had finished, Tomkins admired his work and cleaned the wound again with the antiseptic spray before wrapping it tightly with a bandage. He then offered "G" a vodka and they sat together at the kitchen table chatting away as if they had been friends for life. They talked for ages and for the first time Tomkins told someone what he had done to his mother and her lover all those years ago. He told him all about the bones in the air raid shelter. Tomkins felt a huge weight lift from his shoulders, it was as if he had been to see a therapist for the first time. "G" also confessed to many of his crimes to the professor. He told the professor that it was he who had broken in to the professor's surgery and taken the items from the safe. He also told the professor that it was Charlotte Mobbs who had asked him to do this and that it was she who had given him the key to the surgery and the code to the safe. Tomkins told "G" that he was meeting with Mobbs later that evening to sort out their issues.

"G" showed Tomkins the photos of the letters which he had stolen from Tomkins' safe. Tomkins asked "G" to email these to him as it was his only hold over Mobbs, "G" emailed them immediately.

Tomkins pointed to the body armour and knives on the table. He told "G" that he knew that Mobbs had recently purchased a gun, but that he was prepared. He didn't know that the gun that Mobbs had bought was supplied by the person sitting with him at the table and the person whose arm he had just stitched. "G" did not say a word. "G" had another vodka and thanked the professor for stitching the wound and dressing it. He could see that he needed to keep the professor on his side as he did not know when he may need another makeshift surgery. He told the professor that he would like to help him with the "Mobbs' situation" and would make sure that he would be at the meeting later. "G" left the house and Tomkins watched him walk away. He didn't see him get in to his car as it was parked around the corner and out of sight.

Chapter Ninety-One

"G" left Professor Tomkins' house to walk to his car, which was parked around the corner. He didn't notice that there was a plain clothes police officer in a black unmarked Audi A3 police car on the opposite side of the road from Tomkins' house. Inside the unmarked police car was Detective Harry "James" Bond. Bond saw "G" exit Tomkins' house and took photos with his digital camera with a long telephoto lens. He called his boss, Detective Inspector Chrissy Acton, to advise her what he had just seen. He took the SD card out of the camera, uploaded the photos on to his laptop computer and emailed the photos to Chrissy where they were forwarded to the monitors in the New Scotland Yard operations room. DI Acton called for an additional support team to go to Professor Tomkins' house and instructed Detective Sergeant Bond to follow the Ford Focus. Bond followed the Ford Focus discretely, staying well back and trying not to be seen by "G". It was something that Bond had trained for, and was very good at.

However, "G" was also good at spotting when he was being followed, it was part of his survival nature and, on this occasion, survival beat training. "G" had noticed the black Audi A3 following him as soon as he left Tomkins' house. He did not panic; he was going to have some fun with the Audi. He carried on driving as if nothing was wrong and didn't want to let the Audi driver know. There was a public house ahead of him on the left side of the road. "G" indicated left and slowed the car down before turning in to the car park, all the time looking in the rear-view mirror to make sure that the Audi was still behind him, it was. He parked his car and walked, slowly, in to the public house, making sure not to look back to where the Audi had parked. He touched the bandage on his upper arm and winced with pain as the anaesthetic was starting to wear off. The stitches and wound were starting to hurt. He went in to the bar area and noticed a pretty woman behind the bar, drying a beer glass before placing it on a shelf behind her. "Two bottles of Lager, please luv," he said, with a strong Russian accent to his broken English. "G" ordered two bottles of lager, one for himself and one for the person in the Audi. He gave a twenty-pound note to the woman behind the bar. "Keep the change, I'll be back in a moment," he told her. keeping eye contact with her for as long as possible, before going to the car park. She looked at him and could tell that he liked what he saw, she knew that he would be back.

The woman behind the bar thought that she recognised "G" and when he turned away to go to the car park, she picked up her mobile phone and looked at a photograph. She was right, she did recognise the man. She sent the photograph along with a brief text message to her brother. The message had an emoji of a Russian sickle, followed by the words "my work place in 30!"

"G" took the two bottles of lager and walked out of the bar to the black Audi parked in the car park. He tapped one of the bottles of lager gently on the driver's window, Detective Sergeant Bond pressed a button and the window lowered. "I won't be going anywhere for a while," "G" explained to Bond. "Enjoy the drink," he continued. Bond took the bottle but would not drink it as he was "on duty". "G" walked sprightly back to the bar turning round to look at the detective before he disappeared in to the bar.

Chapter Ninety-Two

Roxana

The woman behind the bar was Roxana. Roxana was from Romania in eastern Europe and had a strong east European accent. She was in her late twenties, five foot eight tall and had long brown hair, tied up at the top. She had a sexy figure, most of which was on show as she was wearing a short white cotton shirt, tied up beneath her breasts and showing a tanned and trim midriff below the shirt. Roxana's long legs were barely covered with a short black leather mini skirt. "G" took an instant liking to her and started talking to her as if he had known her all of his life. Roxana heard "G"'s accent as also being from the eastern side of Europe. It was a stronger accent than hers and after a few guesses she placed it as being from Russia. She had friends and family there too and so the general conversation continued.

Roxana liked strong, confident men and especially those with tattoos. She touched the tattoos on his arms and sexily and suggestively, followed the patterns with her fingers. "I have a few tattoos too," she said, lowering her voice. "Only special people get to see them, as they are in a very private place," she continued. "Would you like to see them?" she asked. "G" nodded. They were laughing and flirting with each other when Roxana noticed that there was blood showing through the bandage on "G"'s upper arm. Roxana looked at the time on her watch and suggested that she could change the bandage for him. She led him upstairs to the staff flat, above the bar. She had taken the key from her purse underneath the drinks bar; unlocked and opened the door to the flat. They walked in and Roxana closed the door behind "G", but did not lock the door.

It was a clean and tidy bedsit style flat with a double bed on one side of the room, a small kitchenette area on the other and a shower room with toilet behind another door. "Sit on the edge of the bed," Roxana told "G". "G" did as he was told and Roxana slowly took the bandage off his upper arm until she saw the stitches. She did not ask him what had happened but could tell that it was serious. The blood on the bandage looked old; the bleeding had stopped and the stitches looked clean, there was no infection. "Whoever did the stitches, did a good job," she said looking impressed.

Their faces were very close to each other and "G" took the opportunity to kiss her on her lips. Roxana froze for a moment and looked at her watch again. She was clearly waiting for something, or someone. "G"'s face was rough with bristle starting to grow as he had not shaved since much earlier in the morning. Roxana pushed him back on to the bed. "Don't move," she told him. "G" did as he was told. He liked Roxana and liked what she was doing to him. She noticed a bulge appear in his jeans and she knew that he was under her spell.

Roxana unzipped "G"'s jeans and pulled them down over his knees, moving his knees as she did this, in order to make the removal of the jeans easier. She had clearly done this before and "G" was not going to stop her. He was impressed by her actions. She completely removed the jeans from his legs and threw them on the floor in a pile. Next were the boxer shorts, they were hiding the bulge and she wanted to see what was being concealed. She was not disappointed as she pulled the boxers off and threw them on top of the jeans. The erect penis that she saw in front of her was one of the biggest that she had seen, and she had seen a few. It was over seven inches long and very wide. She looked at her watch again but, this time "G" noticed. "Are you waiting for something?" He asked. "I've seen you look at you watch a few times," he continued. Roxana did not reply. Instead, she smiled at "G" as she put her lips on to the tip of his penis, licking the tip and shaft as if it was an ice lolly. She played with his penis for a few minutes before looking up from the top of her eyes to see that "G" had his eyes closed. He was enjoying being on the receiving end of what was an amazing blow job; she did not seem to be enjoying giving it, but did not let on. She wanted to bite him, to hurt him, but refrained. She had other plans for him. After a further few minutes of pleasure, she could feel "G"'s body start to tense and knew that he was about to come. She stopped as she did not want him to finish just yet; she wanted him to remember what might be his best, but last, orgasm and was not going to waste this moment. She walked away from the bed to the chest of drawers by the window and pulled out a new fluffy pink pair of handcuffs. She cuffed "G"'s hands to the metal railed headboard, very tightly, making sure that he could not get loose. "We're going to have some fun" she told him.

Roxana stood up and "G" watched as she slowly and seductively took off her white shirt, first untying it at the bottom and then undoing the buttons until her large 34DD breasts were revealed. They were a perfect shape and size and a perfect fit for "G"'s mouth as she walked round the bed and placed her erect nipples in his mouth. She then started to slowly lift her short mini skirt, revealing the moistening crotch of her white panties. She unzipped the mini skirt and let it fall to the floor. She was extremely sexy and had a great figure. She wanted to tease "G" for as long as possible, before showing him everything that she had. After a few more teasing moments, she finally took off her white panties and revealed a short, tidy landing strip of hair above her moist pussy. Roxana had not finished with "G" yet and sat above his bristly face, her naked body facing towards his feet. He placed his tongue onto her until he found her clitoris. She squealed with pleasure as she bent forward and placed her mouth around his still erect penis. "G" was desperate to fuck Roxana, and told her in no uncertain terms.

Roxana looked again at the time on her watch; it had been nearly thirty-five minutes since she had sent the text message and was clearly frustrated, she was wondering if there was a problem. Suddenly her phone lit up, there was a reply to her message, it had a simple message which read "here now." Roxana looked relieved by the message.

"Wait a moment, whilst I freshen up in the shower and get a condom," she told him. He was tied firmly to the bed and could not leave, even if he wanted to. She was only in the shower room for one minute when the door of the flat burst open. Two identical twins, both even taller and more muscular than "G" appeared in the room. One of the twins spoke in Romanian to

Roxana, "are you OK sis?" he asked. Roxana replied through the closed door to say that she was. "I'm OK," she replied. "What took you so long?" she asked, but they did not reply.

The second twin spoke to "G" in broken English before pulling out a pistol with a silencer attached. "This is for our other little sister that you killed, you bastard!" he said as he pulled the trigger and shot "G" in the forehead between his eyes. "G" died instantly. "It's safe to come out now sis," the man said as he looked towards the shower room door. Roxana always kept spare clothes in the shower room and had got dressed in to a pair of tight blue denim jeans and a white crop top. She came out to greet her twin brothers in the room and they huddled together. Roxana looked at the lifeless body of "G", his hands still tied to the metal railed head board. She spat on the body and swore, in both Romanian and Russian. The twins picked up "G"'s body and placed it in to a large body bag which they had brought with them and had left outside the door to the flat.

They turned to Roxana and thanked her for sending them the message that "G" was with her. They had been after him for several months ever since "G" had killed their sister, having sold her cocaine which was mixed with rat poison. Roxana had recognised "G" the moment that he walked in to the bar and knew what had to be done. She was a good actress and, although she had enjoyed the sex, it was just that, sex. She knew that she had to keep "G" there long enough so that her brothers could come and kill him; and what better way was there to keep a man from leaving, she thought. She was right. The bigger picture was the revenge for the death of her younger sister.

Chapter Ninety-Three

Detective Sergeant Bond had been sitting waiting patiently in his Audi in the pub car park for something to happen. It had been thirty minutes since "G" had handed him the bottle of beer. He had placed the bottle of beer in to the cup holder and was eating a ham and cheese sandwich which he had bought at a petrol station on his way to the surveillance at Professor Tomkins' house. The sandwich was starting to curl at the edges and the bread was hardening. He made a mental note of reporting this to health standards, when he noticed a black Transit van pull in to the car park. The van circled the car park and chose a space to the side of the pub, almost out of sight. He thought that it was strange, especially as there were so many available spaces in the car park. It was only his detective's instinct at the moment, based on nothing else. He saw two large men exit the van carrying a black bag and walk to the side door of the bar, away from the main bar area. He thought that this was suspicious behaviour but it was a pub after all, and all sorts of people are allowed to drink in pubs - the money is the same. He carried on trying to digest the stale sandwich and was tempted to drink from the beer bottle by his side, but declined as he had a bottle of water.

After a further ten minutes had passed, Detective Sergeant Bond was starting to get agitated. He called Chrissy who advised him to enter he pub to see where "G" was, but to be careful and make sure that he could not be seen. As Detective Sergeant Bond opened his car door, he saw the two men exiting the same side door of the bar area where they had entered, but this time they were carrying a very large bag, so large that he thought that it might be a body bag. He did not leave his car but closed the door and reached for his camera. He took long range photos of the van and licence number as he watched the men place the bag in to the back of the Transit van and drive away. DS Bond got out of his car and walked to the front door of the pub, looking all around him to see if he could see "G", he could not. He looked around the bar, there were plenty of empty tables. He saw Roxana behind the bar and walked up to her. He flashed his warrant id card and showed it to Roxana.

He then took out his mobile phone and scrolled down to a photograph of Olek Gregorski. He asked Roxana if she had seen the person in the photo. Roxana looked at the photograph of the man who had just been shot to death by her older twin brothers. She carefully considered for a moment what to tell the detective before coolly saying that she had indeed seen the man in the photo. She knew that "G" had bought two bottles of lager and now realised that the second bottle was for the detective, standing in front of her. She quickly adjusted her story to say that the man in the photo had bought two bottles of lager. He had taken them both outside but when he came back, he only had one bottle. She then told the detective that the man had finished his bottle very quickly and left the bar through a back door to the garden area and that she had not seen him since. DS Bond thought it was strange that "G" had not come out to his car and remembered the conversation where "G" told him that "he would not be going anywhere for a while."

Clearly, he had been lied to and assumed that "G" wanted to lose the police surveillance. He thanked Roxana and went back to his car where he called his boss to say that he had lost "G". Detective Inspector Chrissy Acton instructed Detective Sergeant Bond to go back to Professor Tomkins' house and watch Tomkins. Detective Sergeant Bond followed his orders and returned to Professor Tomkins' house. He parked across the road from the house and waited; he did not have to wait too long.

Chapter Ninety-Four

After the excitement of his meeting with "G", Professor Tomkins was covered with blood from the gunshot wound as well as mud, from the fight in his garden. He was only a few hours away from his important meeting with Charlotte Mobbs and could not go to her looking as he was. He took another shower and washed off the mud and blood from the earlier events. He pulled a light brown suit and a white shirt from his wardrobe and put them on. Despite it coming from his wardrobe, the shirt and suit were very creased and there were a few light stains. Tomkins had not had his suits dry cleaned or pressed for as long as he could remember and was not going to start now. The suit was a poor fit, just like his other suits, with his stomach overhanging the waist of his trousers. The shirt was a tight fit with the buttons bulging out. He did not care and admired himself in the mirror.

He went back to the kitchen and picked up his weapons of choice, the six-inch serrated hunting knife along with the eight-inch chef's knife. He kissed the edges of both of the knives and put them in his briefcase; he made sure that they were concealed and covered them with a copy of the Metro newspaper. He put the photocopies of the information that "G" had emailed him into his briefcase. He looked at the recently acquired military grade bullet and stab waistcoat style body armour and realised that he needed to put this under his shirt so that Mobbs would not see it. He re-dressed and put the waistcoat under his shirt, making his shirt even tighter. Tomkins checked all of the windows and doors to make sure that they were shut and locked. He turned the house alarm on and exited through the front door. He opened the garage door and admired his classic 1950 Jaguar XK120 roadster in British Racing Green. He opened the door to the driver's side and climbed in, putting his briefcase on the passenger seat. He turned the key in the ignition but there was no sound. He tried again and the 3.4 litre straight six engines sprang in to life. He revved the engine a few times just to make sure that it was ok, it was. He drove slowly over the shingle driveway to the road and turned left to start the short three-mile journey to Mobbs' house. He didn't notice the black Audi A3 with Detective Sergeant Bond inside, on the opposite side of the road.

Tomkins knew that he was going to be early and decided to stop at the public house further along the road. It was the same public house where "G" had been shot. He turned his Jaguar left in to the car park of the public house and saw the grey Ford Focus parked there. He parked his car two spaces away from the Ford, walked over to it and looked through the window, there was nothing to see except a few drops of blood on the back of the driver's seat from "G"'s recent gunshot wound. The black Audi followed the Jaguar in to the car park and parked several spaces away, so that he was not spotted. Tomkins shuffled towards the entrance to the bar and looked around, it was virtually empty. The bar was more popular at the weekends when families would come along and eat the bar food in the garden, especially if it was a sunny day. He walked over to the bar and asked the lady behind the bar if she had seen the owner of the Ford Focus, he described "G" perfectly. Roxana knew exactly who Tomkins was describing but told him that she had not seen anyone like that. He thanked Roxana and ordered a scotch on the rocks, which he took to one of the empty tables by the window.

Tomkins placed his briefcase on one of the chairs and sat down on another. The window had a view towards the car park where both his and "G"'s cars were parked. Detective Sergeant Bond was taking photographs of Tomkins in the window seat, from his car. As soon as the professor had sat down, Roxana sent a text message to her brothers with an emoji of a car and a message saying "remove from car park, urgent!"

Tomkins waited at the table for over fifteen minutes, planning his meeting with Mobbs, when suddenly a black Transit van pulled in to the car park and drove past the Audi. Bond recognised it as being the same van that was there before. Tomkins watched from the bar, and DS Bond watched from his Audi, as a large man opened the passenger door of the van and went over to the Ford Focus. The man took a key from his pocket and opened the driver's door of the Ford Focus. He got in and adjusted the seat so that he could fit inside; he started the engine and drove off, past the Audi. The van followed.

There was nothing that DS Bond could do; to open a car door with a key and drive off was not a crime. The man with the key to the car may have borrowed the key from "G". Bond took photos of the man opening the car door and photos of the van and forwarded these to HQ.

Chapter Ninety-Five

In New Scotland Yard they were preparing their tactics for the meeting at seven o'clock between Charlotte Mobbs and Professor Clement Tomkins. The photographs sent by Detective Sergeant Bond of the two men at the pub were now on the crime board alongside Mobbs and Tomkins. The photos of Professor Noble had been removed as he was no longer a suspect; the photos of all of the victims were still on the board. The faces of the twins were being scanned through the police computer systems as well as Interpol. After a while of scanning the names appeared on the screen in the list of Interpol's most wanted people. Anton and Bogdan Constantin were twins, in their early thirties, both were wanted for questioning in Romania and Germany for murder. They had two younger sisters, Roxana and Sofia. The photos of Anton, Bogdan, and their younger sisters were sent to all police officers, including Detective Sergeant Bond, who was still in the pub car park.

Detective Sergeant Bond looked at the alert and saw the photographs on his phone; he immediately recognised the photograph of Roxana, the lady in the pub. He called Detective Inspector Chrissy Acton and told her that Roxana was working in the pub where he was watching Professor Tomkins. "Hold back, don't do anything just yet" DI Acton told him. She was working on other information which had just been handed to her. "Boss, look at this," Detective Cross said to DI Acton, with excitement in his voice. "Sofia Constantin had been found dead at a private party in central London only a few weeks ago. It was a bad drug concoction of cocaine mixed with rat poison, which had killed her," he announced. "The drugs had been connected back to a local dealer, Jack Nash, who had been arrested but he had not told the police who had supplied him with the drugs," he continued.

Detective Inspector Chrissy Acton's detective brain started to work at full speed. "Check whether there were any connections between Jack Nash, the local drug dealer, and Olek Gregorski".

She asked Detective Cross. Cross pressed a few keys on the computer keyboard and within seconds the information appeared on the screen. Detective Inspector Chrissy Acton was not surprised to find out that they had both been arrested several years earlier for supplying drugs together at another private party. Jack Nash had served a year in prison whilst Olek Gregorski had been let go, due to insufficient evidence against him. Olek Gregorski had made good use of the time that Jack Nash served in prison. He had expanded his network and created his own local dealers, whilst he took the profits as their supplier.

When Jack Nash left prison, it was Olek Gregorski who met him at the gates and brought him in to his network as a local dealer. Finally, the pieces of the jigsaw puzzle were fitting in to place and starting to show a nearly complete picture. Detective Inspector Acton had connected the death of Sofia Constantin to Olek Gregorski. She then connected that Sofia's sister, Roxana, worked in the public house where Olek Gregorski had been seen. The twin brothers had arrived at the public house with a small bag and left soon after, placing a heavy bag in their Transit van, only to return an hour later to remove Gregor ski's car. "They killed him and disposed of his body and car!" she announced to her team, who were listening with full attention, admiring the brain of their superior officer.

Detective Inspector Chrissy Acton immediately dispatched local squad cars to the public house and told Detective Sergeant Bond to wait for back up before going in to the bar. The local police were told to go in silent, without sirens, and arrived within a few minutes of the instructions received from Detective Inspector Chrissy Acton. Detective Sergeant Bond greeted the officers and took control of the situation as lead detective. He went in to the bar with two of the officers and walked up to Roxana, who was drying glasses behind the bar. Bond had already shown Roxana the photograph of Olek Gregorski but now he showed her the photographs of her older twin brothers. She acknowledged that they were, indeed, her brothers. She told him that they had been at the public house earlier. "They came to see me and help me take some of my belongings away as I am in the process of moving home," she told him, hoping that he would believe her lie.

DS Bond did not believe her story and had a lot more questions for Roxana. He decided that it would be easier to take her to the local police station for official questioning. He asked to see the flat above the bar, but was refused access as he did not have a warrant. He told her that he would get a warrant and return with a forensic team later. A crowd had gathered in the bar, and there were onlookers in the car park trying to see what was going on. Professor Tomkins was watching the situation unfold from his table by the window. He had not made the connection but knew that something was wrong and wondered if it was connected to "G".

Chapter Ninety-Six

The Constantin Family

Anton, Bogdan, Roxana and Sofia Constantin were all born in Bucharest, the capital of Romania, to a poor family. Anton and Bogdan were the eldest and were identical twins. Roxana was born next, and Sofia was the youngest child. Their mother had died soon after giving birth to Sofia and they were brought up by their father. Unfortunately their father died suddenly of a heart attack a few years later; the twins knew that it was their responsibility to raise their younger sisters as best they could. They had friends in London and decided that the best way forward for their family was to leave Romania and go to London, where they lived with their contacts in the local Romanian community.

The twins were heavily built and worked as bouncers for several night clubs and also security at private events in order to provide food and shelter for themselves and their sisters. They had mixed with some influential people, but also with many sinister people who used the muscle strength of the twins in order to settle old scores with their enemies. They were very well paid for the jobs they did and saved their money to protect their sisters. The jobs included killing people back in Romania and also in Germany. They were wanted for questioning for murder and were on Interpol's list, but had escaped capture. The money they saved was used to put both Roxana and Sofia through private education in one of London's top private schools. Many of the children were of famous people, including politicians, film actors and sports personalities.

Sofia had just turned twenty and was enjoying her life in London, when she was invited to the twenty first birthday party of her boyfriend, Justin, the son of a wealthy businessman. Although Justin was a year older than Sofia, they had met at school and kept in touch after leaving. He was her first proper boyfriend and Sofia was in love. Sofia was a younger version of her sister, Roxana. She was a tall and extremely pretty girl with long dark brown hair, and had the face and body of a model. She was also a very bubbly and outgoing person. The room would light up when she was in it, such was her personality. Everyone loved her.

Justin lived in his parent's house in London, it was a five-storey Victorian Villa in Eaton Square, an exclusive road in Belgravia, where the houses cost in their multi-millions of pounds. His parent's lived in their country mansion in The Cotswolds and very rarely came to London anymore as they had both partially retired. They were going to have a separate family party for Justin the following weekend. The party was a masquerade party and the invitation was clear - "No Mask, No Entry" and had a no-entry sign as a mask covering a face. Sofia wanted to impress Justin and had hired a beautiful pink and white Chanel dress which sat just above her knees, showing off her long and beautiful bare legs. She had bought a matching Chanel purse especially for the party. She was wearing a contrasting black mask with feathers and beads, she looked stunning.

Crowds were gathering in Eaton Square as word had got out that there was a party with many rich and famous people attending. Sofia arrived in a chauffeur driven black Mercedes saloon, driven by her brother Anton; the car had been borrowed from one of their associates for the evening. The car pulled up to the pavement in front of the house; part of the pavement had been roped off and there were two burly doormen at the entrance. The doormen were wearing black three-piece tuxedos and each had a basic black eye mask. "Invitation, please miss?" asked one of the doormen. Sofia produced her invitation and was just about to enter when the doorman asked to see inside her purse. He had a quick look and, seeing no weapons, he waved her through. She had been to Justin's house on many occasions before but she did not recognise it this time as it was completely decorated with banners, flags and balloons. Food and drink were in abundance including the finest champagne and caviar. Masked waiters were bringing round canapes and snacks, and there was a buffet arranged for later in the evening. There was a four-piece band playing popular, classical and dance music. There were so many people there and the party was buzzing. Everyone was wearing masks with many different styles including Venetian, Jester, Harlequin masks of all shapes and sizes. Two men took the invitation literally and arrived completely naked, with the exception of wearing a face mask. They were let in but Justin took them to his spare bedroom and gave them some of his clothes to wear, it was not that sort of party.

Sofia had been dancing with Justin and another group of friends when Jack Nash entered the premises. He was part of the pre-planned side entertainment supplying a variety of drugs to the party. Justin saw Jack Nash out of the corner of his eye and gently pulled Sofia by her arm, away from the dance floor. Jack had an assortment of high-end drugs, pre-selected and pre-paid for by Justin especially for the party, in his briefcase. It was part of the service which he offered to an elite group, mainly wealthy people who could afford his drugs. He had been hired by Justin in the past and knew that he was on to a profitable evening. However, he was getting greedy and had cut the cocaine several times using, amongst other things, rat poison.

Sofia and Justin went to one of the bedrooms and made lines of the cocaine on the dressing table. Sofia sniffed the first line with a fifty pound note which Justin had taken out of his wallet and rolled up. Justin was rolling a second fifty pound note for himself when Sofia collapsed on the floor in front of him. He tried to resuscitate her but she died immediately, blood was coming out of her eyes and nose. Justin screamed for help but it was too late. Her eyeballs rolled and had disappeared in the top of her eyes. She was gone. When he heard the screams, Jack Nash picked up his briefcase and ran out of the house trying to get as far away from the house as possible. He knew that his greed had caused the death of the young girl. Police and ambulance teams arrived at the house and a cordon was placed in the street outside. Justin called Bogdan and explained what had happened to his younger sister. Bogdan, Anton and Roxana were incensed by the news and wanted revenge for his sister's untimely death. Within days, Jack Nash Had been arrested and found guilty of dealing class A drugs and was going to serve a seven-year prison sentence. Bogdan and Anton knew that Jack Nash was only the dealer - they wanted to find his supplier, and had made it their priority.

Anton and Bogdan had made many contacts in the drug trade and it was only a matter of time before word on the street got back to them with the name of the supplier, Olek Gregorski, otherwise known as "G". They had a photo of him and had placed this, along with a reward, on the dark web for any information as to his whereabouts. As soon as Olek Gregorski had walked in to her public house, Roxana recognised him and knew exactly what she had to do. She sent a text to her brothers in a code which they had used before. Anton and Bogdan had received the text message from Roxana with the Russian sickle emoji and the words "my place in 30". They knew exactly what it meant. Roxana knew that she had to keep "G" in the bar until her brothers could get to her and, although she wanted to kill "G" herself, she knew that her brothers wanted to kill him too. She took the opportunity of "G"'s gunshot wound to entice him to the flat above the bar, knowing that her brothers were thirty minutes away and had to think of a way to keep him there. She kept him there by knowing what most men wanted, sex, and she was right. As soon as her brothers arrived, she took cover in the shower room.

Chapter Ninety Seven

After Bogdan had shot "G" in the forehead and made sure that he was dead, they told Roxana to go downstairs and back to the bar as if nothing had happened. They would clear the room and dispose of the body. They used their strength to break the bones of the corpse to make it easier to put the naked body in to the body bag. They put his clothes in the bag, making sure to search the pockets and destroy any evidence as to the identity of the body, although with all of the tattoos it would be difficult to hide his identity. They found "G"'s wallet in his jeans pocket and were shocked to see the large amount of cash, they took the cash and shared it between them. They also took his car keys before putting the clothes in to the body bag alongside the body. They looked at the blood on the bed sheets, stripped the bed and put the sheets in to the body bag, before checking to see if there was any other evidence left in the room. Satisfied with their job so far, they opened the door to the flat.

Making sure that there was no-one looking, they carried the black body bag down the stairs to the side door of the pub and in to their Transit van, unaware that they were being photographed by Detective Sergeant Bond. They drove the van to a building site which was being built by one of their associates, Nikola. Nikola was a former Romanian gang member, turned developer, and someone who owed the twins a favour. A very big favour for a job which they had carried out for him some months earlier. The building site was only a few miles north of where they were and it took them only fifteen minutes to get there as the traffic was light.

The building project was a former warehouse unit which had been demolished as part of a redevelopment with sixteen houses and two blocks of flats. Anton had called ahead to Nikola; he told him the situation and what they needed. Nikola agreed to help and arranged to meet them on site. They knew from Nikola that the construction was still at foundation level and would be perfect for their needs. When Anton and Bogdan arrived in the

Transit van, they were met by Nikola who pointed to where they should park the van. They parked the van close to the foundations where one of the blocks of flats was to be built. There was no-one else on the site as Nikola had asked his builders to go for a break as soon as he had spoken with Anton on the phone.

Nikola had already started the concrete pouring machine, making sure that it was ready for when Anton and Bogdan arrived. Anton got out of the van first and hugged his friend before he opened the back door of the van. Nikola was much shorter and thinner than the Constantine twins but held a high position and respect from both Bogdan and Anton. Bogdan got out of the van and walked to the deep and empty foundations of the soon to be constructed flats. He looked down into the vast trenches and could see that they were approximately six metres deep, probably deeper, perfect for their requirements. He walked back to the van to help his twin brother lift the bag from the rear of the Transit van. It took both of the twins to lift the heavy bag and they threw it in to the foundations of the flats, it landed at the bottom of the foundation with a heavy thud. Nikola adjusted the angle of the large spout at the base of the concrete pouring machine so that it was above the foundation trench where the body bag had been dumped. He pressed a button and the machine started to whirr and spin slowly. Concrete started to pour out, completely covering the body bag within minutes.

Not a word was spoken from the initial greeting to the moment that the body bag was no longer visible and the foundation trench was filled to the brim with concrete. As soon as the trench was full with concrete, Nikola turned off the concrete pouring machine and gestured the twins to his site office, for a celebratory drink. Anton and Bogdan were on their way to the site office with Nikola when they received the second text from Roxana with an emoji of a car and a message saying "remove from car park, urgent". They didn't have a chance to have the drink with Nikola but thanked him and agreed that they were now even; his debt from their previous job with him had been repaid, in full.

They drove back to the public house and parked the Transit van next to the Ford Focus. Anton got out of the passenger seat, opened the driver's door of the Ford Focus and started the engine. The Transit van followed the Ford Focus out of the car park. They noticed the Audi with someone sitting in the driver's seat and made sure that he was not following them. They drove the car and van to a nearby breakers yard, owned by another of their associates. They had called ahead and made sure that they would be alone. The Ford Focus was squashed into the size of a small box by the huge machine; any evidence of the car even existing, had been destroyed. The car and "G" were never found.

After several hours of being questioned at the local police station, Roxana was released, without charge. There had been no evidence of the murder of "G" in the flat above the bar and no proof that she had committed a crime of any sort. She called her brothers as soon as she had been released. They picked her up from the police station and returned to the bar where she worked to have a celebratory drink. Anton and Bogdan had a couple of vodka shots and left the bar before the police could catch up with them.

Chapter Ninety Eight

Charlotte Mobbs was pleased with herself as she destroyed what she thought were the last of the camera and listening devices, which had been placed in her house by the bogus drain workmen. She washed her hands and put on more sanitising gel. She had no idea that all of her electronic devices had been hacked by Splinter and that he and his team could see and hear everything that was happening inside her house. She also had no idea that the sound and pictures could be seen by Detective Inspector Chrissy Acton and her team at New Scotland Yard.

Charlotte Mobbs was sitting at the large table in her kitchen, admiring her recently acquired Diamond faced Rolex watch on her wrist. She saw that it was six thirty and nearly time for her meeting with Professor Tomkins. She looked up Tomkins' name on her iPhone and pressed on his name; within seconds Tomkins' phone lit up showing Mobbs as the caller. He was sitting at the table by the window in the bar, still shocked at having witnessed the earlier police activity. He answered her call. "Are you still on for seven?" she asked. "Don't worry, I'll be there at seven," he replied. "Looking forward to seeing you soon," he continued and pressed the red button to end the call. The call ended abruptly and Mobbs got up from the kitchen table. She walked upstairs to her bedroom and moved a chair to one side, revealing a large hidden wall safe. She tapped the code into the safe and the door opened. Inside the safe was cash piled high along with letters, accounts and documents of her victims, from the past and present; as well as future victims. To one side of the cash was the Smith and Wesson SD40 grey frame finish 9mm pistol and a box of bullets, which she had bought from "G".

Mobbs took the pistol and bullets from the safe and closed the safe door behind, making sure that it was locked. She pulled the magazine from the main body of the pistol and loaded it with bullets, until it was full. She replaced the magazine into the pistol and aimed it at the mirror on the wall on the opposite side of the bedroom, admiring herself in the mirror. "A female James

Bond," she thought to herself as she mimicked the action of pulling the trigger.

Mobbs made a few final alterations to her clothing. She was still wearing the long black dress and smoothed it down to remove the creases. She walked back downstairs with the pistol in her hand, and entered her large drawing room. She opened one of the glass fronted mahogany display cabinets on the wall and put the pistol in the cabinet, hiding it behind a photograph of her cats. She opened a packet of wet wipes which she kept in the bar area of the room and wiped the pistol. She then poured herself a large glass of vodka whilst waiting for the arrival of Professor Tomkins. She did not have to wait long.

Tomkins picked up his briefcase from the spare chair next to him in the bar. He opened it slightly, double checking to make sure that the knives were there. He lifted the newspaper and saw the glistening steel of the knives. "My little beauties," he said to himself. They were definitely still there and, in his mind, they had Charlotte Mobbs' name written all over them. He left the warmth of the pub and entered the cooling air outside. The twilight was starting and he knew that it would soon be dark.

He walked back to his shiny Jaguar, admiring it before he opened the door, putting his key in the ignition and listened to the throaty roar of the engine as the car started first time. He was an expert on his car and could hear that there was a slight misfire in one of the cylinders. He made a mental note to himself to check the spark plugs when he had finished his business with Charlotte Mobbs. Tomkins drove the final few miles of his journey to Mobbs' house, taking care not to over-rev, or cause any damage to the engine. After a few minutes he arrived at Mobbs' house in Mill Hill. He turned the Jaguar into the driveway and manoeuvred his car so that it was parked in front of Mobbs' white Mercedes C Class Cabriolet. He parked it in such a way that Mobbs would not be able to move her car without him having to move his Jaguar, the Mercedes was completely blocked in. He turned the engine off, noticing the engine shudder slightly as it stopped. He took his briefcase from the passenger chair, exited the car and shuffled across to the front door. The professor looked at his wristwatch, he was one for punctuality. It was seven o'clock, on the dot. He rang on the doorbell and within seconds he was greeted by the smiling face of his old friend and partner-in-crime, Charlotte Mobbs. She invited him in and gestured for him to go to the drawing room.

The drawing room was a very large, virtually square, room with windows to the side and front and French doors at the rear which opened onto the large rear garden and swimming pool. The doors and windows were closed as it was a cool evening, the room thermostat had automatically started the central heating system to work and the radiators were starting to warm the large house. There were four large Chesterton leather sofas forming a square around a central glass coffee table. Mobbs had clearly been sitting in one sofa and pointed to another sofa for Tomkins to sit in. He sat down and placed his black leather briefcase on the space next to him. Mobbs went to the walk-in bar close to the glass fronted mahogany wall cabinet. She glanced at the pistol in the nearby cabinet, smiled to herself and poured herself another vodka. What would you like to drink?" she asked. "No alcohol for me, thanks, I'm driving," he replied. The real reason was that he wanted to stay sober so that he could concentrate on killing her. Tomkins could tell that Mobbs was slurring her words slightly. He wasn't sure if that was a good or bad sign, or whether she was pretending in order to put him off his guard. He knew that Mobbs had acquired a gun and thought that if she were drunk then her aim might not be too good. He asked for a soda and lime as he had already had a scotch in the bar.

Mobbs went to the kitchen to prepare his drink and, whilst she was gone, Tomkins got up from the sofa to look around the room. The glass display cabinets were full with photographs of Mobbs and her cats. He noticed the Smith and Wesson SD40 grey frame finish 9mm pistol hiding behind one of the cat photos. He picked up the pistol and pulled out the bullet magazine, emptying the bullets in to his pocket and returning the magazine to the pistol. He moved away from the cabinet area quickly, so as not to let on to Mobbs that he knew where her gun was hidden.

Tomkins looked around the room and saw a Steinway Classic Grand piano, standing proud, in the corner of the room. He walked over to the piano and sat in the seat in front of the piano.

He lifted the keyboard lid and played a few notes, touching the pedals with his feet as if he were a concert pianist. It brought back memories of the happier days in his young childhood, when his father would play the piano and he and his mother would sing to the music. He smiled. He remembered the happy moments and then remembered that they were all ruined by his mother cheating on his father. The smile changed to anger as he remembered exactly what he had seen and what he had done to his mother and her lover. He managed to control his anger, at least for the time being as he walked back to the sofa and waited for Mobbs to return with his drink.

Chapter Ninety Nine

When she was in the kitchen, Mobbs opened the door of an eye-level wall cupboard. Inside the cupboard was a row of jars each with a collection of drugs including GHB, Rohypnol, Ketamine and Ecstasy. She assumed that Tomkins wanted to kill her and she wanted to have the advantage over him, by weakening him. She chose the grainy white powder of ketamine and poured a small amount of the powder from the jar in to his drink and stirred it so that the powder could not be seen. Not enough to kill him, or even make him sleep, just enough to make him drowsy and unable to kill her. She left the jar on the worktop, just in case she needed some more.

Mobbs took the drink in to the drawing room and offered it to Tomkins. Tomkins put the drink onto the coaster on the table in front of him, he did not drink it. Mobbs sat down on the Chesterton sofa on the opposite side of the table from Tomkins. She had heard Tomkins playing the piano and liked what she had heard. "I didn't know that you could play the piano," she said to him. "There are a lot of things that you don't know about me," he replied curtly. "I had lessons when I was a child but did not keep it up, my father could play the piano beautifully," he continued. He stopped talking at that moment and Mobbs knew that the mention of his father had triggered Tomkins into a different person from the mild-mannered person who had been in the room with her a moment ago. She changed the subject and talked to Tomkins about their partner in crime, Detective Superintendent Tony Pallett. They knew that Pallett had been arrested. They had not heard any more since then and they assumed that he had not talked about their working relationship.

They discussed the way forward. Mobbs did not know that Tomkins was aware of her doing solo investigations, without sharing the profits with either him or Pallett. Tomkins picked up his glass of soda and lime from the table and brought it to his lips. He could smell that something was not right and looked at Mobbs as he tilted his glass. He saw Mobbs take a swig from her glass of vodka and could see that she was looking at him whilst she was drinking, to see if he was drinking his contaminated drink. The liquid was nearing the edge of his glass but had not reached his lips. He pretended to sip the liquid from his glass but he did not drink. He stopped and asked Mobbs a question. "Why did you do it?" he asked her. "Do what?" she replied. "Why did you feel the need to do solo work when you had the protection of both Pallett and me?" he continued. Mobbs was startled by this question as she did not realise that he knew about her other work.

"She was my niece, you know," he said. "Who?" asked Mobbs. "Doctor Hughes," he replied. "Doctor Hughes was my niece and you went behind my back to line your own pocket." Charlotte Mobbs had not been aware of this and realised that it was now personal to Tomkins.

Tomkins then produced the photograph of the copy of the contents of his safe which "G" had given to him. He confronted Mobbs wanting to know why she had asked "G" to rob his safe. "I gave "G" your address, he should be here at any minute, he's on my side now," he told her. Mobbs was desperate and knew that she had to kill Tomkins; and had to do it now. She slowly got up from the sofa, thinking about how to answer the recent unexpected questions. She didn't want "G" turning up on her doorstep and coming to Tomkins' assistance. Neither she nor Tomkins knew that "G" had been murdered. She walked over to the bar and reached for the grey Smith and Wesson pistol. "Are you looking for anything in particular?" Tomkins asked her as he pulled the bullets from his suit pocket and showed them to her. Mobbs was speechless as she looked at the contents in his hand. She denied that she was looking for the pistol and poured herself another vodka. She was getting nervous and wiped her hands with the sanitiser gel from the drink's cabinet. She was quick witted. "We can sort this out, we both want the same thing. Money," she said. "I've got another investigation booked in, in two days' time. I'll give you a larger percentage of the share of the profits, especially as Detective Superintendent Pallett is no longer part of our team," she said, desperately trying to win back his confidence.

261

Tomkins listened to what Mobbs was saying as he was also very interested in money. He was also interested in revenge for the way that Mobbs had treated his niece. Mobbs picked up Tomkins' glass of soda and lime, and ketamine, and proffered it to Tomkins whilst she went back to the bar and poured herself yet another vodka. He didn't drink from the glass but put it straight back on the table in front of him. Instead, Tomkins quietly opened his briefcase and took out the hunting knife. Mobbs had her back towards Tomkins as he got up from his sofa and walked up to her. Mobbs could see in the bar mirror, that he was approaching her from behind and she turned around, but it was too late. "This is for the way in which you treated my niece, Doctor Hughes!" he shouted with rage as he inserted the knife for the first time. It was the last thing that Mobbs heard and saw before she died.

There was blood dripping from the six-inch serrated hunting knife as Tomkins inserted the knife and pulled it out of the lifeless body of Charlotte Mobbs, before plunging it back in again. Her glass of vodka fell to the floor and smashed in to several shards. "And this is for your deceit to our crime team and for doing private jobs, without sharing the proceeds with us!" he told Mobbs' lifeless body on the second insertion of the knife. The third insertion of the knife was for her having his safe broken in to by "G". The fourth insertion was for having a pistol and wanting to kill him. But he kept on stabbing and stabbing her, with such anger. The same anger as when he had killed his mother and her lover all those years ago. The same anger as when he killed Doctor Harris and Professor Moore. There was blood all over the floor and walls but he didn't care.

Tomkins pulled the knife out of Mobbs' corpse and calmy walked to the kitchen, where he partially cleaned the knife under the running water from the tap over the sink. He would clean it properly, with the love that the knife deserved, when he returned it to his armoury. He dried the knife with a paper towel and slowly walked back to the drawing room where he placed the knife back in to his briefcase. As he was doing this he noticed the jar of grainy white ketamine on the worktop surface, close to the sink and was glad that he had not had the drink which Mobbs had given him. On his way back to the drawing room he could see through the window by the side of the front door, that there were several people standing in front of the house. He could tell that they were the police, and could see that they were heavily armed. He knew that he did not have long and went back in to the kitchen to the jar of ketamine.

Chapter One Hundred

The entire meeting was being watched by Splinter and relayed to the monitors in the police surveillance van close to Mobbs' house. As soon as the first insertion of the knife occurred, Detective Chief Superintendent Robson of SCO19, instructed his highly trained tactical support team to surround the premises. Five officers armed with Glock 17 self-loading pistols and Heckler & Koch MP5 sub machine guns, as well as having riot shields for protection, waited at the front door whilst another five officers went to the back door. The front door was smashed open, with a battering ram. The shouts of "armed police" were reverberating throughout the house as the armed police officers entered the property. They kicked open the drawing room door, announcing themselves as they entered. Detective Inspector Chrissy Acton and Detective Andi Lester, both unarmed, along with uniformed officers, were close behind the heavily armed officers.

Shouts of "clear" came from around the house and Detective Inspector Chrissy Acton and Detective Andi Lester, along with a team from forensics, entered the drawing room. The armed officers left the house; they had done their job. They saw the lifeless body of Charlotte Mobbs on the floor by the bar, there was so much blood that she was not recognisable at first. They looked to the sofa where Professor Tomkins was sitting, he was very still and had an empty glass in his hand. He was dead. Tomkins had taken some more of the ketamine from the jar in the kitchen and mixed it in to his soda and lime. He knew that it would kill him. He was right.

The entire scene was watched from start to finish by Splinter and his team in their office in New York. Hannah was watching the live stream to the Metropolitan Police. What Splinter did not tell Detective Inspector Chrissy Acton was that he was also streaming the live video feed to Hannah's parents, Hilda and Arthur, watching on the TV screen in their flat in Islington. It was also being streamed live to Professor Emerson Noble and

Elizabeth, watching on their huge TV screen, in their Hampstead house. They had witnessed everything, from Mobbs' murder to the police crashing through the door in to her house and finding the two dead bodies in the drawing room. Justice had been done.

Mobbs and Tomkins were both dead, Detective Superintendent Tony Pallett was behind bars, James Hopkiss' life was ruined and Clementine Follows had died in poverty.

Revenge was indeed better than murder.

EPILOGUE

TWO WEEKS LATER

The private function room above the main restaurant at the Michelin Star La JaSte in Mayfair was full. The room could hold up to sixty people with variations on the number of tables but on this occasion, there was just one large round table in the centre of the room, laid out for sixteen people. Sitting around the table were Professor Noble, Elizabeth and their four children Russell, Judith, Steven and Jackie. Chrissy Acton and Andi Lester. Hilda and Arthur Cozin and their daughter Hannah, along with Danno, Kaz, Lucia, Ninja and Markie.

Danno, Kaz, Lucia, Ninja and Markie were staying at The Savoy Hotel in central London whilst Hannah had decided to spend time and stay with her parents. All of the guests had been brought to the restaurant in chauffeur driven Rolls-Royces.

The food and service were even better than usual, especially as the owners, Jackie and Steven, were guests in their own Michelin star restaurant. Celebrations were underway and it was going to be a long evening. Toasts were held every few minutes. The champagne kept on coming, Dom Perignon by the bottle; no expense was spared. On the table was the latest edition of the East Anglia Gazette. The front-page headline read "Exclusive, Cambridge educated Professor re-instated with full exoneration." The article had been written by the local journalist, Patrick Hendrick. Hendrick had been intrigued by the message that Clementine Follows had left for Professor Noble and had been constantly nagging the professor for information. Professor Noble had kept in touch with Hendrick and had kept his word with him.

A few days after Charlotte Mobbs and Professor Clement Tomkins were found dead, Professor Noble had contacted Hendrick and told him the full story of why he had wanted to see

Clementine Follows. Professor Noble had been re-instated with full exoneration by the Royal College of Surgeons but had decided to retire from surgery. Professor Noble was stunned when he found out that it was his supposed friend, Professor Tomkins, who had been responsible for killing his good friend, Doctor Harris. He had lost faith in his old friendships but as a result of the investigations, he had found many new friends. He would continue to lecture but wanted to concentrate on writing a book of his life, including his most recent adventure. He had been promised full compensation for the wrongdoings of Charlotte Mobbs.

Detective Inspector Chrissy Acton had received a commendation for her work in the case and had also received a promotion to Detective Chief Inspector. Detective Andi Lester had also received a commendation and had been promoted to Detective Sergeant. They were also celebrating the fact that their relationship was now out in the open and they did not have to sneak around anymore. They were making plans for their future together.

Hilda and Arthur Cozin were celebrating the fact that their daughter, Hannah and her team, had played such a pivotal role throughout the investigations.

Danno, Kaz, Lucia, Ninja and Markie were celebrating the fact that they had hacked the airline computer system and got free upgrades to first class on both legs of their flights to London from New York. As a result of this, they had secured a contract with the airline to be the sole company in charge of their cyber security, a contract worth many millions of dollars. They had also had a chance to look around London where they, and Hannah, decided that they should start a detective agency working as a team together.

THE END